MAN OF WAX

THE MAN OF WAX SERIES

Legion

Man of Wax

The Inner Circle

End Game

MAN OF WAX

MAN OF WAX TRILOGY, BOOK 1

ROBERT SWARTWOOD

RMS PRESS

Grateful acknowledgement is made for permission to reprint the following:

Excerpt from *The Little Prince*, copyright © 1943, 2000 by Antoine de Saint-Exupéry. Reprinted by permission of Houghton Mifflin Harcourt.

ISBN-13: 978-1945819131
ISBN-10: 1945819138

www.robertswartwood.com

To Holly, My Other Half

In the face of an overpowering mystery, you don't dare disobey. Absurd as it seemed, a thousand miles from all inhabited regions and in danger of death, I took a scrap of paper and a pen out of my pocket. But then I remembered that I had mostly studied geography, history, arithmetic, and grammar, and I told the little fellow (rather crossly) that I didn't know how to draw.

He replied, "That doesn't matter. Draw me a sheep."

—Antoine de Saint-Exupéry,
The Little Prince

PART I

SIMON SAYS

ONE

That morning—the first day the game officially started—the ringing of a phone woke me.

It was a distant, unfamiliar noise that dipped its hand into the dark I'd been floating in and abruptly yanked me out. First I opened my eyes. Then I started to sit up but stopped. My head pounded. It was like a bad hangover only different, making me feel groggy, even shaky.

I waited a few seconds and then slowly sat up, swung my feet off the bed, and reached for the phone on the bedside table.

"Hello?"

"Yes, hello," said the exasperated voice on the other end. "This is your nine o'clock wake-up call."

"My wake-up call," I said, almost a question, but the person on the other end had already hung up.

It was then that I realized something was wrong. Normally I sleep on the right side of the bed, Jen on the left side, and here I was now sitting on the left side of the bed holding a phone that shouldn't be there. After all, we had no phone in our bedroom.

I blinked and quickly stood up.

This wasn't my bedroom. This wasn't even my house.

What the hell?

I was in some kind of motel room. This much was evident by the bed I had just been lying on, completely naked except for my boxers. The air conditioner must have been on high because I was cold, nearly freezing—a fact that came a few seconds later, as I was beginning to catch my bearings. Across from the bed was an old TV, sitting on a four-drawer wooden dresser. The curtains were slightly open, letting in some sunlight. In front of the curtains was a wooden table with an opened bible on top. Beside the bible was a pair of jeans, a plain black T-shirt, white socks, and a black leather belt. Underneath the table on the carpet was a pair of sneakers.

"Hello?" I called out. "Jen? Casey?"

No answer.

I realized I was still holding the phone. I placed it back down on the cradle, feeling a little more awake now but even more confused. Beside the phone was an alarm clock, its digital numbers glowing red. Without my glasses I had to squint to see that it read 9:05.

I took a step forward and leaned over the table and pushed the curtains aside. I squinted through the window at the parking lot beyond. Stepping back, I glanced down at the bible, noticed that its crusty pages had been opened to the Book of Job.

"Hello?" I called again.

Still no answer. The only noise was the air conditioner blowing cold air from the rear of the room, right beside what had to be the bathroom. That door was closed. If my wife or daughter were anywhere, I thought, that was where they would be.

I started that way, my bare feet digging into the carpet. I

hesitated outside the bathroom door, considered knocking, but then just turned the knob and opened the door.

I reached in, found the light switch, flicked it on.

There were fluorescents in the ceiling which blinded me, causing me to squint even more and shield my eyes with my hand. I took another step forward, leaving the coolness of the carpet for even colder tiles. The bathroom smelled strongly of chlorine. It was small and compact, with only a toilet, tub and shower, a narrow mirror and sink.

And on the sink was a pair of glasses. I grabbed them and put them on. They weren't my glasses, not by a far stretch—they were too heavy, the frames thick, and they pinched around the nose—but they were my prescription. At least now I could see fine, I had that going for me, and even though I knew nobody was behind the shower curtain, I still pulled it aside to find only mildew spotting the tiles and drain.

That was when I turned and saw what was on the back of the door. Something skipped in my chest. In crude long letters that seemed to run because of the paint, someone had written:

LET THE GAME BEGIN

I stared at it for a long time. The fluorescents above me buzzed quietly. My heart pounded in my head. I knew what the letters had been written in—some internal voice kept whispering it—but still I walked forward, slowly, until my face was only inches away. I reached out and hesitantly touched one of the letters before snatching my hand back.

Just as I'd thought.

Dried blood.

TWO

The man behind the counter had a scarred face and short hair and looked both alarmed and irritated when I first stormed into the manager's office. He wore a blue polo shirt with a name tag that said KEVIN, but to me he didn't look like a Kevin. A beat-up TV sat on the table behind him, its screen fuzzy, its sound turned low, but still I caught glimpses of Matt Lauer doing an interview as I asked the clerk where I was.

"Are you serious?" he asked, and I recognized his voice at once as the one that had given me my wake-up call. The clock behind him, which continued to tick off the seconds, now read 9:10. "You checked in here last night."

"I—I did?"

Kevin nodded. He reached below the counter and shuffled through some papers, brought out a credit card receipt. He placed it on the counter facing me and pointed down at the scrawled signature. "This is your name, right? I watched you sign it last night."

"Last night?"

It was then that I noticed a small calendar on the counter. According to it today was Monday. Yesterday I'd been home, with Jen and Casey, sitting in my recliner in the living room and watching football. Hadn't I?

"But …"

I shook my head, not understanding any of this. I remembered hurrying out of the motel room, spotting the manager's office and sprinting across the parking lot. I remembered there had been sand on the pavement, the kind of sand we didn't have in Pennsylvania. Then more images and sounds of the outside came floating back to me. Not just the sand, but tall grass, seagulls, the sound of the ocean. I could even smell it now, could feel the salt in the air.

"To be honest," Kevin said, "you looked pretty out of it when you came in. I—well, I thought you might be drunk or something, but I couldn't smell anything on you. You paid with your credit card and then asked me to give you a nine o'clock wake-up call."

And here he slid the credit card receipt even closer, as if begging me to take it.

I didn't take it, though. Instead I looked directly back at Kevin and said, "Where am I?"

Kevin gave me a strange look, realized I didn't want the receipt, and took it back. Behind him, *The Today Show* had cut to a commercial.

"The Paradise Motel," he said.

"No, I mean where *am* I? What"—I swallowed—"what state is this?"

That strange look still hadn't left Kevin's face. When he spoke, his voice had become slow and nervous.

"California."

I shook my head. "No, that's impossible. I—"

But I couldn't think of anything else to say. I was wearing the clothes I'd found on the table, the clothes that weren't mine but were my size. Even the sneakers were size eleven and fit just right. The glasses still pinched my nose and I adjusted them quickly, uncertain what else to do. None of this made sense but I knew that it was true, that somehow I was in California—a state I'd never once visited.

I said, "Where in California?"

"Sir, are you all right? Do you seriously not remember checking in last night?"

"Was I by myself?" I'd begun speaking in a clipped tone. "When I checked in. Was there a woman and a little girl with me?"

"Sir, maybe you should—"

"*Was I alone?*"

Kevin stared back at me, his eyes now wide. I hadn't meant to shout, but things just weren't adding up, they weren't making sense, and right now I didn't know where my wife and daughter were, they were gone and I wanted them back.

"Listen," I said, closing my eyes and placing my hands on the counter. I dropped my head and opened my eyes then, stared at the sneakers that weren't mine. When I looked back up at Kevin, I could tell I'd scared him. In a slow and soft voice, I said, "Please. Just tell me this one thing. Was I alone?"

On the table behind the counter, *The Today Show* had come back, Al Roker now talking to the fans waiting outside the studio.

Kevin said, "Yes, you were alone. At least from what I could see. You checked in at three o'clock in the morning and you were alone. Now, do you want to sit down or something? You look pale."

THREE

The Paradise Motel—the place I had presumably checked into late last night—was U-shaped, the bottom part of the U facing toward the ocean, the sides hugging the parking lot. The motel only offered ten rooms and judging by the parking lot, it looked like the majority was empty. There were only three vehicles: a rusted and paint-flaked Dodge, a pickup truck, and a van. All the plates showed they were owned and registered by citizens of California.

Walking slowly across the sand-spotted pavement, I didn't know what bothered me more—the fact that my car was nowhere to be seen, or the fact that this was California, that I lived in Pennsylvania, where I knew I'd been just yesterday.

Smith River, Kevin had told me, just before the state line that would take me into Brookings, Oregon, and did I want a glass of water or a phone to call somebody?

Actually, yes, I did want to call somebody. I used his phone and dialed Jen's cell but immediately got her voicemail. I listened to her voice and considered leaving a message, but then hung up. Jen always kept her cell phone on, in case someone at the firm or one of her clients needed to get in touch with her, and the fact that it was turned off just wasn't right.

"No luck?" Kevin had asked, and I shook my head, handed him back the phone.

In the end I didn't tell him about the dried blood on the back of the bathroom door. After everything I'd learned from him—and really, had I learned anything?—the last thing I wanted to do was mention blood and alarm him even more. I'd managed to play it off like I just didn't remember checking in last night, that I must have really been exhausted. I couldn't think of anything else to say. The fact that my wife and daughter were now somehow missing was my foremost thought, but I couldn't say this to Kevin. He wouldn't understand. Even I didn't understand, though I was beginning to wonder if maybe it was me who was missing.

Kevin had put me in room six. As I hurried across the parking lot, listening to the ocean's waves off past the dunes, to the seagulls careening through the air, I hoped the door hadn't somehow locked when I left. If need be I could always return to the manager's office, ask for a key, but at the moment looking at Kevin—and forcing the poor clerk to look at me in return—was almost too much to bear.

Stepping onto the walkway, I paused and glanced back toward the highway, what Kevin had said was Highway 101. Probably the most famous highway in California, traveled the length of the state from the top all the way near the bottom, stopped right in Los Angeles. He'd mentioned this as if I should already know it, seeing as how I was obviously familiar with the area (which I most certainly was not), and how I managed to find my way here last night to check in.

Oh yeah? I thought, glancing at the three vehicles in the lot. And what car did I use?

For a couple long seconds I watched traffic pass on the highway. I was putting off the inevitable, which was to step back into room six and check the bathroom. I kept telling myself what I'd seen wasn't real, that it had been an illusion. Maybe I was high on something, though I hadn't smoked since college, that one lonely year I'd been there. Okay, there was that one time after Jen and I had been married, when a friend of ours dropped some off as a surprise, but that was it. The only thing I got high on nowadays were the fumes from painting, but that was on rare occasions, when I was working inside and for some reason the windows needed to be closed or the air wasn't circulating enough, and I always took a break then, stepped outside.

What looked to be a delivery truck was approaching down the highway, its turn signal flashing. I thought maybe I'd stay to watch it make the turn, watch it come down the drive and park in front of the office, but I was being stupid. I was stalling.

I reached for the doorknob, knowing it would be locked. It turned easily in my hand. The next thing I knew the door had swung open, the bright morning sunlight suffusing across the carpet, and I found myself walking inside.

FOUR

I checked the bedside table first, yanking open the drawer.
Nothing there except a phonebook. I took it out, set it on the
bed, and immediately put it back in. Slammed the drawer shut.
I wasn't sure yet what I was looking for but that hadn't been it.

The air conditioner unit continued blowing cold air as I
rushed over to the bolted-down television. I tried the drawers
there, all four of them, but found nothing in any of them, and
it wasn't until then that I realized what I was really doing. Yes, I
was looking for my wallet, my keys, even some goddamn cigarettes though I'd given them up years ago, when Casey was
born, but the real reason was waiting in the bathroom.

"Come on," I whispered, flexing my hands in and out of
fists. I stood in front of the now closed bathroom door. I told
myself that before I did anything else—like call Jen's cell again,
or call home, or do anything to try to track down my family—I
needed to check the bathroom door, to ensure myself I wasn't
going crazy.

Opening the door, turning on the light, stepping inside—it
all happened in one fluid motion that for a second I knew I
was dreaming. Yes, that made perfect sense. This was all a

dream. This entire thing was just a fantasy concocted by my mind, and at any moment I would wake to Jen nudging me or to that annoying spray of sunlight that fell right on my face when the blinds were up. There would be nothing on the other side of the door now, nothing at all except maybe a freshly folded towel. Having anything else—such as, say, four words spelled out in dried blood—would be a nightmare, and I never had nightmares. Jen and Casey did; I sometimes had to coax each of them out of their dreams when they tossed and turned in the middle of the night, and then had to hold them until they drifted back to sleep.

I don't know if I was surprised to find the message still there: those four ominous words, glaring back at me from their place on the door.

At that moment somebody knocked. I jumped. Stood very still then, thinking that it had been nothing.

Maybe it's Jen, I thought (and hoped), but for some reason I knew it wasn't, that it couldn't be.

Before I made my way across the small expanse of the motel room, I made sure to close the bathroom door. My new thought now was that it was Kevin, checking to see if I was really okay, and I didn't want him to see the blood. Because if he saw what was there he'd become even more alarmed, might even call the police, and then what was I going to tell them? That while Kevin claimed I'd checked in early this morning, the last thing I remembered was being at home with my wife and daughter and watching the Eagles game?

The knock came once more, insistent.

I went to the window and peeked through the curtains. It was a young woman, dressed in a blue uniform. Her truck was parked just outside my room.

I glanced down at the bible on the table, its crusty pages still opened to the Book of Job, then went over and opened the door.

"Benjamin Anderson?" She was chewing something that smelled like strawberry bubblegum. She held a package in her hands, a plain brown box that looked as if it could hold a pair of my sneakers. Her face was plain but somehow pretty, marked by a smattering of freckles. "This is for you."

"For me."

She nodded, handed me the package, and grabbed an electronic device she'd been keeping underneath her arm. She extracted a black stylus from the device and handed both to me. I just stood there for a moment with the package in my hands, the box that didn't feel as if it had a pair of sneakers in it at all. No, it was much lighter, which for some reason felt wrong—shouldn't it at least be heavy?

I set the package on the ground and grabbed the device, signed my name and handed it back.

"Thanks," she said, the word clearly automatic, then punched a few buttons on the device and turned away.

I watched her go for a few seconds, walking down the steps to the parking lot, pulling herself up into the truck. When I finally felt strong enough to pick the box up off the ground and take it to the bed, where I set it down on top, I realized the door was still open. I went to it, peered outside again. I smelled the ocean, felt the salt in the air, then shut the door and turned back around.

The box just sat there, staring back at me.

Waiting.

FIVE

I had no scissors, no knife, not even the jagged edge of one of my keys to open the tape that kept the box sealed. Instead I had to work one of the ends with my fingernail, working it back and forth, until I had enough to start tearing it away. Minutes passed. I was aware of the time, knew that I was again stalling, but I felt more inclined to do so now than before. The four words on the back of the bathroom door and what they'd been written in was enough to prove that this was no dream, no nightmare, which meant I had no reason to kid myself into thinking whatever was in this box wasn't real as well.

The first thing I saw when I had the box open was that it was filled with Styrofoam peanuts. I reached in, hesitantly, imagining the angry tips of knives and syringes, the tiny mouths of spiders—but what I touched first was a leather wallet. Pieces of Styrofoam rained down around the box onto the comforter as I pulled it out.

I opened the wallet and found only money inside. No credit cards, no driver's license, nothing else. It definitely wasn't my wallet, though—the wallet my dad had given me for high school graduation, filled with a thousand dollars, a small fortune to a man who only made twenty thousand dollars a year and who had been saving this gift ever since I was in middle school.

The money in this wallet came to five hundred dollars. All of it twenties. I set them aside and reached back in the box, a little less hesitant now. I wasn't expecting any insects or glass shards to bite me anytime soon.

Next thing I pulled out was a cell phone. It was a small simple black phone—half screen, half keypad. There was no company name on it, no provider logo. There was only one button on the top, presumably the power button, and that was it. No volume switch, no slot to plug in a power adapter, nothing. A note taped to its screen said in typed letters TURN ME ON.

I didn't hesitate at all, pressing the power button and watching the phone light up.

The phone's main screen was blank, offering no menu or contact list or even clock. Then, quite suddenly, the phone started vibrating. On the screen, the words INCOMING CALL flashed on and off.

I immediately went to press the green send button and hesitated. Someone was calling me but I didn't want to answer it. For all I knew it could be Jen, telling me that this was all just some joke, one big surprise, but a feeling in my gut told me that wasn't the case, just as that same feeling kept telling me not to answer the phone.

But I knew I had no choice. I'd been sent this package for a reason. I'd followed the simple directions in turning the phone on for a reason. Now I had to answer it to find the sum of those reasons.

I hit the send button, placed the phone to my ear, and said, "Hello?"

"Benjamin Anderson," said the voice on the other end, a

cheerful yet somehow unctuous voice that I was already beginning to hate. "Greetings."

"Who the hell is this?"

There was a pause, and though I had no reason to suspect this, I knew the speaker on the other end was grinning.

The voice said, "You can call me Simon. I'm sure you've played Simon Says before. Because that's exactly what we'll be playing now."

"The fuck are you talking about?"

"Didn't you already get the message? You know, the one on the back of the bathroom door?"

At that moment it was as if time had stopped. I even glanced at the clock on the bedside table, as if to confirm this fact, but it was digital and didn't show the seconds so it was still stuck on 9:38. I could feel the bathroom door behind me, urging me to look at it, to maybe even walk over and open it so I could step inside, stare again at what had been placed there.

"What the fuck is going on here?"

My pulse had quickened; I could hear the blood pounding in my ears—then, just as fast, the low chuckling of the man on the other end of the line.

"Just like the message says, Ben. May I call you Ben? I hope so. It'll make things easier if I do. Just think of me as a friend. That's probably the only way you and your family are going to get out of this alive."

I was staring at the alarm clock, at those red glowing numbers reading 9:38. They now changed to 9:39.

Simon said, "I know this is difficult for you, Ben," and I hated to hear what sounded like sympathy in his voice. "It's always difficult for a new player. But once you accept there's nothing else you can do, it gets easier. Trust me, it does."

"I don't . . ." I swallowed, shook my head. "I don't believe this."

"It doesn't matter what you believe. Nowadays belief means

nothing. Seeing, however, is everything. Go ahead; look in the box. There's something at the very bottom."

I wanted nothing to do with this fucking box anymore. In fact, I wanted to throw the goddamn cell phone across the room, smash it against the wall. But I was powerless, something I knew not just from what this psychopath was telling me, but from that small internal voice that always speaks to us when we're in a time of struggle, that gives us the best advice possible. That voice told me I really had no choice in this matter, and that if I ever wanted to see Jen and Casey again, I should—and God help me for even thinking it—do as Simon says.

"Okay," I said, both to the voice on the other end and to the voice inside my head.

I reached into the box, felt through the peanuts, until I touched something at the very bottom. It was a piece of paper, that's all it was, but when I brought it out, more Styrofoam peanuts raining onto the comforter, I saw it wasn't a piece of paper at all.

As it turned out, I was seeing my wife and daughter much sooner than I'd anticipated. In the glossy photograph they were both staring back at me, gags in their mouths. The camera's flash could be seen in the tears falling from their eyes.

"No," I whispered, staring down at my family that stared helplessly back at me. "You sick son of a bitch."

"Watch it, Ben. Remember—call me Simon. And right now, you're going to do everything I say, or else."

"Or else what?"

The red glowing numbers on the clock changed from 9:39 to 9:40, proving that time had in fact not stopped.

Simon chuckled. "Or else they die."

SIX

As there was no apparent key for the room, I didn't even bother locking the door. I just grabbed the money on the bed and shoved it in the wallet, and shoved that wallet into my left front pocket. Then I shoved the cell phone into my right front pocket.

Outside, the three vehicles—the rusted Dodge, the pickup, the van—were still parked in their places. I marched straight toward the Dodge, the one that Simon said would be unlocked. I glanced at the manager's office on the other side of the parking lot, thinking for some reason that Kevin was inside watching me. I should have taken that credit card receipt. I should have looked more closely at that scrawled signature. Anybody could forge a signature. It didn't take much.

For a moment I even considered veering off course toward the office. What I'd do once I got inside I had no clue, but the idea of reaching across the counter and squeezing the clerk's neck until there was nothing left to squeeze was quite appealing. While nearly all of this didn't make sense, some of it was beginning to, and Kevin (if that was even his real name) was one of the things that stuck out as being WRONG. Just like the message in blood on the bathroom door, the picture of Jen and Casey now folded and stuffed in my back pocket, and the fact that yesterday I'd been sitting peacefully at home in Lanton and now found myself all the way across the country.

But I didn't end up going to the office. Maybe things would have been different had I gone along with that initial thinking. Then again, maybe things would have just turned out the same. It's impossible to say, even now, but I continued toward the Dodge, glancing briefly through the dust-coated windows. There was nothing in the back, nothing even in the front. I wanted to check the trunk but knew it didn't matter. Not like it was going to change anything, and Simon had already given me a deadline, telling me the first part of the game was to get on the 101 and head south. Don't call the police, don't call the FBI, don't even call the boy scouts—"Do you see a pattern yet?" he'd said. When around others—no matter if they were children or geriatrics—I was to act like nothing was wrong. Just a man going about his business like normal, nope nothing wrong here, thanks for asking. Do all that, Simon said before he disconnected, and as long as I played along with the game and followed the rules, I would see Jen and Casey again.

"Alive?" I'd asked, and I could almost see the smile on his formless face as he said, "Of course, Ben. What do you take me for—a monster?"

The driver's door squeaked angrily when I opened it. Hot air rushed out. The outside temperature itself wasn't that bad, maybe mid-eighties. I could still hear the ocean beyond the motel, the seagulls crying out in the sky. The traffic continued on the highway, none of its drivers remotely aware just what kind of hellish circus I was being put through. Well, good for them, and fuck you too.

I got inside and shut the door. The seat squeaked the way old fake leather does when it gets hot. The car reeked of dust and hot rubber, and I rolled down the window for some fresh air.

Simon had said the key was under the seat, but I didn't reach for it yet. He'd also said there was a surprise for me in the glove compartment. Just a surprise, nothing else, so I should obey the speed limit and not do anything stupid, because there was no registration or proof of insurance. Still, whatever that surprise may be, I didn't want to look. I was still thinking about the trunk, about what might be inside it. Images kept invading my mind, grisly snapshots of my daughter's twisted body: her legs snapped backward, her arms bent at awkward angles. Or maybe it was Jen's body instead, in all the same positions, just taking up more space.

Never mind, I told myself, shaking my head and blinking the images away.

I reached down and found the key, right where Simon had said. For some reason I didn't expect the engine to start, figured I'd have to try it a few times before it finally turned over, but it roared to life at once. I let it idle for a few moments, feeling the entire thing tremble around me, which made me realize I hadn't yet begun to tremble myself.

"That's strange," I murmured. I held my right hand out in front of me. Nope, it was just there in front of my face, completely still.

The gas gauge told me I had three quarters of a tank left. The odometer read close to eighty-seven thousand miles. The radio was turned off. My eyes still kept darting at the glove compartment.

After about a minute or two, when I was certain the car wasn't teasing me, I backed up and started down the drive toward the highway. I glanced only once at the manager's office. For some reason I expected to see a face watching me from one of the windows, the face of a man who may or may not be Kevin, but there was nobody there. Traffic continued toward me, headed south, and I waited a minute before there was a break large enough for me to pull out.

Though I was within just a few miles of the coast, it was another fifteen miles or so before I passed through a place called Crescent City and the highway got close enough and I saw past the houses and trees and tall grass. There it was, the Pacific Ocean, stretching toward the horizon. I'd never seen it before, having always been satisfied with the Atlantic. It really looked no different. Jen had been out to California many times before, back when she was younger and her life was different. Once she married me everything changed for her; she went from being unbelievably rich to being moderately poor. No more glitzy and exotic vacation spots where everyone spoke another language. No more staying in famous and elegant hotels where the help knew your name and smiled and nodded and wished you a good day. No more flying first class, or even coach. For our honeymoon we hadn't even gone to Florida, where most middle-income couples go. Instead we'd gone to Virginia Beach, and that was only because it was in reasonable driving distance and just within our budget. Thinking of it I remembered our wedding night, while we lay together in our hotel room, and I had broken down, felt like a complete asshole and cried because I couldn't give her everything she'd had before, and she had held me and told me everything was fine, that she loved me and didn't care if I had no money at all.

"If you could only see me now, Jen," I whispered, not even realizing it until a few seconds later and feeling quite ridiculous. Then I thought: *The only money I have now is five hundred bucks. That and—*

And again my eyes darted to the glove compartment. I decided enough was enough. Keeping my left hand on the wheel, I leaned over and—now realizing I was trembling —opened it.

SEVEN

I'd been driving for close to an hour and a half when I decided to stop for food. My stomach had been growling ever since I passed through Redwood National Park. I'd considered pulling off the highway to find something then but kept remembering what Simon had told me, how I had a deadline. And so I continued driving, ignoring the Pacific even when it was nearly touching me. I kept my eyes forward, on the cars in front of me, on the cars passing me. I maintained my speed at an even sixty. The Dodge had no cruise control, and my legs were starting to cramp. I kept my mind on Jen and Casey, on the prospect of seeing them again. It was the only thing that kept me going, the only thing that helped me to forget the revolver in the glove compartment … that was until, every five minutes or so, my eyes would dart once more to my right and I would remember all over again.

My mind tried to process everything that was happening to me, formulate some kind of reasonable explanation. But it was impossible. There were no numbers in the phone, no way for me to contact Simon if and when I needed to.

And so I drove.

And drove.

And drove some more, until finally my stomach's steady growl became a roar. This was when I spotted a sign for Arcata Airport, then a few moments later saw a plane making its descent from the pale blue sky—a pale blue that nearly matched my wife's and daughter's eyes.

Five minutes later I passed a sign for McDonald's, where I eventually ended up. The parking lot was fairly full, even for a Monday in early October, but what the hell did I know? I pulled the Dodge into a space, got out and stretched my legs, my arms, my back. It felt good being outside, even if it was in a strange place. At least the Golden Arches were a comfort, an Americanized symbol that said in not so many words it didn't care who I was, where I was going, or what I'd done; as long as I had money, they had grease-fried food with my name on it.

But when I started toward the entrance I found myself stopping almost immediately. Staring at the building and its familiar white and red and yellow motif caused an ache in my heart. I suddenly remembered all the times Casey had playfully pestered me and Jen to take her to McDonald's, how she wanted, *needed*, a Happy Meal. Sometimes we gave in; sometimes we didn't. We'd decided early on to keep our daughter away from unhealthy foods, though there had been a series of weekends last year where we went to McDonald's every Saturday, after Casey proudly proclaimed McDonald's hotcakes were her all-time favorite food in the whole wide world. So Jen and I had decided to make a morning of it, sitting out on the colorful tables of the Playland, surrounded by the watchful gazes of Ronald McDonald and Mayor McCheese, Grimace and the Hamburglar, watching our daughter happily eat her syrup-drenched hotcakes. Sipping our coffees and clasping hands beneath our table, we talked about whatever—movies, books, Jen's recent cases, Casey's upcoming preschool—both so happy to be together as a family and warmed by the simple knowledge that we would always be together, all three of us, no matter what.

Inside, I went to the bathroom first. At the sink, washing my hands, I realized I hadn't yet showered. The men's room door opened and an old guy walked in, his gray hair wiry, shuffling his way past the two hand dryers to one of the stalls. I waited until I heard the satisfying click of the lock before pinching the collar of my T-shirt and pulling it out, lowering my nose so I could take a whiff. Wasn't any B.O., but it didn't smell that good either, and I decided I wasn't apt to get many strange stares while I waited in line along with the general public.

I stared at myself for a moment in the mirror. I didn't look like me, at least not the me I remembered. The glasses were what really threw me off. They just didn't fit my face in the right way, and thinking of them, I became conscious of just how much they were pinching my nose.

In the farthest stall, the old man was mumbling, telling himself he could do it, that he really could.

There was no line at the counter, and the woman who waited on me had crooked teeth but somehow managed to pull off a nice smile. She pressed a button on her register screen and looked up, asked if this would be for here or to go. I glanced down at my arm, realized I wasn't wearing my watch.

"To go," I said, and pulled the wallet that wasn't mine from my pocket.

Back in the Dodge a few minutes later, a large paper bag now on the passenger seat, containing two Big Macs, large fries, and the largest size Coke they had—which didn't occur to me at the time how stupid that was considering I was on some kind of road trip with a deadline—my stomach had quieted

down. It knew it was getting what it wanted and didn't intend
to rush me any further. Still I didn't reach for the food just yet,
thinking I had to make up for the time I'd lost on my little
detour.

The phone started vibrating in my pocket the moment I
backed out of my parking space. I wasted no time pulling it
out. The same INCOMING CALL was on the screen.

Simon said, "Did I say stop at McDonald's? Because, quite
frankly, I don't remember ever doing so."

I closed my eyes briefly, cursed myself. I thought of Jen, of
Casey, and remembered I hadn't yet looked in the trunk.
Which one of them was crammed back there right now?

"Ben? When I ask you a question, I expect an answer."

"I'm sorry." For some reason it didn't even occur to me then
to ask just how the fuck he knew I'd made a pit stop.

"You're not forgiven. But that's okay. I guess I'll allow it,
considering you're no doubt hungry. Besides, you're going to
need all the strength you can get for what's in store."

"What's in store," I said. I'd come to the parking lot exit,
was just waiting there with my foot on the brake. "What does
that mean? Where're my wife and daughter? What have you
done with them?"

"Relax, Ben. They're safe. And as long as you follow the
rules, and do everything I tell you to do, they'll remain that
way. Now why don't you do those nice people behind you a
favor and quit sitting around? Head back onto the highway.
Take 299 east."

I glanced up at the rearview mirror, saw the Buick there
behind me. An older man (the one from the restroom?) and
an older woman in the front, the man hunched over the
wheel, the woman shaking her head and raising a frail hand, a
wordless gesture expressing she had no idea what I was
thinking.

"How the fuck can you see them?"

"Don't worry about it, Ben. Just get going. Time's a-wastin'."

"But what—" I started to say, but by then Simon had already disconnected. I cursed myself again. I realized I was trembling. I'd already begun to hate that voice, to loath it so much my mind had created a face for Simon just so I could imagine myself smashing it. This wasn't fair. This wasn't right. None of this made sense.

Relax, that small internal voice of mine said. *It'll do neither you nor Jen or Casey any good getting pissed right now. You need to stay in control.*

Yes, that's right. I needed to stay in control. But just how the fuck was I supposed to do that when I had the least control possible?

The Buick's horn sounded out behind me, a very high-pitched sound, and without hesitation I pulled out onto the road. Minutes later I was on 299. The phone was still in my hand. I knew better than to even fool with it again, but I had to know, needed to know, and so I dialed the house even though I'd already tried Jen's cell, even though I knew there would be no answer.

I placed the phone to my ear and listened to the rings. It rang four times before the answering machine picked up: Jen's voice saying, "You've reached the Anderson's, sorry we're not home," and then Casey's voice, her soft and gentle voice, beaming in with, "Leave a message!" There was a beep and I started to say something but stopped. Instead I disconnected the call and placed the phone between my legs.

"Think," I muttered to myself. "Come on, *think*."

I was now a part of a sea of traffic heading in a new direction. At least I was pointed east this time, though I knew that changed nothing. Home was still thousands of miles away, and I grabbed the phone again, intended on trying the house one more time. Instead another number popped into my head and

I dialed that one, waited three rings before Marshall Gibson, a friend and fellow painter, answered his cell.

"Hello?" he said, hesitant and unsure like any person would be when a strange number appears on the screen of his cell phone.

"Marshall, it's Ben."

A slight release of breath on his end. "Oh my God, Ben, where—where are you? Where are you calling from?"

"Listen," I said, but at once the phone started beeping. I pulled it away from my ear to see the screen. I had another incoming call. Of course I had another incoming call. Had I really been that stupid?

Marshall said, "Ben? Are you still there?"

"Hold on a second," I said, then switched over. Simon didn't even wait for me to say hello or anything. He started right up, his voice angry and petulant.

"What the hell do you think you're doing? Goddamn it, Ben, are you an idiot? What did I tell you before? You talk to *nobody*."

"Where's my family?" My body was beginning to tremble again, though I managed to keep it hidden from my voice—or at least I hoped I did. Stay in control, I kept telling myself, stay in fucking control. "I want to talk to them."

"You don't get shit, Ben." Simon paused, took a calming breath. "Now switch back over and tell your friend Marshall that you're away on vacation, or something to that effect. Make it good."

"How did you know I was using the phone?"

"My God, you really are an idiot, aren't you? I see everything you see. I hear everything you hear. I know everything you goddamn know. So quit screwing around or you can kiss your family goodbye."

"Okay, okay," I said, a bit too quickly. My body was still trembling. My eyes kept darting from the highway and the cars to the glove compartment. While in McDonald's I'd managed to forget what was inside, now it came back at me, slapping me across the face. "Hold on," I told Simon, and switched over, said, "Marshall, you still there?"

"Yeah, I'm here. So what's up? I heard you canceled on the Johnsons today. You feeling sick or something?"

And just like back in the motel room—room number six, with those four letters in blood on the bathroom door, which I doubted were advertised in the brochure—time stopped again. Of course, nothing actually stopped—the cars around me continued driving, the Dodge maintained its speed, and my body continued to shake, but that internal sense of time had stopped. I was to start on William and Cassandra Johnson's Tudor house today. They were having the entire second floor remodeled, had commissioned me to do the walls and ceiling. And supposedly I'd canceled. Son of a bitch.

Then, just as quickly, time started up again and I said, "Yeah, I actually am feeling sick. I probably won't be around for the next couple days."

"Shit. Well start feeling better, man."

"Thanks, Marshall. I'll talk to you later."

I switched back over to Simon.

He said, "That's going to cost you, you know. Otherwise how are you going to learn that rules are rules?"

I was silent. I'd put my window back up when I left McDonald's and the car now reeked of French fries and oil.

Simon said, "Your wife or your daughter."

"What?"

"Your wife or your daughter. Which one do you love more?"

"You fucking son of a bitch."

"No, Ben, my name is Simon. I'd asked you to remember that. Because from now on, every time you call me something else, either Jennifer or young Casey will lose a body part. Do I make myself clear?"

I felt a tear push itself from the corner of my eye, start rolling down my cheek. I blinked it away, tried to remain cool, calm, as if I was in control. What a fucking joke.

"Now, Ben, answer the question. Between Jennifer and Casey, which one do you love more?"

"I—" But I couldn't go on. I couldn't continue with what I wanted to say, which was that I wouldn't tell him what he wanted to hear. I wasn't going to choose between my wife and daughter like that.

"I understand, Ben," Simon said. "You need time to think about it. It's a tough question. In the meantime though, it appears as if you're getting quite low on gas."

My eyes, instead of darting from the highway to the glove compartment, now darted to the gas gauge. It was hovering right above E.

"There's a gas station coming up," Simon said, "which means the first part of the game is very close."

"What ... what are you talking about?"

"Shoplifting, Ben. Don't tell me you've never stolen anything before. Please don't tell me you're that self-righteous."

"You want me to ... steal gas?"

He said, "Why no, Ben, of course I don't want you to steal gas. I want you to steal something else, something much simpler."

"What's that?"

"A Snickers bar."

EIGHT

As per Simon's instructions, I went inside the station to pre-pay. The place was like any ordinary highway gas station, well lit with white tiled floors and racks of potato chips and pretzels and other snacks. The one wall was lined with sodas and bottled water and milk and orange juice, all kept nice and cold behind glass, where static clings announced sales and specials on Pepsi and Coke and Gatorade.

There was one person in line, a guy in jeans and a denim jacket telling the clerk which numbers he wanted to play for tonight's lottery, so as I waited I made it a point to study the candy aisle. It was just one row over, positioned so the clerk had a good view. Shit. Not only that, there were cameras in every corner, all with small signs below them saying SMILE, but that didn't really mean anything. The monitors for those cameras were probably in the back, where nobody was right now, and even if somebody did happen to be there, it wasn't like they had their eyes on the screens all the time, right?

The clerk was an old black man, his hair and mustache gray, who looked at me tiredly when I told him I'd like fifty bucks on pump three. He took my sixty dollars, handed me back ten, and then I was back outside. I was farther away from the ocean now, from the beach, so I no longer smelled the salt in the air. What I smelled instead was gasoline, oil, and that ubiquitous odor of exhaust, which can be found in every major city around the world.

I walked to the Dodge and lifted the handle to the pump, unscrewed the gas cap and inserted the nozzle. Luckily there was a catch, which allowed me to keep the nozzle pumping on full so I could grab the McDonald's bag off the passenger seat. Standing outside, watching the numbers cycling through on the pump, I had a couple of the fries, took a few bites into one of the Big Macs. All of it was cold so I tossed it in the garbage can beside the pump, and just waited.

A woman was on the other side of the island, conversing with the use of the Bluetooth in her ear while she gassed up her SUV. She wore sunglasses and was shaking her head, saying, "No, that's wrong, that's wrong," again and again, making me suspect that she didn't quite agree with the party on the other end.

Eventually the nozzle kicked, dislodging the catch. I replaced the nozzle on the pump, screwed back on the cap, and just stood there. The woman was still talking, waving her hand around now as if to prove a point, but I was barely listening. I'd been trying to think so far how I wanted to go about this. All I had to do was lift a Snickers bar, that was all, just one simple candy bar, place it in my pocket, and leave. Easy as cake. The only problem was I'd never stolen a thing in my life.

I headed back inside, an electronic bell sounding as the door opened and closed. The clerk hadn't moved from his spot behind the counter. He wasn't waiting on anybody—in fact, I was the only customer in here—and he looked at me with his tired eyes, as if to ask what I wanted now.

"Bathrooms?" I asked, and he lifted a hand, pointed a finger, and I started toward the back. I purposely went down the candy aisle, keeping my head straight while glancing at the candy at the same time. The Snickers bars were sandwiched between the Milky Ways and Butterfingers. Just waiting there for anybody to grab.

It appeared the last person who'd used the toilet in the men's room hadn't flushed. The smell of shit was rank, and I had to put a hand to my mouth and nose to keep from retching. An idea came to me and I pushed open the stall door, peered inside. Yep, just as I'd thought.

Back out in the store, the woman with the sunglasses who'd been very adamant about something being wrong was at the counter. She was purchasing two bottles of water. The Bluetooth was still in her ear but she wasn't shaking her head or waving her hand around as much as before, which meant she was probably talking to someone else. I walked up right behind her, waited the few seconds before she collected her change and grabbed the bottles. As she turned away she was saying, "Yeah, see, and that's just what I told her." Then she was gone, the electronic bell dinging twice, and it was just me and the clerk. He was giving me that look again, the one that said he'd never planned on ending up in this gas station, standing behind this counter, but shit happens and that's life, and what can I do for you now?

I said, "The toilet's clogged," jerking my thumb back toward the bathrooms, as if I'd been talking about the toilet down aisle three instead.

The clerk—his name tag announced him as Frank—gave a long, heavy sigh. "All right," he said, nodding his thanks to me, and started to turn away.

I was ready. I was set. Now was the time, and I could feel the blood pounding away in my ears, palpitating even louder than before. Once Frank headed back there, plunger in hand, I'd hurry over to the candy rack, grab a Snickers, and get the hell out. Screw the cameras. If they were going to hunt me down over a dollar-something snack, the world was a lot more fucked up than I cared to admit.

At my sides my hands flexed in and out of fists, anticipating, waiting for the right moment, the moment when—

"Elliot," Frank shouted toward the backroom, staying where he was behind the counter, "check the men's, will you?"

He turned back to me, that same tired look in his eyes, and forced a small smile just as a young Mexican man emerged from the back. He had a plunger in his hand and started down the aisle, muttering to himself in Spanish.

The electronic bell sounded again—*ding, ding*—and two middle-aged men, both dressed in slacks and shirts and ties, walked in. They were talking together, in the middle of a discussion that seemed to hinge on the importance of a particular golf course. They headed toward the wall of cold beverages.

I caught Frank watching me again. That look of tiredness had changed, had become almost quizzical, and he said, "It should just be another minute or two. If you need to, use the women's."

A moment's thought, a simple nod, and then I was headed toward the back again. Shit, this really wasn't turning out as I'd hoped. And now I was angry. Just what the fuck was this all about anyhow? My wife and daughter were God knows where, held by God knows what, and the person who called himself Simon said that if I didn't follow through with his instructions to the letter then they would be killed. And after all that, after all that build up, he wanted me to lift a fucking candy bar?

There was no answer behind the women's door when I knocked. I stepped inside, not because I needed to use the toilet but instead to keep up appearances. I stood there for a very long time, staring at myself in the mirror dotted with watermarks and trying to decide just what the hell I was going to do now.

Eventually I ran the water, wet my hands, cranked the

towel dispenser. Came out of the women's room just as Elliot came out of the men's. He gave me a brief curious stare but then seemed to decide I wasn't worth the bother and started back toward the counter. The plunger at his side kept a constant trail as it dripped, dripped, dripped on the linoleum floor.

"Fuck it," I whispered.

I walked over to one of the long glass refrigerated doors. I grabbed two bottles of water, the same size and brand as the SUV woman, then turned around, grabbed a bag of pretzels. Next was the candy aisle, and I glanced toward the counter, itching my chin on my shoulder so it wouldn't look completely obvious. The two men who'd been discussing golf were there now. They were talking to each other still, barely even paying any attention to Frank as he began ringing them up on his register.

I didn't hesitate another second.

I reached out and grabbed a Snickers bar and placed it in my pocket. One smooth motion, the candy going from place A to place B. Simple as that.

I approached the counter like I would any other time, not feeling guilty at all. Because I knew that if I felt guilty, I'd look guilty, and something told me Frank had been behind that counter long enough to spot a guilty face among a hundred faces. He probably told stories about it at home, eating dinner with his wife. Telling her about the crazy customers, the asshole customers, then of course the kids who thought they were hot shit and sometimes tried lifting bags of snacks and bottles of soda. But Frank knew what they were up to, he could always tell, and my, let me tell you about this guy I caught today. Looked to be in his thirties, had on these glasses that didn't seem to go right with his face, and he had a Snickers bar in his pocket. Can you believe that? A goddamn Snickers bar.

Frank said, "Find everything you need?"

I started nodding but stopped. After setting the two bottles of water and pretzels down on the counter, I motioned at the cigarettes behind him. "Marlboro Reds too, please."

Frank turned, grabbed a pack, and placed it on the counter next to the rest of my stuff. Then he started punching numbers into the register. The electronic bell sounded again, this time a young kid, couldn't be more than sixteen, strolling in with his cap reversed on his head and a chain hanging from his pants.

"Anything else?" Frank asked, his hand already extended to take my money, and I thought: *Is it really this easy?*

Then something else occurred to me.

"Actually, yeah," I said. "Do you have any maps?"

NINE

Not even ten minutes later, back on the highway, the phone vibrated in my pocket.

By then I'd already smoked one of the Marlboros, was working on my second. I hadn't smoked since Casey was born, agreeing with Jen that a new baby shouldn't have to be exposed to secondhand smoke. I hadn't even tried bargaining around the issue, asking if I could at least smoke outside, or when I was out on a job (which, I knew, I could have done without Jen ever finding out, but still didn't). Now that I had a daughter my life had changed even more—I finally felt I had a purpose —and I intended to stay around as long as possible. Now, after all this time, I needed the cigarettes because otherwise I knew I'd lose it, and so far, the shakes hadn't come back.

"Yeah," I said, propping the cell phone between my ear and shoulder, so I could keep one hand on the wheel, one hand on my cigarette. My window was down just a couple inches, where I tapped the ashes. "I did it. I got you your Snickers bar."

"I know, Ben. Remember, I see everything you see, I hear everything you hear. But you didn't really follow the rules properly, now did you?"

I glanced at the stuff on the passenger seat: the Snickers, the bag of pretzels, the two bottles of water, the pack of cigarettes, and the folding map of California.

"What do you mean?"

A pause on Simon's end, a kind of sigh, then: "What's the point of lifting something if you're going to buy other items too? You were supposed to lift the candy bar. That was all. Lift it and walk right out."

"But you never said that. All you said was steal the Snickers. You never said I couldn't buy anything else."

"Ah, I see. So you want to play semantics, do you, Ben? Well, okay. Then when I say I'm going to kill your daughter and make your wife watch, does that mean I'm not going to rape your daughter too?"

"Jesus." The cigarette was finished now, down to the filter, and I flicked it out the window. "She's barely even four years old. A fucking baby. You … you …"

"Yes, Ben? What am I? Go ahead—say it. But keep in mind what I told you before. You call me anything else but Simon and either Jennifer or Casey will lose a body part. A finger, an ear, a toe. Or maybe an eye."

The highway was curving all over. I was passing trees, mountains, even an occasional river.

"You've already broken one of the rules. Probably the easiest rule of them all, which makes me doubt your ability to even continue. Then you went and pulled that shit at the gas station. Well, fine, I understand you don't quite believe this is real. That's why I'll have something waiting for you when you arrive at your destination."

I swallowed, barely had a voice when I asked, "What is it?"

"Can't tell you that, Ben."

"Where am I going?"

"Can't tell you that either. Spoils the fun."

I grabbed the pack of cigarettes, stuck one in my mouth,

punched the Dodge's lighter and waited the few seconds for it to warm. Then I had the cigarette lit, took a very long pull, let it out. Closed my eyes briefly, tried to remain calm. I told myself I should have bought another pack of cigarettes back at the station, maybe even a carton.

After several seconds when I did my best to calm down, I said, "Can I ... can I speak to them?"

"Which one, Ben? I asked you before which one you loved more. Telling me which one you want to talk to now will answer that question, don't you think?"

I said nothing. I took another pull. The road curved again, and I followed it, entering shadows which blessedly hid me from the glaring sun.

Simon said, "Okay, I think I can arrange something. After all, you need proof that this is real, right? Not like the blood on the door back at the motel was real or anything."

"It wasn't?"

But Simon had already disconnected. I dropped the phone between my legs. The road curved, the shadows fell back, and the sun found me again. Just a simple game of peek-a-boo, something every parent is familiar with. I remembered playing it with Casey when she was just a year old, the smile on her face brightening every time I showed my face from behind the blanket. I'd have played that simple game with her for hours, but then again I would have done anything for her. My precious baby. My little princess. My only child who would constantly draw me into a debate on how *Shrek 2* was twenty times better than the original, a little thing we had between us because Casey loved the *Shrek* movies (well, the first two) and we watched at least one of them once a month, if not more, just the two of us with a bowl of popcorn. I don't know how it started between us, that never-ending debate, but I knew how much Casey loved arguing the point, how she was so much like Jen in that respect. And for that reason alone I maintained that I found the original *Shrek* the better movie, and would not be swayed no matter what kind of support Casey provided (the addition of characters like Puss-in-Boots and Fairy Godmother, the singing, how Shrek saved the day in the end), though internally I was always proud of her for never faltering.

Five minutes passed and the phone vibrated. I didn't even bother to glance at the screen when I answered.

"Ba—Ba—Ben?"

It wasn't Simon's voice.

Time seemed to slow down once again and I whispered, "Jen? Jenny, is that you?"

"Ben, oh my God." She burst out sobbing, and even though she was God knows where I could see the tears in her eyes. "Tha—tha—they cut—they cut off—they cut off my—"

She started crying out even louder then, and the sound fell away, until it was hardly even there at all. I started saying her name, again and again, asking if she was all right, if she was there, but there was only silence. Then, out of that silence, Simon spoke.

"Satisfied?"

"You," I started to shout, but kept myself in check. I just closed my eyes, slammed my left hand against my forehead, ran it through my hair. Stay in control, I kept telling myself. Stay in control.

"Go ahead, Ben. You deserve to call me something now. I'll give you a free pass."

But I didn't call him anything, though my mind was running through a continuous list of names. I kept hearing Jen's voice. I kept seeing those tears.

They cut off my—

Cut off her what? Good fucking God, what did they cut off?

"Now," Simon said, in an almost chipper tone, "maybe

you'll start taking this more seriously. This is for real, Ben. Don't doubt that for a second."

"Why are you doing this?"

"To be one hundred percent honest," Simon said, "I'm not really doing anything. I'm just the mediator. As far as everybody else is concerned I don't even exist. You're the main attraction. You're the entertainment."

"What are you talking about?"

"Do you spend much time on the Internet, Ben? Checking your email, looking up websites. Anything like that?"

"I ... what does that have to do with anything?"

"You're addicted to porn, aren't you? You sometimes spend hours on the computer looking at it. You've been addicted ever since you were in high school. When you got married you thought you'd stop but you didn't, and you never once told your wife. Why couldn't you confide in her, Ben? Maybe she could have helped you stop. Who knows, maybe she would have wanted to watch it with you."

"How"—I swallowed, my throat suddenly dry—"how the fuck do you know all this?"

"I can't say I blame you. Going out to the bar, trying to pick up a woman, either she's going to say yes or no. And even then there's no guarantee you'll get any pussy. But porn? Porn will never turn you down. Isn't that right, Ben?"

I said nothing, my hands squeezing the steering wheel.

"Do you ever think about those girls on those websites? Not the ones that are posing in their skimpy lingerie, touching themselves and whatnot, but the other ones. You know, the ones with the cocks in their mouths and pussies. Even the ones with the cocks in their asses. You get off just seeing them being gangbanged, that look each of them gets on their faces when they get close to climax. Go ahead, Ben, tell me you don't. Tell me that doesn't make your dick go hard."

The road continued to curve. The sun continued to fight

with the trees and mountains in an endless game of peek-a-boo.

"You're a man of wax, Ben." There was something different about Simon's voice, the unctuousness gone, now filled with what almost sounded like concern. "That's okay, because I'm a man of wax too. Everybody is, even if they don't want to admit it. They sit in front of the television for hours at a time, never moving their asses. Or they sit in front of their computer screens. None of them ever look away, no matter what they're seeing, and do you know why? It's because we can't. The same reason cars get backed up when there's an accident. We need to see that pain. We need to fulfill that desire in our hearts and souls. Right now, Ben, you're simply playing a game to fill the desire in others' hearts and souls. You're giving them what they want, just like those countless girls with cum all over their faces were giving you what you wanted."

I was listening but at the same time I wasn't. I was remembering all the nights I'd spent on the computer in my den, while Jen was fast asleep. I'd always done so well at cleaning up my tracks, of deleting files and the history. Never once did Jen suspect anything, just as never once did I try telling her what I really did late at night.

"It's nothing to be ashamed about. We all have our needs, our dark desires. We all have our fetishes we never want to tell anybody else about, not even our wives or girlfriends. It's what makes us human, Ben, what sets us apart from the rest of the animals in the world."

"How ... how do you know all of this?"

"It's possible to know everything about anyone, if you have the proper resources. Your full name is Benjamin Jacob Anderson. You're thirty-two years old. You were born into a poor family, your father a painter, your mother a dry cleaner. You went to high school in York, Pennsylvania. You got pretty good grades, graduated with a three-point-four. You ended up going to Penn State's York campus for English, because you wanted to be a lawyer. But you were only there for two semesters. Though, actually, that's not quite true, is it? You went one full semester, then only a few weeks into the second before dropping out. Something happened that made you question everything. What happened there? I already know, but I want you to tell me. Come on, Simon says tell me what happened."

I opened my mouth, started to speak, shut it. Just kept my attention on the road.

"I understand it's difficult for you," Simon said. "Her name was Michelle Delaney. She was a sophomore. She was at the same party you went to, she and her boyfriend. I'll at least give you that much. But tell me what her boyfriend did. Tell me what *you* did."

"There's … there's no way you can know that. There's no goddamn way."

"Keep telling yourself that, Ben. Keep telling yourself that none of this is real."

On his last couple words his voice had made a strange sound. I glanced at the phone, saw that it only had one bar left.

"You're cutting out."

"Am I? Well, I'm surprised it hasn't happened yet. I should go now anyhow. Give you some time to think. Turn the phone off in the meantime. I don't intend on talking to you for the next couple hours. Besides, all you have is driving ahead of you. Stop for gas when you need it, buy whatever you'd like, but remember: I see what you see, I hear what you hear, I know what you know. Use the map you bought at the gas station to get you where you need to be headed. Turn the phone back on when you start passing through Doyle."

The road was beginning to straighten out some. Ahead the endless stretch of trees of one of California's many national forests rose in the distance.

"Where am I going?"

For some reason I didn't expect Simon to answer me, but he said, "The Biggest Little City in the World: Reno, Nevada."

"And what"—I swallowed again, my throat still dry—"why am I going there?"

Again, I didn't expect him to answer. I expected him to give me some bullshit about how it wasn't any of my business to know. But then, right before he disconnected, he told me, that grin once more palpable in his voice.

"There's a young woman there just dying to meet you."

TEN

From where I'd entered Six Rivers National Park near Willow Creek, to where I finally started seeing signs for Doyle, California, roughly six hours passed. I took 299 all the way to Redding, the first true solid sign of modern Americana in the past couple hours. I stopped for gas and then took a long piss in the bathroom, having downed both bottles of water. I stocked up on snacks while I was inside, more pretzels and soda and even some beef jerky. I also bought a Snickers bar, if not to spite Simon, then to at least make amends for the one I'd lifted and then eaten. The wrapper—the only evidence of my crime—lay in the trash out by the pumps, along with the pretzel bag and the empty pack of smokes. At the counter, I thought long and hard, and asked the girl for a carton.

Outside, I paused by the payphones. I considered calling Marshall again. Just what I would tell him I still wasn't sure—Simon saying *I hear what you hear* kept reverberating in my head—but I wanted to tell him something. Maybe have him stop by the house, just in case, though I knew that would be a waste of time. Hadn't I heard Jen's voice? Hadn't I heard her screaming?

They cut off my—

Yes, Jen? Yes, my darling? Just what the fuck did they cut off?

Besides the obvious, I wished she'd never gotten that much out, because in the last six hours all I'd been doing was filling in the blank. While I'd originally thought there wouldn't be that many possibilities, I quickly realized that wasn't true. Seems that when you're under extreme pressure and stress, your mind will think up anything.

Then again, I wasn't being quite truthful with myself. There was something else I'd been thinking a lot about, too, a girl I hadn't really known in college but a girl who'd haunted me ever since. Michelle Delaney. Son of a bitch, how the hell did Simon know about her? The only person I'd ever told was Jen; even my parents, when they asked why I had dropped out of school, were given some bullshit response that it just wasn't for me.

Another annoying revelation that had dawned on me in the past few hours was I'd been kidding myself before, back in room six of the Paradise Motel, waiting to open up that bathroom door. I'd called it a nightmare and said I'd never had anything like that before, but it was a lie. Nightmares came to me every so often, most times while I was asleep, other times while I was awake. A nightmare so clear and precise it was as if I were reliving the scene again and again. I'd see her there, I'd see Michelle Delaney, and I'd be forced to watch no matter how much I wanted to wake up. It seemed, just like in real life, I had no control over the matter.

Two hours later, now on I-395, I turned on the phone. Doyle was just another mile or so away.

For some reason I expected Simon to call in a minute or two of having turned the phone on, but he didn't. Instead it was in another ten minutes, as I was entering the Doyle State Wildlife Area, that the phone started vibrating.

He said, "Having fun yet?" I didn't answer, just waited, and it took him a few beats to say, "Oh come on, Ben, don't be like that. We're friends."

"We are not friends."

"Fine then. We're acquaintances. Does that sound better?"

It was close to seven o'clock in the evening. The light had already been retreating for an hour now, the sky darkening. I'd never driven so long before in my life. Both my legs were starting to cramp; my neck was starting to hurt. I'd done only one road trip with my parents when I was younger—we'd gone down to Orlando, after my parents had scraped enough extra money over the years to do something nice for my birthday— but then I'd been in the backseat, simply a passenger, and had slept or read comic books most of the way.

"Ben, it won't do you any good to not talk to me. After all, I am Simon, and what I say goes."

"What do you want now?"

"Now? Now I just want to talk. I figure since you've been driving so long you might be feeling lonely."

I didn't say anything and just continued driving, gripping the wheel tightly with my left hand as I kept the phone glued to my ear with my right.

Simon said, "So, Ben, I've been wondering something. I want to know why, after having such ambitions to become a lawyer, you instead went back and worked with your father as a painter. Quite a different field of work arguing cases in front of a judge and jury as opposed to mixing paints because the owners don't exactly like the tint of the beige from the can, isn't it?"

"People are going to realize we're gone, you know. I might not be a lawyer, but Jen certainly is, and her firm's probably wondering right now why she didn't show. The same with Casey's preschool."

"Relax, Ben. All of that has already been taken care of. You really think we'd forget something like that? Now answer my question. Why painting?"

"I just—" I shook my head. "I don't know. It was something to do. I'm good at it."

"I don't buy it. There has to be more to it than that."

The highway stretched out before me. Cars coming in my direction in the other lane, cars in front of me, cars behind me: they were all headed home, to a friend's, out to eat, to maybe their own work. None were in the same position as me, their family held hostage, some kind of madman on the other end of a cell phone that wasn't even theirs, that instead belonged to whoever had set this fucking thing up. For some reason, I hated each and every one of them.

I closed my eyes for a moment, pictured the one summer when I was a boy and went up to my father painting the backdoor. Heard the question I asked him, listened to his response.

"You know, Ben," Simon said, "it won't do your family any good giving me the silent treatment. I'm just trying to make conversation anyway, to ease the tension. It doesn't really matter to me what makes you tick."

"Then why'd you ask?"

Simon didn't answer, but I could see that grin there on his goddamned face, and it made me grit my teeth. I pinched the cell phone between my ear and shoulder again, gripped the steering wheel with my left hand, while with my right I reached over and found the opened pack of cigarettes on the passenger seat.

Once I had the Marlboro placed in my mouth and lit, I said, "Let me talk to my wife again."

"I don't think so. You've already talked with her."

"My daughter, then."

Silence. Then, "Hmm."

I kept my eyes on the road, following the glow of red taillights, my foot lifting off the gas pedal.

"What?" I asked, my voice all of a sudden more cautious and tense than before. I flicked the cigarette out the window. "What is it?"

Simon said, "It's just your daughter," and paused. Took a few seconds, as if thinking of something. There was complete silence on his end, which made me wonder if maybe I'd lost the connection, or if maybe he'd hung up. Finally he said, "You haven't checked the trunk yet, have you?"

ELEVEN

There was no real shoulder along this particular spot of 395 but I pulled over anyway. Except pulled over isn't quite right, seeing as how once I threw the phone down I gripped the wheel tight and slammed on the brakes. The Dodge protested immediately, its brakes screeching, the back of the car fishtailing. Luckily nobody was tailgating me, or else there may have been one ugly crash. As it was, a tractor-trailer was about one hundred yards behind, its driver not at all impressed with my driving skills, because a low horn blasted out right as it passed.

I barely noticed. Instead I just sat there, staring forward at the dash, and wondered just what I really wanted to do now. My mind had been feeding me blurry images since the beginning of what might be in the trunk, and now, with Simon's help, those images had begun to gain focus.

More cars passed by on my left, what seemed just inches away. I ignored them all, debating what I wanted to do, until finally I cut the ignition and grabbed the key, started opening the door but then heard the rush of oncoming traffic and hesitated. Good thing too, because somebody else decided they weren't impressed, and another horn shouted out into the night. I waited until there was a break in the cars and got out and started toward the rear of the Dodge.

"Please no, please no, please no," I whispered.

More cars passed by on the highway, the rush even louder now that I was standing just feet away from them. The sky was clear, the temperature cool, and somewhere in the grass by the trees insects chirped.

And I kept whispering, "Please no, please no, please no."

Somehow I made myself stop. I don't know how long it took, how many minutes (or hours) passed, but eventually I fell quiet and just stood there in front of the trunk. The key was in my right hand, hovering just inches away from the lock. Nothing was holding me back, nothing except the images that flashed through my mind. Like a series of jump cuts, I saw my daughter's battered body, her tangled arms and legs, her smashed face. Like she'd been hit by a tank and then placed in this trunk, just waiting for her daddy to bring her back out.

When I decided enough time had passed that it was clear I was stalling, I lowered my hand holding the key. It slid right into the lock. A second went by, another second, and I turned it. There was an unsatisfying click as it unlatched. I was aware that the trunk had risen just a bit, whatever springs there were trying to force it to lift up into the air.

I wasn't ready for that quite yet.

And so I stood there, holding it down, traffic sporadically surging past me. There were houses close by, many with lights on in their living rooms and kitchens, and in one of the back-yards a dog started barking. The insects in the grass kept up their constant symphony.

I opened the trunk, took a step back, and stared down at the bloodied remains of my three-and-a-half-year-old daughter.

TWELVE

When the doctor told us we were having a daughter, I'll admit that something broke in my heart. Any father who says he doesn't want a son is a liar. Because there is some part of him, some part deep down inside, that wants his baby to be just like him, to grow up idolizing him and carrying on his name. I'll admit I was more than just disappointed.

But then the day came when Casey was born. I stood in the delivery room, holding Jen's hand, and watched as my own child took her first breath. Jen had been too exhausted to hold Casey, so our daughter had been given to me. I remember crying as I held her, wanting to wipe my tears away but at the same time wanting to never let go of my baby girl.

Jen had only been allowed so much time off work, so after a couple of weeks, Casey became my responsibility. I would change her, play with her, even took naps with her. A favorite book of mine growing up had been *The Little Prince* by Antoine de Saint-Exupéry, and I made it a point to read it to Casey at least once a month. I'd read other books, but I always came back to *The Little Prince*. And, somehow, the book became Casey's favorite too.

When she was just two and a half years old she started drawing pictures. She spent hours hunkered over blank sheets of paper with an opened box of Crayolas beside her, until she was finally done and came running to me with the finished product. And each and every time I'd pull her up onto my lap, inspect the latest picture, and say, "That's a hat," to which Casey would giggle and say, "*Da*-dee." A year passed and the ritual never changed. The only thing that changed was that her pictures got even better, so much so that I hoped she might be a prodigy.

Reading *The Little Prince* to her at least once a month never changed either. I'd read a little to her before bedtime, while Jen was downstairs working on yet another stack of briefs. Every once in a while Jen would poke her head in, listen while I read, but Casey always nudged me and pointed, letting me know we had an intruder. This was our own special time and Casey wanted nobody else involved, not even her mother. One time Jen actually exploded at me about this, calling me a bastard for trying to take her daughter away from her. But she was just venting, stressed out because of her workload. She knew that wasn't the case. She and Casey had everything else; besides our ongoing debate of *Shrek* and *Shrek 2*, Casey and I only had *The Little Prince*.

No matter how many times we read it, Casey giggled when we came to the part about the little prince visiting the king, and then the very vain man—she couldn't decide which tickled her more. Then her smile would always fade when the little prince came to the fifth planet on his journey to meet the lamplighter, who was constantly lighting and extinguishing his lamp.

Like most children her age, Casey couldn't really read yet, but she memorized her favorite parts of the book. So when we got to the part where the little prince arrived to earth and came in contact with the fox, she wanted to read his secret.

" 'Good-bye,' said the fox," she'd say, her soft voice light but full of energy. " 'Here is my secret. It's quite simple: One sees clearly only with the heart. Anything essential is invisible to the eyes.' "

Yet no matter how often she read it aloud, she always had trouble pronouncing *essential*. I could never decide whether this was really a problem, or whether she did it just so she could get my help.

Then near the end, she'd want to read what the little prince said about how the important thing is what can't be seen.

" 'If you love a flower that lives on a star, then it's good, at night, to look up at the sky. All the stars are blossoming.' "

We'd go on from there to the very end, until that final picture on the last page and the note from the author saying to him it was the loveliest and saddest landscape in the world. Casey would always have tears in her eyes, but they were good tears, happy tears, and I always handed her a tissue, and she always took it from me, smiling. And if the sky was clear and the temperature just right, we'd go outside and stand in the middle of the backyard. I'd hold her in my arms and we would stare up at the sky and the stars and ask aloud, "Has the sheep eaten the flower or not?"

And though I claimed to never hear it (because I couldn't), Casey always said she could hear the stars.

She said they sounded just like the book said.

She said they sounded like five hundred million bells.

THIRTEEN

I may have cried out, I don't know. I may even have screamed, though until then I'd never actually screamed a day in my life. Who knows, maybe I did scream but the scream was silent and all that I did was just stand there with my mouth open, my throat making a weird sound where it tried to work but kept failing. Whatever the case, I didn't do it for long until what little was in my stomach churned once or twice and started up the way it had entered.

I doubled over and vomited into the grass. At first it came out easily, like in a spray, but the longer I stayed doubled over, the longer I retched, and the more the bile became just little bits and chunks. The pretzels, the beef jerky, the two Snickers bars—they were all there somewhere, partially digested, now soaking into the ground.

The images that had risen up in my mind before had ceased. Now I had an actual image of what lay in the Dodge's trunk. No tangled arms and legs, no head bent backwards. It was just Casey's body, lying there almost peacefully, except covered in blood.

The traffic continued on the highway, everyone oblivious

that my daughter lay dead just feet away. It made me hate those people even more, those people probably waiting to make it home in time to catch their favorite sitcoms or dramas, who maybe picked up a DVD at Redbox and just wanted to relax for the rest of the night. They might have had a run-in with the boss today, who berated them in front of their coworkers, or maybe their boyfriend or girlfriend broke up with them and they were thinking that their life couldn't get any worse.

No, I wanted to tell them, I'm sorry, folks, but believe me it can. It can get a whole lot fucking worse.

I stayed that way for a long time: doubled over, my hands on my knees, staring at the ground. I noticed, even in the dim light, that some of the vomit had gotten on my sneakers. Something wet was on my face, something I didn't realize were tears until I started wiping them away. I was crying but I wasn't sobbing, and I told myself I was a terrible father for being that way. My daughter, my own flesh and blood, was now dead, and I couldn't bring myself to break down. Instead tears were all I could give her, and that sad simple fact was enough to make me want to rip my hair out.

Eventually I got myself under control. The trunk was still open, its contents free for anybody to see, and the last thing I needed now was a concerned citizen catching a glimpse inside and calling the police. If that were the case, Simon or whoever it was that did this might as well have thrown Jen in there too.

I wiped at my eyes, at my mouth, then stood and turned back around. I approached the trunk slowly, not wanting to look back inside but knowing I had no choice. One step, two steps, three steps, and I was standing right where I was minutes earlier, the Dodge's key hovering just inches above the lock.

I took a breath, braced myself, and peered again into the trunk.

This time it wasn't my daughter that lay in there amongst all the blood. My mind was able to contemplate that in the matter of only seconds. Before, I'd just glanced, and my mind had already known it was Casey, so Casey was what I saw. Now, after accepting that the body was my daughter's, my mind wasn't working in the same way. Instead it was working properly, and it told me, *Sorry, Ben, guess I was wrong on this one.*

Yes, I thought, standing there and staring into the trunk, I guess you were.

It wasn't my daughter's body lying in there at all. It wasn't even a real body. The only light there belonged to the dim bulb hanging just within the trunk, but staring long enough made me see that what lay inside was maybe four feet long from head to toe. And plastic.

"Oh my God," I breathed, and took a very long, deep breath.

It was a mannequin. Nothing more than an oversized doll. The pink fake flesh stood out among the blood … which, I started to think, wasn't really even blood at all.

I started to reach forward, to touch the stuff I'd first thought was blood but couldn't be blood because it looked like some of it was still wet, and that couldn't possibly be so if I'd been driving this car for almost eight hours already, and the car had been in the parking lot for God knows how long before that.

But before my hand could lower itself any further—it was about twelve inches or so from being swallowed by the trunk—headlights splashed the back of the car and trunk, headlights so bright that it made me realize they didn't belong to the traffic out on the highway.

And along with the headlights, other lights as well. Flashing blue and red lights, a kaleidoscope of patriotic colors that filled the night.

Without thinking I lifted my hand and grabbed the top of the trunk and slammed it shut. I turned around, raising my other hand to my face to shield my eyes from the blinding glare of all the lights. An unmarked police car was parked just twenty feet away, the cop inside already opening his door.

Oh shit, I thought, and continued it in a kind of mantra: *oh shit oh shit oh shit oh shit oh shit oh shit.*

I remembered Simon's first rule, no talking to the police or the FBI or even the boy scouts, was I seeing a pattern?

The cop stepped out and shut his door. He glanced out at the traffic and started walking toward me. I couldn't really see his face, which was nothing more than a circle of darkness, but from the size of him he looked to be about six-foot. He walked slowly but steadily, his one hand on his holstered pistol, his other hand holding a flashlight. Its beam was shining right at me.

"Evening," he said, his low voice coming to me above the rush of traffic and insects and the dog, which continued to bark nonstop. "You realize there's not much of a shoulder here, don't you?"

"Yeah, I do," I said, nodding, thinking to myself come on come on come on *think*. Then, all of a sudden, I said, "It's just that I popped a tire about a quarter mile back. Tried to ride it out to the next gas station but I got too nervous. I wanted to change it now. You know, better safe than sorry."

The cop had stopped walking about ten feet away. He still stood in the same position, with his right hand on his holstered pistol, his left hand holding the flashlight, but instead of the flashlight's beam striking me right in the face, it was doing an entire sweep of my body. Shirt, jeans, shoes, back to jeans … and then back to shoes.

"What's that?"

The beam was centered right on the few spots of bile that had splattered there.

"It's vomit," I said, as casually as possible. "Had some fast food earlier today. Wasn't settling too good with me, and got even worse in the past hour. I would have taken some Tums or something had I had some on me, but as it was I just wanted to keep going. Then after I changed the tire, it really hit me and I … well, you know."

And I pointed, almost as an afterthought, to the side, where the bile had begun to dry together with the grass, looking like some poor kid's failed science experiment.

The beam swung over there, only briefly, then came back, this time at my face. I raised my hand again to shield my eyes.

"Look, officer," I said, really feeling the part I'd created for myself now, "I'm sorry if I shouldn't have pulled over here. I kind of figured there wasn't much room, but the tire that blew was on the passenger side, so I knew my ass wasn't going to be sticking out in traffic. If you need to give me a citation or something, I completely understand."

Traffic continued to rush by on the highway, this time a tractor-trailer that sounded like it was shifting gears. The dog, which had been barking this entire time, was now silent.

The cop stood there for a moment, considering, then clicked off the flashlight. From the light of the oncoming cars, I saw him shake his head. "No," he said, "I'm not going to give you a citation. But just be more careful next time, okay?"

I nodded. "Thank you, officer."

He stood there, as if waiting on something, and it didn't occur to me until a second or two later that he was waiting on me. And so I nodded once more, told the cop to have a good night, turned and waited for a break in traffic before I started toward the front. As I did I wiped my hands on my jeans, as if wiping away grease, something that had been absent on my hands but which I hoped the cop had missed. A moment later I was inside the Dodge, turned on the engine, and waited for another break in traffic before pulling out. In the rearview mirror the unmarked car had turned its flashing lights off. But it just sat there, waiting, until the car was nothing more than a dot in the mirror, and then gone.

FOURTEEN

I didn't recognize the noise at first. I'd been driving for almost five minutes, having already smoked one cigarette. I had passed through Doyle, which wasn't much of a town, and now it was just me and the road. This noise had started the moment I first pulled back on the highway, but I figured it was just the Dodge. Then the noise stopped, just to start again a minute later. I was now working on my second cigarette, relishing it even more than the first, when I looked down at the foot well on the passenger side and saw the cell phone lit up.

My left hand on the wheel, I kept the cigarette stuck in my mouth to reach down and grab the phone. INCOMING CALL, the screen said. I pressed the green send button.

Simon said, "I'm not sure which was stupider. Your reaction to what was in the trunk or how you handled the cop. Though, I must admit, both were quite entertaining."

"My reaction? You said it was my daughter in there!"

"Oh, Ben, now you're putting words in my mouth. I never said it was your daughter. You just happened to ask about your daughter, and I happened to ask if you'd checked the trunk. Simple coincidence."

I took a long pull of the Marlboro, tried to remain calm. Was having a hell of a time pulling it off, though I was more than relieved that it had just been a mannequin and not really Casey.

"You bastard," I said. "I thought … I thought she was dead!"

"Of course you did, Ben. Why else do you think we put it in there? I'll have to admit, the expression on your face was perfect. But the fact that you then threw up—well, that just made it priceless."

I didn't say anything and kept my eyes on the road. It hadn't really occurred to me before, but at that moment it struck me hard that I was on camera. The only question was, where the fuck was the camera and were there others?

"Ben? What's wrong? You have a strange look on your face."

I glanced around the car, at the dash and the rearview mirror and the passenger side foot well. I shook my head. "It's nothing."

"No, it's definitely something. Spill it."

"I'm just—I'm wondering how you can see me, is all. Like where the camera is and everything."

"It doesn't matter how I can see you, Ben. What matters is that I can. Just like how I saw you handle the cop. I must say, while you did do something quite stupid, you handled yourself well."

The road stretched out before me. The sky had darkened even more. I wanted another cigarette but told myself not yet.

"What did I do that was stupid?"

"The first rule I explained to you was don't talk to cops. Now in that situation, I can understand you had no choice. But asking him to give you a ticket? Are you joking?"

"Guilty people never ask to be punished. They're too

worried already obsessing over it. Innocent people have nothing to worry about."

"I see. So your asking for a ticket was your way of pleading innocence. Sure, makes perfect sense. And all the while you weren't thinking about how maybe the cop wouldn't help you out?"

"How the hell is he going to help me out? This car's not even mine. If he ran the plate it would probably come up stolen anyhow." I paused. "What would happen if he ran the plate?"

Simon said, "I wouldn't worry about it, if I were you. All you need to worry about is getting to Reno. Should take you less than an hour if you don't stop."

"Where am I going to go once I get there?"

"I think you fail to understand our relationship, Ben. You don't get to ask questions. But to answer you, just this once, I'll call you when you get there. In the meantime though, I do want to ask you one more thing."

Finally I couldn't take it anymore. I grabbed the pack of smokes, stuck one in my mouth, punched the cigarette lighter.

"What's that?"

"I'm just wondering," he said, "has your wife ever let you cum on her face?"

FIFTEEN

I reached Reno a little over an hour later. I drove straight through, even though the gas gauge told me the Dodge had less than a quarter tank left. I wasn't worried. By that time I had already concluded that if anything were to happen to the car, Simon would provide. He'd somehow know about it, would give me a call, and tell me to hold on. Who knows, maybe he'd send a limo. Add to the entertainment, whatever the fuck that meant.

Roughly five miles past the Nevada state border I started seeing signs of solid civilization again. Just like when I passed through Redding, the trees dropped away from either side of the highway to reveal the lights of buildings and houses and stores. Even billboards for gas stations and fast food places were lit up along the highway, reassuring any weary traveler that their money is always welcome.

I continued down 395, headed toward the heart of Reno. As I passed over some train tracks the phone started to vibrate. I waited a couple long seconds before picking up the phone. Then I waited another couple long seconds before answering it.

"What's wrong, Ben?" Simon asked. "Don't you want to talk to me?"

I said nothing. I'd already smoked two packs of cigarettes. The inside of my mouth felt raw, and I wished I'd bought some gum the last time I stopped for gas.

"The Grand Sierra Resort," Simon said, his voice now low and serious. "Tell the front desk you're Romeo Chase. They'll have a room waiting for you."

I didn't bother answering him. Just like at the end of our last conversation, it was me who disconnected the call. But instead of throwing the phone down at the floor, this time I tossed it over on the passenger seat. Traffic continued surging around me, cars passing me, me passing cars. I'd become sick of driving hours ago but figured I could do it for a little longer. I didn't know what was going on but I still had the hope Jen and Casey were both alive. It was what kept me going. It was what kept me from ignoring that urge in the back of my mind to take the gun from the glove compartment and end this once and for all.

SIXTEEN

To say I was overwhelmed by everything that'd happened in the last twelve hours would have been an understatement, but the moment the Grand Sierra Resort came into view I was completely beset. This was just too much, I kept telling myself, and after I'd parked I stared up at the gigantic white building that rose higher and higher into the night. I couldn't seem to will myself to blink. From waking in the crummy cramped room of the Paradise Motel, to now this—it just seemed wrong, and it made me think of Jen. She would have felt completely at home in a place like this, having stayed in these types of hotels ever since she was young. She'd stayed in the Plaza Hotel at least two dozen times, she once told me when we visited New York in December, and when I told her I'd never once stepped foot inside the place, she laughed and told the cabdriver to take us to Fifth Avenue.

I cut the Dodge's ignition, the car immediately going silent except for the soft ticking coming from beneath the hood. I tried to picture Jen's face every time she laughed. I tried to picture her smile when she led me up the steps to the Plaza Hotel, where the doorman opened the door, and we entered the lobby. She said, "Well, now you can't say never," and reached up on her tiptoes, kissed me on the lips. That had been Jen, wanting me to experience everything I possibly could. She always said she envied me, the simple life I'd led, though I never truly believed her.

How long I sat in the Dodge, surrounded by the sea of vehicles much flashier than the one I'd driven almost four hundred miles, I couldn't say. There were luxury cars made by those foreign companies like BMW, Mercedes-Benz, and Lexus, as well as what I always thought of as Common People Cars, those made by Ford and Toyota and Honda. And of course there were RVs. All were vacant, their owners inside playing poker or blackjack or keno or the slots, or else maybe taking in a show. I myself had never once been inside a casino, my upbringing in a poor family one that taught me to always save money, to never waste it.

The passenger seat was a mess of trash, all of which I ignored except for a pack of cigarettes and the phone. Those I stuck in my pockets, right there along with the wallet that wasn't mine. I opened the door but hesitated, thinking about the gun in the glove compartment. I didn't want to leave it there, worried it might fall in the wrong hands if someone tried breaking into the car. Then I laughed, realizing out of all the cars surrounding me, this rusted and beat-up Dodge would be the last thing somebody would want to steal.

I headed inside, where I was immediately bombarded with noise and brightness. I kept my head down, wanting nobody to see me. I felt completely out of place in my jeans and black T-shirt, wearing those sneakers that still had the spots of vomit on them. Damn it, I'd forgotten to clean those off. I really hoped nobody would notice, but the fact that it was all I thought about made me certain everyone was seeing it.

At the front desk, a clerk named Jason smiled and asked how he could help me this evening. The look in his eyes said that he'd been trained to use the same smile and expression on every person that walked through the hotel's doors, no matter how rich or poor or in the middle they happened to be.

I said, "Yes, hi, my name's Romeo Chase," feeling at once like a complete jackass, and all of a sudden I realized that this was just another one of Simon's jokes. Jason might pause to check his computer, but there would be no room waiting under that name. No, there would be no room at all, and then I'd just be standing there, with vomit on the toe of my right sneaker, looking like an idiot. Would they have security escort me out? I thought about the wallet. Was there even enough cash to stay one night in this place?

Just as I'd guessed, Jason began to check his computer. He typed something, moved his mouse once, looked back up at me. The smile never wavered.

"Ah yes, Mr. Chase, we've been expecting you. Your bag arrived earlier today."

I said, "My bag," completely oblivious. Then quickly nodded. "Yes, my bag."

"Hold on one second." Jason picked up a phone. He said a few words and then hung up, gave me another one of his plastic smiles. "It'll just be another minute."

I thanked him, started to back away, but thought of something and leaned forward. "I'm sorry, it's been a long day, but can you tell me how long I'm booked for? I forget what my secretary told me."

He glanced at the computer screen again. "Looks like two nights."

I nodded, thanked him again, and started to turn away just as a bellhop was approaching. In his right hand he carried a suitcase—a large black suitcase which seemed to express to anyone who cared that its contents belonged to someone with money, and a lot of it.

"Mr. Chase?" the bellhop asked, and I nodded. "Follow me, sir. I'll take you to your room."

He turned and led me to a bank of elevators. We waited along with a few other people until one opened up. An older couple—both who looked as if they'd traveled here via Winnebago—were discussing how much money they'd won playing the penny slots. Ignoring them, I stared forward at the panel of floor numbers. The one the bellhop had pressed was 7.

Eventually we reached my floor. The bellhop stepped aside, motioned for me to step out first. I obliged him then waited so he could lead me to my room. In his other hand a plastic keycard had appeared. He used it on the door, an electronic beeping sounded, and he pushed it open. Once again stepped aside so I could enter first.

The room was large and impressive. I immediately had the sense of someone who's someplace he really can't afford to be. Two nights I'd been booked here. What was I going to do in Reno all that time? Shit, what was I doing here to begin with?

The bellhop followed me into the room. He carefully set the suitcase on the luggage rack. Then he stood there, his hands clasped before him, asking if there was anything else I should need.

"No, I'm fine," I said, looking about the room. Then I noticed him just standing there, and I understood. I reached into my pocket for the change I'd gotten back at the gas station in Redding. I had a five and three ones, along with a scattering of change. I stared at them awhile, thought really hard, and ended up handing over the five.

"Thank you, sir," the bellhop said. He left without another word. The door closed behind him.

Leaving me alone with the suitcase.

Like the bathroom door, like the glove compartment, like the trunk, I didn't want to open it. But yet I knew I had no choice. This was just another part of the game, and while

Simon hadn't specifically told me to do anything yet, it was inferred. Besides, hadn't he said something to me before, after I'd lifted that Snickers bar? Something about having a package waiting for me at my destination?

In my head, Jen's voice echoed as she cried, *They cut off my—*

That was it. Just those four words. I heard her cry it again and again, like a broken record. I knew whatever filled that blank was waiting now in this suitcase. And I knew that as long as I could, I would refuse to open it.

SEVENTEEN

At some point the cell phone vibrated. By then I was seated in one of the chairs on the farthest end of the room, right beside the window. Curtains obstructed the view—a view I had yet peeked outside to see—but they for some reason reminded me of the curtains back at the Paradise, and though the air wasn't on full blast I was feeling quite cold.

The cell phone was in my pocket. I pulled it out, pressed the green send button.

Simon asked, "What are you waiting for?"

I didn't answer for the longest time. The room was completely silent. Earlier, I'd heard the muffled voices and foot-steps of people out in the hallway, but those had faded away what seemed like hours ago.

"I don't want to open it."

"Relax, Ben. The package I mentioned earlier hasn't arrived yet. The suitcase you've been staring at for the past fifteen minutes has been waiting for you since this morning. It's all part of the game." A pause, an invisible grin, then: "Nothing to worry about."

Simon disconnected before I could say—or not say—anything else. I held the phone to my ear for a while longer. I pushed myself out of the chair, staggered the few steps it took me to reach the bed, and stared down at the suitcase.

Like before, images had been invading my mind, different possibilities of what lay cramped inside the Samsonite. Questions like: *If all her bones were broken, could Casey's entire body fit in there?* and *If they just cut off Jen's leg and stuck it inside, would they have used packing material to keep it from moving?* Insane, terrible thoughts, yes, but I couldn't help myself.

Finally I leaned forward, undid the two clasps, and opened the suitcase.

It could have belonged to anyone, as far as I was concerned. Nothing like what had greeted me in the Dodge's trunk was inside here. Instead there were clothes: khakis and a white long-sleeved dress shirt, both encased in dry cleaning plastic; a pair of nice dress shoes, a belt, a red silk tie. Even fresh boxers, a fresh undershirt, and a leather bag which was all too familiar, sporting the Eagles logo, because it was my travel toiletry bag (something my parents had gotten me for Christmas when I was in high school and which I had kept ever since). Inside it was a stick of my deodorant, a small bottle of my shampoo, my toothbrush (and here you have to understand it wasn't a toothbrush that resembled mine, or was the same brand, but *my* toothbrush) as well as a tube of Crest. Even my—*my*—electric razor.

Beneath all of this was a small paper-wrapped package which contained two cell phone batteries. Below this, a folded piece of paper, the letters typed.

Ben:

   Hope you're having fun. I know everyone else is. A car will pick you up at 11:30. Dress appropriately.

Cheers,
Simon

I glanced at the clock on the bedside table, saw it was now almost eleven. I cursed, threw the note down, grabbed my Eagles travel bag, and headed for the bathroom.

EIGHTEEN

A half hour later I stepped back onto the lobby floor. I felt like a totally different person than the one who'd first walked in here with his head lowered. I'd shaved, showered, and the clothes fit just right.

Even though it was almost midnight on a Monday in October, the place wasn't dead. People were wandering around, some headed for the casino, others headed back to their rooms. Everyone looked happy, so much so it pissed me off, but at least the noise and brightness wasn't as intimidating as before.

Jason was still at the front desk. He was dealing with somebody on the phone, talking and nodding as he stared at his computer screen. I approached, dreading what I wanted to ask him but knowing I had no choice.

He noticed me standing there, smiled and raised a finger, waited thirty seconds until he was done with his call, then said, "Sorry about that, Mr. Chase. How may I help you?"

"Has a"—I cleared my throat—"package arrived for me?"

He didn't even hesitate, shaking his head at once and saying, "No, but I'll make sure to keep an eye out for when it arrives."

I thanked him, a sudden conflicting emotion of relief and dread flashing through me, and began to turn away.

"Oh, Mr. Chase?" Jason said. "Your car's waiting outside."

It was a black Lincoln Town Car, an older model but very well cared for. Its driver, a young guy with a mustache decked out in a black suit and driver's cap, opened the back door with a smile and a nod.

I slid in and the man closed the door and for a moment I was alone in the car, just sitting there staring ahead at the dash at the driver's name—Gerald—and picture ID and the car number in the usual spot. Over in the corner by the speedometer and gas gauge were two wallet-sized photographs. One showed two little girls, their brown hair in pigtails; the other showed the same two girls with a woman who was no doubt their mother.

The front door opened and Gerald slid in behind the wheel. Before he had even fully turned on the car and placed it in drive, I asked:

"Is that your family?"

He paused, at first not sure what I meant, then a second went by and he nodded. "Sure are."

"I couldn't really see the pictures well, but they look beautiful."

Gerald was quiet for another half-moment before he said, "Thank you," and got us rolling forward.

I stared out my window and didn't speak right away. I had made the man nervous, which hadn't been my intention. What I had intended, I wasn't even sure, but I wanted to say something, strike up some kind of conversation, and had royally messed that up.

"Where are we headed?" I asked.

Again, that half-moment pause, and then he said, "I'm not supposed to tell you."

"You're not?"

He shook his head, gave me a warm smile in the rearview mirror. "It's a surprise."

We drove for awhile on the expressway in silence, not even any light music playing, and when he took an exit I said:

"I have a wife and daughter, too."

He gave me another look in the rearview mirror, didn't say anything.

"You look surprised."

He shook his head.

"Why?"

He opened his mouth, shut it, opened his mouth again and said, "I just thought this whole thing was for your bachelor party. Like, your friends set this up and everything, based on where I'm taking you."

"Where are you taking me?"

He smiled again. "Remember, I'm not supposed to tell you."

"You can tell me."

"I'd rather not."

"My daughter's three and a half. How old are yours?"

He was quiet for another moment, no doubt debating whether he should continue the conversation, and I wondered just how strict Simon's instructions had been.

"Seven and nine," Gerald said finally.

"They must be a handful."

"At times. Still, I wouldn't trade it for anything in the world."

"How long have you been doing this type of work?"

"What does that mean, this type of work?"

"Just, you know, driving."

He gave me another look in the rearview and for a moment I thought that I'd screwed up whatever little friendship I'd made with this guy.

"Fifteen years," he said, "give or take."

"Do you like it?"

"It has its moments. What do you do for work, if you don't mind me asking?"

"I'm a painter."

"Like an art gallery painter or house painter?"

"House painter."

There was another moment of silence as we passed the buildings and cars in the city, the few people on the street, the area not quite looking like it was the best place to be at midnight.

I asked, "So where are you taking me?"

The smile in the rearview mirror again. "Sorry, you know I can't tell you."

"Sure you can."

"I can't. But it's actually not that far now anyway."

"How much farther?"

"Maybe ten blocks."

Eight blocks later I said, "Can you stop the car?"

"What?"

"Just let me out here."

"Uh …"

"You're not going to get in trouble. In fact"—I dug into my pocket, pulled out a twenty—"this will be an extra tip for your trouble. I'm sure you and your wife are already saving for your daughters' college tuitions, right? This could help."

We were stopped at a traffic light, and Gerald was turned, glancing back at me, still uncertain.

"Come on, take it," I said. "It'll be fine. I just hate surprises, so this way I can prepare myself."

Gerald didn't do anything for a couple long seconds, and then he took the twenty and said, "It's the Sundown Saloon, just two blocks up."

I thanked him, opened my door, stepped outside. The light changed and he moved forward, went down another block, turned and was gone.

I just stood there for another minute or so before I realized I had begun to shake. Whatever Simon had next in store for me, it was at the Sundown Saloon. Even from where I stood I could see the neon sign—an orange setting sun—but I didn't want to move. Not yet.

In my pocket, the cell phone vibrated.

I closed my eyes, cursed myself, pulled the phone out and answered it.

Simon said, "What do you think you're doing?"

"I needed some air. It was getting stuffy in the car."

"That wasn't what I told you to do."

"You really didn't tell me anything."

"Oh, I see. So we're playing semantics again, are we?"

I started walking forward. "I'm going, all right?"

There was a silence, and then Simon said, "O Romeo, Romeo. Wherefore art thou Romeo?" before he clicked off.

I paused, staring down at the screen, not sure what to make of this latest development. Whatever it was, it made me dread going into the Sundown Saloon even more. But I knew I had no choice, not if I ever wanted to see my family again, so I slipped the phone into my pocket and kept walking.

I hadn't even gone another ten steps before they came for me.

NINETEEN

They came at me from behind. They were strong and they were quick and one second I was on the sidewalk, headed toward whatever awaited me at the Sundown Saloon, the next second I was shoved forward and went sprawling down onto the pavement.

I reached out just in time so I didn't land right on my face but still I scraped my hands pretty bad on the sidewalk. Before I could get up one of them grabbed the glasses off my face and pressed my face against the sidewalk, keeping me down while someone else searched my pockets. I thought they were going for my money but it was the phone they grabbed and took away and I may have said, "Hey, don't," or something like that, I can't remember, but I said something and then one of them said, "This is for your own good," and before I knew it both of them grabbed me and lifted me to my feet just as a black utility van screeched up beside us. The side door opened and one of my assailants—there were two of them, one black, one white—said, "Come on, let's go," and they pushed me toward the van.

Suddenly they stopped and I didn't realize why at first—I could barely see a thing without my glasses—but then I heard the *dink!* and *ping!* of something against the parked cars and then, an instant later, a window shattered and the men pushed me down and reached into their pockets and pulled out guns and returned fire at whoever was shooting at them.

The shooting wasn't loud, not as loud as I thought it should be, and it took me another moment to realize that these men and the men they were shooting at had sound compressors so the gunshots sounded like nothing more than claps.

I was on the ground in a fetal position, my head ducked, my arms over my head, when suddenly there was a lull in the gunfire.

I risked a peek and saw one of my assailants heading for me but then the shooting started up again—*clap! clap! clap!*—and he turned away and dove into the van along with the other guy and the van's tires screeched as it sped away into traffic. There was honking and shouting and then the van was gone and footsteps hurried toward me and someone else grabbed me, someone I couldn't quite see.

"Are you okay?"

I nodded, thinking that this was the police, that Simon's number one rule was not to speak to the police, not if I ever wanted to see my family again.

"Shit," someone else said. "They got both the glasses and the phone."

A car suddenly pulled up. The two men dragged me toward the car. One of them opened the back door and the other threw me inside and climbed in after me and the door closed and the front door opened and the other guy climbed in and then the car was moving again, picking up speed into traffic.

"What happened?" I said, looking at the man in the back with me, at the driver and passenger up front. "Who are you?"

"Relax, Ben. Everything is going to be fine."

"How ... how do you know my name?"

The man touched his ear and said, "Yeah ... I know ... I

figured they might try to make a play, too ... I think we should switch locations ... I understand ... I'll let you know," and the entire time I sat there, breathing heavily, shaking worse than ever. The man's voice sounded familiar but I couldn't place it, not then, not after everything that had just happened.

I said, "Simon?"

The man ignored me. He said to the driver, "Head back and we'll drop him off. He wasn't that beat up."

The driver turned at the next intersection. The man looked back at me.

"Unfortunately all we have right now is an extra pair of glasses. We'll have to get a new cell phone to you later."

"Simon?"

The man ignored me again, reaching out and grabbing my chin and moving my head back and forth as he inspected my face.

"There really isn't any bruising, so you're lucky in that respect. Still, once you get inside, go to the restroom and clean up. Then go to the bar and order a Budweiser. Sit at the very end of the bar and wait. Got it?"

I nodded dumbly.

The man in the front passenger seat handed a black eyeglass case to the man in the back, who opened it and took out a new pair of glasses and handed them to me.

"See how they fit."

I put them on. Just like the other pair, these felt awkward and pinched my nose, but at least I could see clearly now.

"Simon?" I said again.

"Would you shut the fuck up? Get your head in the game. If you want to save your wife and daughter, play by the rules and don't try to mix things up again. Got it?"

I nodded dumbly again. The man's voice was still familiar but I couldn't place it. It wasn't Simon's voice, though; I knew that for a fact. Still, how did I know this man?

The car slowed and stopped and the man opened his door and stepped out and motioned me to do the same. I got out, realized we were right in front of the Sundown Saloon. Two blocks down, a police cruiser sat with its roof lights flashing, two officers on the sidewalk talking to witnesses.

"Don't even think about it," the man whispered.

"I'm not."

"Sure." The man stepped back, touched his ear—I now saw he wore a Bluetooth—and said, "Start the transmission." He got back into the car.

I stood there, watching the car pull away and drive down to the next block, disappear around a corner, then turned and stared at the two cops down the street just as another police cruiser pulled up. It hadn't been too long ago that the shooting occurred; they had made decent time, though it hadn't been soon enough.

Don't even think about it.

Right.

I entered the Sundown Saloon.

TWENTY

For lack of a better word, the Sundown Saloon was a dive. It was smoky and dim, people at tables and booths and the bar, talking and listening to what sounded like country music or just watching one of the half dozen TVs posted around the room.

I went directly toward the back where the restrooms were located. I stood at the urinal acting like I was taking a piss but was really waiting for the two guys who were already in here to finish up and leave. Once they were gone, I turned away and approached the sinks and stared at myself in the mirror.

Like the man in the car said, there wasn't much bruising. Mostly just some dirt on my cheek which had been pressed down onto the sidewalk. I took off the glasses, set them aside, turned on the water and cupped some in my hand. I splashed my face twice, wiped it with paper towels, went to put the glasses back on but stopped.

This is for your own good.

That was what one of my assailants had said to me right as they tried to get me into the van. Right before the shooting started and Simon's men came to my rescue.

The restroom door opened and an old biker came in coughing up a lung.

I slipped the glasses back on my face, left the restroom, and headed for the bar.

Just like the man that wasn't Simon told me to do, I ordered a Budweiser and waited at the end of the bar. I waited for nearly ten minutes, nursing the beer, before she arrived.

She was the type of woman that literally made heads turn. She came in through the entrance and everyone looked her way, even the women. She was tall and blond and gorgeous, wearing a tight black top with a short black skirt and black four-inch heels. She had the kind of flawless, beautiful face you'd expect to find on glossy fashion magazines at the checkout lines at the grocery store.

And she walked directly up to me.

"Romeo?" she asked.

For a moment my mind was a complete blank. Then I nodded.

She smiled and extended her petite hand. "I'm Juliet."

I shook her hand but didn't say anything. I *couldn't* say anything; this woman's beauty literally made me speechless.

The smile didn't leave her face. It was the kind of smile that knew it had power over people, especially men.

She asked, "Don't you want to buy me a drink?"

I nodded and motioned at the bartender. He came over almost instantly, eager to take the woman's order.

"A Cosmopolitan, please," she said.

The bartender gave me a wicked grin before he turned away to mix the drink. Amid the country music and all the talking, I heard the faint ringing of a telephone behind the bar.

"So," Juliet said, climbing up on the stool next to mine. "How long are you in town?"

Before I could answer (assuming I could even find my voice), the barman called out, "Are you Chase?"

I looked over to find him standing there with a portable phone held against his chest. I nodded and he said, "Call for you," and handed me the phone.

I sat there with the phone in my hand, not sure what to do. I glanced at Juliet and she smiled back at me and said, "I think I'll go freshen up," leaned over and kissed me on the cheek before standing up and heading toward the restrooms. I watched her go, unable to take my eyes off her swaying ass, still smelling a waft of her perfume left behind, and then placed the phone to my ear.

Simon said, "You're embarrassing yourself."

"What do you mean?"

"This isn't middle school, Ben. The time for shyness is over. Be a man and at least make conversation."

"What do you want me to say?"

"Oh, I don't know. Maybe start with something simple like 'How are you doing?' "

"Who were those people from earlier?"

"Trouble," Simon said, distaste in his voice. "Let's not worry about them right now, okay?"

"What do they want?"

"Didn't I just say let's not worry about them?"

I knew pushing Simon wasn't the best idea, so I decided to switch gears.

"The guy that gave me the glasses, I recognized his voice. He's the cop that stopped to check on me before I reached Doyle, isn't he?"

Simon chuckled. "Very good. You didn't think we'd chance an actual encounter with a real police officer now, would you? Too many ways things could go wrong."

"Then why have him there at all?"

"To keep you moving. If he hadn't shown up, you would probably still be there crying your eyes out."

The bartender came over with the Cosmopolitan. He set it on the bar and gave me another wicked grin, this time with a wink, before he turned away to take someone else's order.

"Does the bartender work for you too?"

"No."

"How about that driver from earlier?"

"No."

"And the girl?"

"No. But she is a pro, if it's not obvious already. And she's very expensive."

"I'm not going to sleep with her."

"Again, Ben, you're embarrassing yourself. Don't be such a boy scout."

"I will not do anything with her."

"What's the difference if it's your wife or this woman? A pussy is a pussy is a pussy, as Gertrude Stein once said."

I opened my mouth to say something else but then my eyes —which seemed to have been darting most of today, mostly to the glove compartment as I drove endlessly—darted now to my left hand. At the finger just between my middle and pinkie fingers. The one that should have had my wedding ring around it right this instant.

It was gone. In almost six years of marriage I'd never once taken it off, not even when I worked. I'd had the superstitious fear that if the ring were to come off I'd somehow wake up from whatever magnificent fantasy I was daydreaming, because surely my life couldn't be this great, this complete, surely a woman like Jen would never marry a guy like me, and surely the two of us would never produce a child as amazing and perfect as Casey.

I'd worn it ever since Jen put it on my finger, and it had become so much a part of me that I was so used to seeing it, so used to feeling it, I hadn't even noticed it was missing earlier today when I first woke up, or on the miles and miles and miles of driving. Did that make me a terrible person? Did it make me a terrible husband?

Simon said, "Well, Romeo?"

"I refuse."

"Your mouth says that but what about your body? You're only human. You have wants, needs, desires, just like everyone else. And like everyone else, those desires are sometimes dark. Sometimes they're very dark."

"I want to speak to my wife and daughter."

"If you care anything for your wife and daughter, you'll stop being a pussy and go fuck this woman. I don't even know why you're fighting me on this. You've seen all the different ways they do it on those websites. You have your own fetishes, the little things you always wanted to mention to Jennifer but always failed to in the end. Now here's your chance."

At the other end of the bar heads began to turn again and a moment later I saw Juliet emerge from the restrooms, headed directly my way. Her eyes were on me as she walked, that seductive smile on her face. She was just a girl, only twenty-one, maybe twenty-two, and even though I was just thirty-two I kept telling myself this was wrong. I thought of Casey and reminded myself that Juliet was somebody else's daughter, just another little girl who'd once thought herself a princess before the dark reality of the world came crashing down all around her and she began to sell her body for sex.

"Why are you doing this?" I asked, doing everything in my power to make my voice as calm and collected as possible, while inside I wanted to tear myself apart, I wanted to break-down and cry right here in front of everyone.

Simon said, "Goodbye, Ben."

There was a click and he was gone, and then the music and the talking and shouting of the bar enveloped me once more.

I set the phone on the bar and glanced up to see the barman walking toward me. I handed him the phone, wanting to say thank you while at the same time wanting to spit in his face. Instead, just before Juliet returned to her stool, I heard myself asking him for two shots of Southern Comfort.

"For you and the lady?" he asked, already reaching behind him for two small tumblers resting upside down on a towel. There was no reaction when he said *lady*, no disapproval or resentment at all in his eyes or face, which maybe meant he was used to men coming in here looking to hire pussy.

I shook my head, thinking of Jen, thinking of Casey, thinking of being with them just yesterday. I tried remembering everything we'd done together, everything we'd talked about, but it was all coming up blank.

"No," I said, ignoring Juliet as she climbed up onto the stool next to me, leaned over and kissed me again on the cheek. This time, out of nowhere, her hand touched my inner thigh and didn't leave. "Just for me." I threw three of the twenties down on the bar. "And keep them coming."

TWENTY-ONE

I don't want to think about what the rest of the night consisted of, what happened after several hours passed and Juliet asked if I was ready to go. We ended up going to some place, what may have been a motel or apartment or something, I can't even remember because by that point I'd been smashed.

She led me into the room and sat down on the bed, where she started undressing. I went immediately for the bathroom, where I fell beside the toilet to throw up. Nothing came. I just dry-heaved for the longest time, got up, looked at myself in the mirror and didn't recognize the man who stared back. Finally I washed my mouth, wiped my face, and stepped outside.

Juliet had taken off her nylons, had stripped off her top and skirt, and just lay there in her black bra and panties. And heels.

Christ, I remember thinking. *She still has on the heels.*

Shaking my head, I turned away, went for the door, opened it.

The man from earlier was standing there, the man who had impersonated a cop. He was standing off to the side so I couldn't see him full on, reaching out and holding me in place with a meaty, powerful hand.

I looked at him. He looked at me. He shook his head and pushed me back into the room and shut the door behind me. I turned back around to find Juliet still on the bed, now with her hand down her panties, pleasuring herself.

Okay, that's enough. Simon forced me to do what I ended up doing, but he can't force me to relate the events, so I won't. I've tried so hard keeping it from my mind—that terrible act of forced adultery—and I want to keep it gone. Besides, just as I'd soon learn, all of it was being broadcasted over the Internet anyway. Everything I did with that girl is out there somewhere. And even though I didn't know this at the time, I still thought about those two men who'd jumped me, what one of them told me before the shooting started; I thought about everything Simon had said he knew about me spending time on the Internet, and I felt like one of those girls. Why, I'm still not even sure, because Juliet should have been the one to feel like that instead. To feel like an object, just a simple means to an end. But no, for some reason I felt that way, and it made what I ended up doing to her feel even worse.

Eventually I found myself in a taxi, headed back to the Grand Sierra Resort. The city was lit up all around me but I barely noticed. I was in a daze, even more so than before when Juliet first walked into the Sundown Saloon and forced all those heads to turn. I was still feeling drunk but I kept thinking about everything I'd just done. I thought about Jen, about Casey, and I hoped wherever they were, they were safe.

When the driver dropped me off at the hotel, I gave him all the money I had left. I don't know how much that was. I'd spent all my money at the bar and was using some money Juliet had given me as I left, the girl saying that she'd been paid more than enough.

I wandered through the lobby toward the elevators but stopped when Jason called my name. He still stood behind the front desk, on the phone again, the mouthpiece against his shoulder to keep it muted. In his free hand was a small cardboard box.

With the worst dread I had ever felt, I approached the front desk.

"The package you mentioned before," Jason said. "It was delivered a few hours ago by courier."

He held the package out to me but I refused to take it.

"Sir?" There was sincere worry in his voice. "Are you okay?"

I nodded and took the package and hurried away toward the elevators.

A minute later I was on the seventh floor, inside my room. It felt much colder than before, just like in room six at the Paradise Motel. I sat down on the bed and held the small cardboard box in my hands. Like before, if I wanted to open it, I'd have to use my nails because I had no knife or scissors or key. And like before, I didn't want to open it.

But I knew I had no choice.

And I remembered I did have a key—the Dodge's, resting right on top of the TV along with the black and white glossy photograph of Jen and Casey bound and gagged. I opened the box and let the Styrofoam peanuts fall all over the place. I pulled out what was inside.

I dropped it at once.

It was a finger. A human finger. Delicate and slight, it still had something attached to it at the end, right near where it had been cut off from its hand. Something that matched the thing that hadn't been on my finger when I woke up this morning, in the middle of what could only be called hell.

A wedding ring.
My wife's wedding ring.

PART II

NO OUTLET

TWENTY-TWO

Meeting the woman who would become my wife was just one of those auspicious events that make us believe the world may not be a completely random and chaotic mess after all. She was a friend of a friend; I was a friend of a friend. There had been other girls there, girls who'd acted stuck up and refused to introduce themselves to me, to instead have Clive Goldman— one of my closest friends from high school, who'd invited me out to visit the spring after I dropped out of college—or one of their friends do the introductions. They were good-looking and, below their well-manicured façades, nice and a few could even have been called sweet. Clive had even told me which girls were the easiest to talk to and who were just the easiest, and while normally I would have taken his advice to heart, this time I didn't.

This time my eye was on one girl in particular.

Her name was Jennifer Abele and from what I understood she didn't go to DePaul like Clive but someplace else, some Ivy League school. She came from an extremely rich family, her father being an important figure in the city of Chicago. We met briefly one day and I'd been perplexed, just staring at her because she was so beautiful and I knew it was one of those things where I was bound to wake up any moment, because occurrences like these just don't happen, or else are so completely rare that they might as well not happen. I'd say it was love at first sight, but that would not only be cliché, it would be wrong, because there really is no such thing when you think about it. Still something had been there, something that caused us two days later to start talking. A group of us had decided to walk the city and went down to the Lincoln Park Zoo. I'd been meaning to go up to her but kept losing my nerve until eventually it was she who made the first move, Jennifer Abele, daughter of the renowned Howard Abele who would someday offer me half a million dollars to break up with his daughter and turn my back on her forever.

"I don't know about you," she said, coming up to stand beside me, "but I'm not a big fan of elephant shit. I mean, it just reeks, don't you think?"

At first I didn't even think she was talking to me. Then I looked over, saw her staring back at me, trying to keep a straight face, and I just burst out laughing.

"I know we were introduced before," she said, "but I'm Jen." She extended her hand and I shook it, not being able to find my voice for the longest time. Then finally it came, and I said, "I'm Ben," and that was how it started, how we began talking. But it wasn't like there were any instant fireworks. Far from it. As it turned out she had a fiancé, a guy named Jeremy she'd dated since high school and who now attended Yale. She was getting married in the fall, would probably get pregnant and have to settle down, which would play hell on her career, because she wanted to be a lawyer. No way, I told her, I want to be a lawyer too—but then caught myself a few seconds too late, when she asked me if that was true. Well no, I had to admit, the defeat apparent in my voice, I had *wanted* to be a lawyer. Oh really? she asked. What happened to change my mind?

But of course I didn't tell her. That would come years later, about a year after I learned her little dark secret, feeling as if I owed it to her … though, to be honest, I never did tell her the whole truth.

By the time the week of my visit was up Jen and I had grown a strong rapport. The woman I'd first thought was an angel would turn out to be nothing more than a friend, and a long distant friend at that, because on the last day we exchanged email addresses, Jen telling me to stay in touch, and while I had hope, I also knew she was just being nice. Still, on the long drive back home, she was all I thought about.

I tried forgetting her, shoving the scrap of paper she'd written her email address on in the bottom of my desk with no intention of contacting her, but she emailed me that first week. We stayed in touch, talking about random things, until one day months later the phone rang. My mom answered and she called for me, and I took it in my bedroom, expecting one of only a few friends from high school I still kept in contact with. It had been none of them, had instead been Jen, who was in tears, who had just found out her fiancé had cheated on her, had in fact *been* cheating on her, and she wanted to get away, just wanted to leave Chicago, and could she come visit me in Pennsylvania?

I almost told her no. I don't know why, but for some reason I thought I was dreaming and that I might as well not allow this dream to continue any further, because eventually I would wake up and realize just how pathetic my life really was, and to tell her no now would at least keep the majority of my pathetic existence at bay.

"Yes," I said, sitting on the edge of my bed, "of course you can."

She flew out a few days later and stayed at a Holiday Inn (which was no doubt the first Holiday Inn she'd ever stayed in). I took time off work, taking her down to Philly, down to Baltimore, up to Harrisburg. Hershey Park would be closing for the season in a month and we spent a day there too. Things felt just as they had back in Chicago, like we had been friends since we were born, and that friends was all we were ever going to be. Then, just two days before she was supposed to leave, I couldn't stand it anymore and found myself leaning in to kiss her. We were leaving the mall, walking through the parking lot, and I'd just unlocked her door. I tried to stop but had apparently lost all control over my body and continued, sealing the deal and ensuring our friendship would not continue from this moment onward.

But the strangest thing happened: she kissed me back, and like that, the world began to have meaning again.

The kiss, while deep, didn't last long, and when we both pulled away she peered up at me and smiled.

"I was wondering how long I was going to have to wait for that."

Long distance relationships, as a rule of thumb, almost never work out (this was the reason why my girlfriend the last two years of high school, Marissa, broke my heart just days after we graduated). Somehow ours did. Jen had to finish school, then had to go to law school, because her life's dream was to become a lawyer. The fact that we were together and that I was a painter and would always be a painter, no matter what happened, never bothered Jen in the slightest. Which, as my dad told me one night, right after he'd been put in the hospital because of his angina, meant Jen was one special lady and I would be an idiot to think otherwise.

I met her father only three times, the first on one of my few visits to Chicago, when Jen brought me over to the mansion she'd grown up in.

Howard Abele was always a busy man, so much so he barely glanced at me when Jen introduced us. He was short and slim, wore glasses and had his hair combed to the side; he had a beak nose and piercing eyes and seemed to have been born in a suit. He didn't shake my hand and hurried past, saying he was late for a meeting.

The second time came three years later when I approached him to ask for his permission to marry his daughter. He'd simply shaken his head and said no, walked away without a glance back. I had stood there stunned, speechless, unsure what to do next, but then Jen's mother came to the rescue. She told me of course I had permission to marry her daughter; as long as I made Jenny happy, then she didn't care what we did.

Unfortunately Claire Abele never attended our wedding, which was in Pennsylvania. She was killed in a hit-and-run only a few months later. I'd gone with Jen to the funeral, which was the third place I saw her father, and which afterward he'd taken me aside and handed me the check for five hundred thousand dollars. It was more money than I would ever see at one time in my entire life. More money than my parents would ever hope to earn even if they worked every day of their lives and saved every dollar and penny. I briefly thought about all the debt my parents had, about all the debt I had, and how even a tenth of this check would help improve things. Then, with these thoughts running tandem in my mind, I ripped the check up right in front of him. For some reason I hadn't wanted to tell Jen, but she'd gotten it out of me sensing I was holding something back, and from that day forward she cut off all ties with her dad. Refused to speak to him again. Suffice it to say on our wedding day, her side of the chapel was quite sparse, so our guests had been encouraged to sit wherever they pleased.

I'm not sure what else I want to say about Jen. Obviously I could go on forever, and that doesn't even include the three and a half years after Casey was born and our family really became complete.

But there, speaking of completeness, I should mention about the night, only a month before we got married, where Jen and I were lying in bed and I said something about us being soul mates. I don't know what we were talking about but I said the words and immediately felt stupid, thinking they were beyond cheesy.

"Soul mates don't exist," she whispered. We were spooning, my arm around her, holding her close.

I said, "Oh," a little more than just disappointed (wanting to kick myself, really), and she had turned over so we could stare at each other. Around the room were a half dozen scented candles, and in the soft light I stared at the curve of her face, her dimples, the slight birthmark just beneath her chin.

She said, "Don't say it like that. We're so much more than soul mates."

And then in the dark and quiet of our apartment bedroom, Jen told me the story of Plato's Symposium, which was a recreation of a discussion among Greek philosophers concerning love. One of the philosophers there, Aristophanes, said that originally there weren't two sexes, but three. That at the beginning of time there had been men, women, and beings of both man and woman, an androgynous sex. All of these creatures were round, with four hands and four legs and two faces on opposite sides of one head. They were strong and mighty, and it was said they dared to challenge the gods. Naturally Zeus wasn't too pleased about this, and he came up with a plan to stop these creatures. He decided he would allow them to exist, but would weaken their power by cutting them all in half. When he did this the male creatures he cut apart became homosexuals, who pursued other males. The same with the female creatures. But the androgynous sex was split up so one half was male and the other half female, and pursued each other. So, according to the myth, we search the world for our other half, so when we find each other we can become whole again.

"But isn't that just like soul mates?" I asked, once she was done speaking. I loved listening to her talk, the soft lilt of her voice, the way she always knew which words to speak and in which order to say them. It was what made her such a great lawyer, because it never took her long to formulate her argument, and to stick by it no matter what.

"Maybe," she whispered. She leaned forward and lightly kissed me on the lips; I could taste the lip-gloss she'd applied earlier, still present after our lovemaking. "Either way you're my other half."

"Oh yeah? And how do you know that?"

"You laughed at my stupid elephant manure joke when no one else did."

The next day I went to the jewelry store and asked if I could change the inscription. I didn't even know if it would be possible. If it was possible, I figured it was going to cost a lot, probably more than I could even afford, but luckily they hadn't done Jen's yet, which had been a simple and generic: TO JEN WITH LOVE and our wedding date. Instead I had them change it to: TO JEN, MY OTHER HALF.

It was the first thing I looked for that Tuesday morning, sitting in my room on the seventh floor of the Grand Sierra Resort, as I held my wife's finger in my hands.

I gently took off the ring the same way I'd first put it on, not trying to squeeze it over the flesh that had been so savagely cut off. It had gone pale in the hours it took to ship and didn't feel like a living human finger at all. But still I knew it was hers, and when I finally slid the ring off and set the finger down on the bed, I moved close to the lamp on the bedside table to check.

And yes, there it was, the inscription I'd had put there the night after Jen told me the story she'd heard in one of her classes at school. That had also been the same night she woke from just one of her many nightmares. It was the first time I became aware of them at least, and she said she hadn't had them for the longest time, not since we'd been together. She had assumed, or maybe just hoped, being with me kept them away.

While we'd been together almost four years she finally came out with something she had been holding back, what she said had been a dark period in her life. How in high school she'd been heavily into drugs, so much so that one night she actually tried to kill herself. Her parents had gotten her help, forced her to talk to psychiatrists, but all that eventually happened was that she was put on permanent antidepressants. Just a chemical imbalance in her head, the doctors told her, and that imbalance combined with the medication sometimes caused her to have nightmares. These nightmares would, over the course of the next eight years, become as much a part of my life as they were Jen's, because it would be my job to wake her up in the middle of the night when she began thrashing around. No bogeymen attempted to kill her in these nightmares, no obscene monsters chased her down endless dark passages. In these nightmares the monsters were those of the real world, serial killers and rapists who chased her, and who I eventually had to save her from. I'd wake her and hold her and tell her everything was okay, just as I soon ended up doing with Casey when she would cry out in the middle of the night. Though my daughter never told me what chased her in her nightmares, I began to suspect they were not the unnatural kind. That really, in all nightmares, the bogeymen and monsters are not unnatural at all, but are merely façades for the real monsters of the world. And to each of them, to Jen and to Casey, holding them and comforting them as best I could, I had told them that the monsters weren't real, that they couldn't hurt them, that everything would be okay.

But now it seemed I'd been lying to them this entire time, because the monsters had come. They had come and now they'd taken my family, they had cut off my wife's finger and sent it to me in a box. Only God knew what else they'd done, what other packages were just waiting to be shipped my way. And the worst part was these monsters wanted me to do things, do these terrible things to save my family, and the more I thought about it, the more I was beginning to believe I would never see them again.

TWENTY-THREE

Exhaustion must have knocked me out. The last thing I remembered was sitting on the bed and holding Jen's ring and crying. This was followed by darkness, a darkness which thankfully brought no dreams. Then, in that darkness, the soft and faint ringing of a telephone.

I opened my eyes.

I was lying on top of the comforter, still in the clothes from last night. I'd put my tie back on when I left wherever Juliet had taken me, something I didn't even remember doing. Jen's ring was on the comforter, just inches away. At the foot of the bed were the cardboard box and Styrofoam peanuts. And a finger, which from this far away didn't even look real—though I realized a second later why this was: I wasn't wearing my glasses.

The lamp beside the bed and the lamp in the corner were still on, but their light was now enhanced by the sun, which was fighting to get past the closed curtains for all it was worth.

The phone continued ringing, in the same spot as yesterday —to my right, on the bedside table, right next to the alarm clock.

I sat up but immediately lay back down. My head, which had been pounding since I opened my eyes, began pounding even harder. I rolled over and squinted at the clock. Almost noon.

The phone continued to ring, almost the same pitch and tone as the one back at the Paradise Motel. When I answered this one, I didn't expect to hear a desk clerk's voice giving me my wake-up call. Score one for me, I was right.

"Well, well," said Simon, his voice sounding joyous and refreshed, "good afternoon to you, Ben. Did you sleep well?"

Despite the drums beating in my head, I slowly sat up. "You fucking cut off my wife's finger."

"Again, semantics. Physically yes, I did cut off Jennifer's finger, while technically no, you did. Remember what I said about following the rules? You just needed a little, let's say, unfriendly reminder. By the way, we were also going to include her engagement ring but it was just so … pathetic. Seriously, what did you spend on it, fifty bucks? I really can't believe she accepted it."

"Fuck you."

Simon chuckled. "Speaking of which, did you enjoy yourself last night? I'd wanted to call you when you got back but liked watching you cry even more."

I was silent, refusing to give him what he wanted. Out in the hallway, I heard the soft shushing of footsteps, the murmur of voices. The pounding in my head had subsided some, bringing on the pounding in my entire body. My back, my legs, even my arms: they were all sore.

Simon said, "It is a shame what happened to that poor girl. She seemed like such a sweetheart, didn't she? I mean, underneath all that moaning and grunting."

"What the hell are you talking about?"

"Turn on the TV. Channel six."

I hung up the phone and in one fluid motion got up and

made my way to the television. The remote was lying on top, right beside the black and white photograph of Jen and Casey. I paused just momentarily, staring at the picture for a couple seconds, before realizing I couldn't really see them at all. Not without my glasses, which I had to go back to the bed for. They'd come off sometime during the night, and at first I couldn't find them. A few moments later I spotted them on the carpet, in the space between the bed and the wall, and I grabbed them and put them on and went back to the picture.

My wife and daughter, both staring at the camera, their mouths gagged, tears in their eyes and running down their faces. Had they cut off Jen's finger then, or had they merely promised her it would happen when I failed to comply with whatever crazy demands they gave me? What had they promised would happen to Casey?

Hands shaking, I replaced the picture on top of the TV, grabbed the remote, and seconds later had tuned into channel six. The news was already in progress. But it wasn't Juliet's face that was currently on the screen as a newscaster spoke.

"Police have already identified the man as Gerald Newcomer, a thirty-three-year-old cab driver. The victim, a young woman who police haven't yet identified, was brutally assaulted and then strangled to death."

Gerald's face—it was there only briefly, what looked like his driver license's photo—disappeared as the second newscaster went on to the next story. I had missed most of the segment that Simon wanted me to see, but I had seen enough.

I lifted the remote—my hand still shaking—and turned off the TV just as the phone on the bedside table began to ring.

I made it there in five strides, tearing the phone out of its cradle, and growling, "You piece of shit."

"Careful now, Ben. For all you knew I was room service asking if you wanted your burger medium or rare."

"Why did you kill her?"

"Simply tying up loose ends."

"And Gerald?"

"His unfortunate demise is all thanks to you."

I sat down on the edge of the bed, facing the closed curtains. The little lines of sunlight that fell on the carpet and walls had stretched.

Simon said, "He was supposed to drop you off right at the Sundown Saloon. Those were his instructions, plain and simple. But greed changed his mind."

"He had a wife and two daughters."

"You say that like I should give a shit."

"He"—I shook my head—"he had nothing to do with this."

"And what is 'this'? Is 'this' life? Is 'this' the game? Enlighten me, Ben."

I just sat there on the bed, watching the lines of sun.

"You need to understand that we're not fucking around here. We will do whatever it takes to make sure you play by the rules. Yes, that man had a wife and two daughters, and right now that wife believes her husband raped and murdered a prostitute before killing himself. Trust me, the crime scene is very clean. The detectives working it aren't going to lose a second of sleep over it. As far as they're concerned, it's an open-and-shut case."

"And what if I were to call the police right now and tell them the truth?"

I said the words before I could even think twice about them —my body shaking even more, adrenaline coursing through my veins—and immediately shut my eyes and cursed myself.

"Don't be an idiot," Simon said. "You may be the star of this show, but you're not a hero."

"What are you talking about? What show?"

Simon ignored me. "Downstairs when you check out there will be two items waiting for you—a package and an envelope.

The package will contain a new cell phone and a new wallet, with enough money to get you to your next destination. The envelope will contain a valet ticket for your new car."

"I want to speak to my wife again."

"I'm afraid at the moment that's not possible."

"Then let me speak to my daughter."

"Sorry, can't help you there either."

"Who were those men from last night?"

"Trouble," Simon said, sounding more irritated now than ever before. He waited a beat and said, "You still want a chance to win back Jennifer and Casey, don't you?"

"Yes."

"Then I suggest you take a shower and get dressed."

"What else are you going to make me do?"

"You say that like you aren't enjoying yourself. But I saw you last night, Ben. You were enjoying yourself quite a lot, weren't you?"

"Last night …"

"Yes?"

"The police are going to find my DNA."

Simon was quiet for a moment, then chuckled and said, "You mean when she sucked you off? I wouldn't worry about it. She was a prostitute, for Christ's sake."

I closed my eyes, didn't say anything. My head had begun to pound again, those drums stressing the fact that the natives were getting restless. The soreness in my body had seemed to dissipate, but I knew the moment I stood it would return.

"I'm not here to reassure you," Simon said. "I'm here to tell you what you need to do if you ever want to see your family again. But ask yourself this—have you ever been to jail? Have you ever been arrested for anything a day in your life?"

"No," I said, shaking my head slightly. I was staring down at the carpet, watching those lines of sunlight grow longer and longer.

"That's right. Which means your prints are not on some police database. Neither is your DNA. You've spoken to the police before—how could you forget your time at college?—but again, they don't have your prints. God, Ben, you have to stop watching *CSI*. This is the real world."

I was silent again, my eyes now closed. The pounding had subsided even more.

"Okay, get yourself cleaned up. Make sure to flush your wife's finger, unless you want the maid to find it. Keep the ring if you want, I don't care. But the last thing you need right now is for anyone from that bar last night remembering what you look like."

I opened my eyes, stared down at the carpet, at those growing lines of sunlight.

"That would be bad, Ben. That would be very bad. Despite Gerald being the prime suspect in an open-and-shut case, there's always the chance the police might want to speak to witnesses."

I stared down at those growing lines of sunlight and thought of those two men from last night.

This is for your own good.

Simon said, "Are you following me so far?"

I swallowed. "Yes."

"Good. Now before we say goodbye, I need to ask you one more thing."

"What?"

"Are we having fun yet?"

TWENTY-FOUR

Jason wasn't at the front desk when I checked out. Instead it was a young woman named Marni who smiled at me as she handed me the package and envelope.

"Leaving a day early, are we?" she asked pleasantly as she took my keycard. It was an innocuous enough question but still it unsettled me. I had been booked for two nights. Clearly Simon had had other plans for me.

I nodded but said nothing. The package—a small cardboard box—was not heavy at all but still felt like it weighed a ton.

"Did you have a pleasant stay here in Reno?"

The lobby was much busier than I'd seen it last night. I was wearing the same thing I'd worn yesterday on my drive, the same boxers and socks, all the way down to the sneakers—which, before leaving, I'd cleaned and scrubbed off any traces of vomit. The rest of the clothes were in the suitcase, along with Jen's finger that I hadn't found the heart to flush. (I think I was still under the impression that, when this was all over, the doctors might be able to reattach it.)

I nodded again. When she asked if I would like a receipt, I said, "No thank you," and turned and walked away.

By a pair of empty chairs, I set the suitcase aside and inspected the items. Both were addressed to Romeo Chase. I opened the cardboard box, thinking it might be another body part even though Simon had already told me what was inside. Just like he said, another cell phone and a wallet. The wallet contained five hundred dollars in crisp twenties.

I put the wallet in my pocket. Turned on the phone. Waited a minute for it to fully power up and find a signal, then waited another minute for it to vibrate.

Simon said, "Are you waiting for an invitation?"

I glanced around the lobby, at the people walking back and forth, at the employees, at the cameras near the ceiling.

"What's going to happen to the Dodge?"

"Don't worry about it."

"And the gun?"

"I said don't worry about it."

"Not worrying about it isn't as easy as you make it sound."

I stuffed the cardboard box in the closest trashcan and headed toward the main entrance. Two valets were waiting there, and I handed one of them the ticket.

As I waited, I said into the phone, "Should I expect any surprises in this car's trunk?"

"You should always expect surprises, Ben. That's the true meaning of life. But no, besides a spare tire and jumper cables, there will be nothing waiting for you back there. We've already gotten past the establishing part of the game."

"The establishing part."

"Well of course, Ben. You watch movies, don't you? You watch TV. You know that if the viewer's not sucked into the presentation within the first minute or so they're bound to change the channel. And do you know what that means? Ratings go down, advertisers jump ship, and soon that show's canceled. Or that movie's yanked from the theaters. That's all it comes down to nowadays, you know. Advertising."

I glanced around, made sure the other valet and any patrons were out of earshot before I said, "So that message on the bathroom door, that doll and all the fake blood in the truck, it was all just, what, for ratings?"

"You could say that. But it's mostly for the audience's benefit. Keeping you on your toes keeps them on their toes. Now that we've established just what kind of game this is, how far you're willing to go to save your family, we have our set audience. They're excited to see what will happen next. That's how producers keep any show going. By the promise of what's to come. And believe me, with the stakes raised like they are, the next part of the game is a doozy."

A black Ford Taurus pulled up, and the valet who'd taken my ticket got out. I had nothing but twenties in the wallet so I tipped him with one of those.

"Thank you, sir," he said. "We hope to see you again at Grand Sierra Resort real soon."

I said nothing and got in the car. The mileage showed less than one hundred miles and the interior still had that new car smell. I put the car in gear and drove out toward the highway.

"Where am I going now?"

"Do you really think I'm going to answer that question?" Simon chuckled. "You just don't get our relationship yet, do you?"

"We don't have a relationship."

"Perhaps. But as long as you remember that I tell you what to do, you do what I tell you, then everyone will be happy. Because otherwise, how are you going to know what to do next? Do you even have the slightest clue what it is?"

"I can only guess."

"Come on now, Ben, have I gotten that predictable? If so, maybe we have started a relationship after all. I mean, even though your wife and daughter are being held captive, there's no reason you and I can't be friends."

I came to the intersection and stopped and in a bored tone said, "Left or right?"

When Simon spoke again, the fun was gone from his voice and he was all seriousness now, all business.

"Get on 80 and head east. Keep driving until you can't drive anymore. If I were you I'd get something to eat first. You're looking pale, Ben. The last thing we need right now is you falling unconscious behind the wheel."

I must have pissed him off, or maybe just irritated him enough so he was closing in on disappointment, because he didn't wait for me to say anything else, he didn't even say good-bye. There was just a click and he was gone. I was alone, just me and this new car. I set the phone aside and pulled out into traffic, doing everything I could to forget Gerald's warm smile last night when he told me it was a surprise, and Juliet's seductive smile when she asked, *Don't you want to buy me a drink?*

TWENTY-FIVE

I spent the next eleven hours driving. Yesterday I'd thought I was sick of the endless roads and highways, but it was nothing compared to the miles and miles and miles I was seeing now.

Hoping for a distraction, the radio kept me company. When I found a station I liked—these were mostly hard rock stations, the kind that played Zeppelin and Floyd and Cream —I'd stick with it until it started cutting out so much I could hardly tell what song was playing. Then I'd do another search, find another station, and keep it on again as long as I could. Really it wouldn't have mattered what songs were playing, just as long as there was something in the background that took my mind off the past forty-eight hours. But it didn't work. I kept thinking of Jen, Casey, Gerald and Juliet. I kept thinking of the two men who had jumped me, who had taken my glasses and the cell phone, and who had said it was for my own good. And then there was the life back home, the world that was constantly going no matter what was happening to me and my family. William and Cassandra Johnson had no doubt found a new painter by now, had contracted him out to make the Tudor look just like they dreamed. Marshall was probably doing his thing too, figuring nothing was wrong. The same about the people at Jen's work, the people at Casey's preschool.

I no longer had the carton of Marlboros I'd bought yesterday; those had been left in the Dodge. I picked up a new carton at the first gas station I came to, smoked every twenty minutes.

The desert was endless, nothing on the jagged horizon except the promise of more rock and sand and dead looking grass. Sagebrush dotted the view along the highway, a busy cover of silver-gray. The sky was mostly clear, an occasional aimless cloud blocking the heavy and angry glare of the sun for a few minutes at a time.

I was approaching Elko around seven o'clock when the sky was really starting to lose its light and the sun was lowering into the horizon. I wasn't even hungry but forced myself to stop anyway, to gas up and use one of the many twenties at a nearby restaurant. For some reason I expected the food to taste better because it was in a place where there were car dealerships and movie theaters and doctor's and dentist's offices. It didn't.

Back on 80 then, passing through Deeth, Wells, Oasis. I entered Utah, went through Wendover, surrounded by more sagebrush and desert. The radio, while proving a close but unreliable companion, was beginning to get on my nerves. I kept glancing at the phone on the passenger seat, waiting for it to ring. As much as I hated Simon I could at least put up with listening to his dark and unctuous voice than to be left with my own thoughts.

Then, just as I was passing the Great Salt Lake, he called.

"Miss me?"

"What do you want now?"

"Oh, nothing. Just figured you were lonely. How's the drive so far?"

I didn't say anything. As I was nearing the city, traffic had begun picking up. There was less distance now between me and everybody else, and like usual, the assholes going five miles below the speed limit blocking lanes.

"Are you a Mormon, Ben?"

I'd been wrong before, I realized. I would have been content with my own thoughts.

"Is there a right or wrong answer?"

"No, just curious."

"Then no."

"Ah, but do you believe in God?"

"I don't know. I used to go to church. We sometimes still do."

"But going to church and believing are two different things, no? Besides, in our modern age, God is all but nonexistent. Yes people go to church and say they believe in God, but He's not what they worship. Do you have any idea what they worship instead?"

I was silent, already tiring of Simon's voice.

"Speaking of church and God," Simon said, "I meant to ask you what you thought of the bible back at the motel? Did you get the Book of Job reference? Maybe it was a bit too much, but I thought it added nice foreshadowing. Don't you?"

Still I was silent.

Simon sighed. "Do you really want to make this difficult?"

"What do you want me to say?" I asked.

"For starters, how about you answer my original question. Do you have any idea what people worship instead of God?"

"I have no idea," I said. The radio was still on, attempting to numb my mind in the background. I switched it off.

Simon said, "Sure you do," the grin clear and proud in his voice. "We live in a celebrity-driven world. We worship actors and singers and even politicians who are just like us, who set their hearts on becoming famous and just managed to catch a break and now bitch and moan about being in the constant spotlight. It's quite pathetic, really, when you think about it. Oh, by the way, a few of them are even watching you now."

"Explain what that means. You said before that I'm playing a game to fulfill the desire in others' hearts and souls. What desires are those?"

"Please, Ben, don't be stupid. You know exactly what they are. Which brings us to what else people worship. Television, music, computers, even automobiles. Tell me, which porn stars do you worship? I'm sure you have at least one or two you think about when you're jerking off."

"I don't want to talk to you anymore."

"Yeah, well, Simon says you have no choice, so you have no choice. Now spill it. And don't tell me Jenna Jameson. Please be more original than that."

I said nothing and just continued driving. Now that I'd entered a place where the population was over one hundred thousand I'd taken off the cruise control.

Simon said, "All right, how about you at least tell me something else. I'd asked you before why you went back to painting. And you never did answer me."

"I want to speak to my wife and daughter."

"Soon, Ben. You'll speak to them soon. But that won't be for at least another day. Depends on how long and how far you drive. You're doing quite well, by the way, not going too much over the speed limit and such. Last thing you need right now is for some cop to pull you over, yes?"

"My wife and daughter," I said. "Let me speak to them."

"Sure, Ben. But first tell me which one you love more. Tell me that and I'll have them on the phone in a minute."

I disconnected the call and tossed the phone on the passenger seat. The action didn't hit me until a few seconds later, when my mind caught up with everything, and I thought: *What the fuck did I just do?* I could already picture them approaching Jen with wire cutters, could picture her crying and screaming for them to stop.

"Stupid," I murmured. I punched the top of the steering wheel. "Stupid, stupid, stupid."

The cell phone vibrated. I grabbed it at once.

Simon said, "What the fuck do you think you're doing?"

"I don't want to play your stupid mind games."

"I understand that, Ben, but the thing is, you don't have a choice. Unless, that is, you want either Jennifer or Casey to die. Is that what you want?"

My voice was hardly a whisper: "No."

"What was that? I can't hear you."

"No." A little louder now, but not quite.

"That's better. I'll let this one slide, because your little stunt took balls, and I respect that. I'll tell you, no one's ever hung up on me like that before."

I didn't know what to say to this, so I said nothing.

"Okay, Ben, you win. I'll talk for a little. I'll educate you on the nature of human beings. I'll even give you a brief history of television and reality TV. Say, you watch reality TV?"

I knew just what kind of risk my hanging up on him was before; it had been stupid and reckless and I'd been convinced for a minute there that both Jen and Casey were as good as dead. Now I had to step cautiously. Simon said he was giving me a free pass but that didn't mean shit. He was irritated—this much was clear from his voice—and I had to do everything in my power to calm him down.

Simon said, "Well?"

I started to speak, realized my throat had gone dry. Glanced down at the two empty water bottles on the passenger seat, wished I'd picked up more during my last stop. "Sometimes," I said finally. "Seems like nearly everything on TV today is a reality show."

"Yes, it does seem that way, doesn't it. And do you know why that is?"

"I have no idea."

"Well, Ben, I'm sure you do have *some* idea. But regardless, reality TV has been around since the beginning of TV. It's simply showing humans acting natural. It's called the news."

"The news."

"That's right. What does the news do? It reports ongoing events. And nine times out of ten, what are those events based on? Come now, Ben, you can do it."

"I … I'm not sure."

"This is pathetic. You're not even trying." Simon did another one of his over dramatic sighs and said, "Crime, war, corruption—that's what makes up nine out of ten news stories, give or take. Ever since the beginning we humans have been intrigued by the suffering of others, the corruption of others. Basically, anything that's happening to anybody else but ourselves. We love to watch that, and do you know why?"

A yawn hit me, the first sign that I'd been driving much too long. What I really needed, I decided, was another cigarette, which I'd light up the moment I was done with this fuck.

Simon was waiting for me to respond, so I took a long moment to think about it and then said, "Voyeurism."

There was a sound in the background, an echoing sound that at first made no sense. Then it hit me. Simon was clapping.

"Excellent, excellent. You get a star for today. That's exactly right. We're the only species that likes to watch others without those others knowing it. That's what the news is. That's what reality shows are all about. But remember, we're a celebrity-driven world, so these stupid producers think we want reality shows with celebrities, but that's not really the case. Voyeurism is what it's all about. Watching normal people, just like you and me, and seeing how they react to different situations."

I'm nothing like you, I wanted to say but didn't. Instead I asked, "So that's what this is, huh? Just another reality show? When do I get to sign the release forms and negotiate my contract?"

"I'm sorry, but what was that? Was that a *joke*? Did Benjamin Anderson just make a *joke*?"

I was silent. I'd begun miles and miles back—mostly in my hotel room at the Grand Sierra Resort—to understand Simon only wanted to push me as far as he could. If I started pushing back there might be problems, and not just for me, but for Jen and Casey. And with the constant touch of my wife's wedding ring in my jeans pocket, it was enough to keep me quiet when Simon started up.

"No," he said, after a couple of beats, "this isn't another reality show. Far from it. Reality shows are never ever really real. That's the fault in them."

"But all of this," I said, keeping my voice steady, "is being set up by you and whoever else. None of it's real. You're just a … a producer telling me what to do."

"Perhaps I am a producer, Ben, but you are so much more than an actor, or a contestant. You are a true and real human being. You're a man of wax, for Christ's sake. You stealing that Snickers bar was just as real as you fucking that now dead prostitute. A few strings were pulled in the pro's case, but you were the one that stuck your cock in her."

"But I had no choice," I said, my teeth now gritted. "You forced me to do … to do all of that."

"Did I force you, Ben? Did I really? I don't think so. The gun was, figuratively speaking, at your wife and daughter's head, not yours. You could have refused anytime."

"But—"

I stopped myself, knowing it was a lost cause. He was trying to get under my skin again and I wasn't going to give him that. Let him go ahead thinking whatever the fuck he pleased. I didn't care just as long as I got through this and saw my family again.

Simon said, in a musing voice, "You know, it does go back even further. This obsession of ours to watch other people, our lust for seeing violence. Do you know anything about the Roman Empire, Ben? Over two thousand years ago, the greatest civilization to ever rule the earth? Believe it or not, they were attracted to extreme violence. It was entertainment to them, a way to pass the time, and they couldn't get enough of it. Historians have scratched their heads trying to come up with a reason how an empire so civilized could love watching what they did. But we know the truth, don't we? We know why they did what they did. We know what made them so great."

I remained silent, just watching the cars in front of me, the dark red of their taillights.

"Well, I guess that's enough for now," Simon said. He suddenly sounded bored. "For the time being, just stay on 80. Stop whenever you feel like you can't drive any longer. In the morning get back on 80 and keep heading east. I don't suspect you'll reach your destination by tomorrow, but stranger things have happened."

I asked, "Can I please speak to my family?" saying the words without really thinking, and Simon's chuckling response was no surprise.

He said, "You'll just never learn, will you, Ben," and then he was gone.

TWENTY-SIX

I ended up staying at a Motel 6, just off the interstate in Rock Springs, Wyoming. By that time it was one o'clock in the morning and I didn't think I could go any farther. I'd been picking up maps at every gas station I came to, because God only knew where Simon was having me go and I wanted a reference if I happened to get lost. From the Wyoming map I saw I could keep going to Wamsutter, but that was at least another hour, if not more, and I just wanted sleep.

In my room, I stripped out of my clothes because they'd begun to reek of sweat and body odor. Of course I'd applied the Old Spice Simon had provided, but I'd been sitting in a car for the better part of eleven hours and was beginning to become sick of my own smell. In the morning I'd find a store, buy some clothes, even a jacket.

In the meantime I crawled under the covers in my boxers and just lay there in the dark. I'd taken out Jen's wedding ring and now cupped it in my hands. It was the only thing besides the black and white photograph that proved to me my wife and daughter actually existed. I didn't even have the pictures I'd kept in my wallet (the frayed one my dad had given me so long ago, that gracious gift he'd been planning for over ten years) to remind me of what their faces looked like, and all my memory gave me now was the image that had been seared from that black and white picture.

"I won't forget you," I whispered to the cold dark room. "I'm coming for you. I love you both so much."

And I just lay there and tried keeping my thoughts focused on my wife and daughter, on the promise of seeing them again. It was enough to keep me steady, to keep me calm, and to keep my mind off what else was happening so that I eventually drifted off to sleep.

TWENTY-SEVEN

One nightmare fades into another, and I'm in college again, just a lowly freshman trying to do well in his first semester of classes. My roommate's name is John Keel and he smokes too much pot and plays too many video games, but somehow he's maintaining a B average in all his classes, which just blows my mind. I'm studying every night, going to guest lectures even when they're not mandatory, and somehow I still just barely manage to keep my head above water. John's cool with a bunch of the upperclassmen, knows them somehow (it doesn't really occur to me the reason for this until much later), and he's always going to parties on the weekends, keggers mostly where you pay five bucks for a blue plastic cup and an unlimited supply of warm and skanky beer. John invites me every weekend and I go a few times but just stand in the corner, content to watch the juniors and the seniors talking and laughing, the guys hitting on the girls, the girls hitting on the guys. I haven't been with anyone since Marissa dumped me, and to be honest I'm still kind of nervous at starting over. John says all I need is to dip my dick and everything will be okay, but that's just the kind of shit he says, the way he lives his life.

For fall break I go home and help my dad on a house over the weekend. Both my parents ask how school's going and I smile and give them the thumbs-up, because my grades aren't bad though they could be better. I know that if I want to go to law school my grades have to be phenomenal, they have to stand out above everyone else's, and I'm starting to wonder why I even bothered with this crazy dream to begin with. That I was born poor and that I will always be poor, no matter how hard I try to change my station in life.

Back at school, I go to classes, I go to the library to study when I'm not in classes. John's always at the room, the sweet scent of marijuana constant, playing his Sega or Super Nintendo, having a great time. Halloween's coming up and he invites me to a costume party this one fraternity's having, and John's thinking of going as Super Mario, do I want to go as Luigi?

Halloween rolls around and our costumes suck but we go anyway. We pay our money and get our blue plastic cups and try to have a good time. They have Jell-O shooters, dyed orange and black, and I have one or two but that's about it, I don't feel like getting trashed for some reason. I only have two beers anyway, and I'm just standing in the corner like usual, watching everyone else in their togas and gorilla suits and cowboy getups, the girls in French maid and nurse and angel outfits, their skirts so short and tight that I think maybe I'll head back to the dorm, get on the Internet and look up some porn. I've been doing it ever since high school, have been surfing the web because on it there's an endless supply of naked chicks doing naughty things, and sitting in front of the screen with a box of tissues beside me always calms me, always gets my head straight.

So I decide to leave the party, but first I want to try to find John to tell him I'm headed off, since he's Mario and I'm Luigi (though we make terrible Mario Brothers, the fact neither one of us is Italian), but I can't find him, he probably went to another party or is selling his stuff right now to a few happy upperclassmen. So I drop my cup in the trash and head outside, where the sky is dark and cloudy and the temperature cool. Across the way a house has been toilet papered, white lines drooping everywhere. It's enough to at least make me grin and I start off through the grass, taking the short cut toward my dorm.

That's when I hear the shouting coming from the side of the building I've just left, a man's heavy voice shouting and cursing and a woman's soft voice begging him to stop. I hurry toward the noise, my shoes getting wet in the early evening dew. I'm not drunk at all, only a little buzzed, and what I'm hearing now has sobered me up. I glance down at myself, realize just how ridiculous I look, but then I'm around the corner and I'm seeing it.

Please, stop, don't, the girl shouts, pleads, cries.

Her name is Michelle Delaney and she's dressed as an angel, wearing a long white dress and white wings and even a small glowing halo. She's being dragged out of the same building I've just come out of but from a different exit, she's being dragged out by her boyfriend who's wearing—surprise, surprise—a devil costume. He's on the football team, his arms cannons, his shoulders broad, and his face is screwed up in anger, in fury, in rage. He's bellowing at her, calling her a slut, telling her nobody cheats on him and she sure as hell ain't gonna to be the first, and she's pleading with him, trying to pull her arm away, slapping at him with her free hand though it makes no difference in the matter, no difference at all.

Please, Mike, she sobs, and even in the dim light I can see the tears in her eyes. Please don't, I'm sorry, I swear I am, I'm so sorry.

Shut up, cunt! he shouts, and slaps her—and like that, my body jumps, feeling the slap too.

I want to say something, to do something, but I just stand there, helpless, as helpless as Michelle Delaney. Hey, I try to shout, but I have no voice, I don't even think I'm breathing. I just stand there alone, the only witness to what Mike the Devil's doing right this moment. He's beyond drunk, staggering as he drags Michelle, and she keeps on hitting him, trying to get away, trying to free herself. She's crying and sobbing and even screams when he squeezes her arm too tightly.

Please, she keeps saying, keeps pleading, but Mike doesn't seem to hear her, or if he does he doesn't seem to care. He jerks her forward, trying to keep her walking with him, but when she pulls back once more he finally has enough. He turns and throws her to the ground, falls on one knee and just starts raining down punches. Her face, her stomach, her arms—every place of her body is kissed by the rough touch of his fists, and she does her best to cry out for as long as she can until she's exhausted her voice, until the blood gushing from her nose gets caught in her throat and she can do nothing else but gurgle her pleas.

Do something, my mind tells me, and I do want to do something, I really do. But I just continue standing there and watching as Michelle Delaney is beaten into unconsciousness, beaten by her drunken boyfriend who saw her talking to another guy and thought they were sleeping together so of course in his own mind his actions are reasonable, of course they are just.

Pluh, Michelle Delaney gurgles, her last attempt at pleading her case, before she falls silent. And still Mike the Devil continues punching her, kicking her, calling her a bitch and a cunt and a whore while she just lays there, her body now motionless, taking it all.

Do something, I tell myself again. Help her.

But I just stand there and watch. I can't do anything else. I can't even move.

TWENTY-EIGHT

I spent all Wednesday driving. I got up around eight o'clock, shaved and showered, then went out looking for clothes. I found a Walmart and got the essentials—new underwear and socks, a new pair of jeans, two T-shirts, and a sweatshirt. I even bought a winter jacket, which from its bulk promised to keep me warm in case the Taurus broke down and left me stranded in the middle of the desert at night. Later, after a good and hearty breakfast at a nearby diner, I was back on 80 and headed east.

It took me four hours to reach Cheyenne, where I stopped for lunch and to gas up. It had also started to rain, which was a change, and I began to tap my fingers to the constant back and forth of the windshield wipers. It continued to rain the entire way to the Nebraska state border, where it stopped all of a sudden and the clouds broke and the sun shined down again.

The radio kept me company, as did the Marlboros and the snacks I stocked up with at the gas stations. I'd even picked up some sixty-four ounce plastic cups to piss in so I didn't have to stop. The urge hit me twice and I kept putting it off, knowing Simon and whoever else was watching, but after everything I'd already done so far I thought fuck it and unzipped my pants. It's difficult taking a leak in that position while you're doing seventy miles an hour, but I managed and then set it aside, to dump out the next time I stopped for gas.

I began ignoring everything that wasn't the highway or the cars in front of me. The road signs, the billboards, even the horizon—it had all entered into a background that was eclipsed by my inexorable desire to win back my wife and daughter. A tractor-trailer, doing at least ninety, passed me and I followed in its wake for a good twenty miles or so, until it got off onto 76 at Big Springs. Then it was just me again, driving and driving and driving.

The cell phone chirped outside of Paxton, telling me its battery was low, and I changed it, not wanting to miss it when Simon called. It was strange—as much as I hated his fucking voice and seeing his fucking grin in my mind, I felt lost and directionless without him.

By the time I passed Kearney it was close to eight o'clock at night. I was sick of driving and stopped for something to eat. I chose the first restaurant that didn't look like a complete dive, and I sat at a booth, staring down at my plate of meatloaf and mashed potatoes and gravy and cranberry sauce. I'd asked for a cup of coffee which the waitress did a good job of coming back again and again to refill. She was an older woman, in her late-fifties, early-sixties, who had a smoker's voice and skin like a lizard's. Her name tag said DAWN and she seemed pleasant enough, the kind of woman you wouldn't have minded having as an aunt around the holidays, because you knew she would bake the right kind of cookies and pies and volunteer to do the dishes while everyone else sat in the living room watching TV or listening to music and enjoying themselves.

"Long day at work?" she asked me, when I declined dessert, and I glared up at her, told her with my eyes I wasn't in the mood and that she would be wise to just walk away. She didn't take the hint, or maybe she did and wanted to leave me with some final words of wisdom. Whatever the case, she slid into the other side of the booth and leaned forward, glanced around at the other patrons at the tables and booths to make sure no one was watching. She whispered with her mid-western twang, "You know what I find works? Go home and draw a nice hot bath. Even put in some bubbles if you like. Then just sit yourself in there and close your eyes and lose yourself to the soak. Relieves all the stress, believe you me."

She gave me a wink, still oblivious to the rage in my eyes, to the desire to punch her in the face, and leaned forward.

"Yeah," she said, smiling, her teeth stained from coffee and nicotine, "looks to me like a soak's all you need and everything will be just right."

TWENTY-NINE

Simon called early that Thursday morning. I'd stayed at the Days Inn of Lincoln that night, had thankfully had no dreams. It was close to eight o'clock when the phone on the bedside table rang and I answered groggily.

"Everything's set for the next part of the game," he said. "Are you ready?"

I slowly sat up. I grabbed my glasses from off the bedside table, then Jen's ring which I had placed there last night before falling asleep. I held it in the palm of my hand, thinking of her, thinking of Casey, thinking of all the things I would change if I could go back and do it over again. Then I remembered what had occurred to me for the first time last night—how it was possible Jen was being denied her medication.

I asked Simon about this.

"Her Paxil?" he said. "What about her Paxil?"

"She needs it."

"Yes, I'm sure she does. But at this time I'd suggest you not worry yourself about that. Her mental well-being is far less important than her physical well-being, no? Now listen closely, Ben, because I'm only going to say this once."

It took me less than three hours to get to Creston, Iowa, so I got there just before eleven, when the sun was beginning to reach its apex in the sky. Once there I headed directly for the Amtrak station, found a place to park, and went inside. Came out five minutes later, carrying a black leather briefcase that had been waiting for me in a locker, its key hidden in the bottom of (what else?) a Snickers box on the candy rack at the newspaper stand. The locked briefcase beside me on the passenger seat, I headed straight for 34.

It took me close to another four hours to reach Illinois, and at roughly three-thirty I passed through Burlington and drove over the Mississippi River. Eventually I got onto 67, followed that south all the way past Roseville and Good Hope. I came into Ryder, what looked to be just another small American town surrounded by farmland. An ornate sign posted on the way into town educated anyone who cared that it was named after some corporal in the American Civil War.

I found a place to stop at a gas station and parked. I cut the ignition and then just sat there, staring at the plate glass window. There was a rack in front of it filled with propane tanks. A couple minutes passed where I was beginning to think this might not work, but then the cell phone vibrated.

Simon asked, "What are you doing?"

"I want to speak to my wife and daughter. I won't go another mile until I do."

"You're hardly in the position to negotiate. But I did promise you before that I'd let you talk to either one of your family members. And besides, I think by now you could use the extra motivation, am I right?"

I said nothing and just waited. The presence of the briefcase —which wouldn't open, just like Simon had said, no matter how much I tried—and whatever was inside it was as palpable as Jen's wedding ring in my jeans pocket.

"All right," Simon said, almost sighed, "one moment."

There was a silence that seemed to last an hour. I wanted a cigarette but put it off.

After about a minute there was noise again on the phone. A voice said something, a single word that I couldn't make out completely. But it didn't matter. I recognized the voice at once.

"Casey?" I said, almost breathless. My heart had begun beating rapidly in my head, my body had started shaking. "Casey, are you all right?"

"Daddy?" she said again, her voice so soft and so weak, yet so alive, that I wanted to start crying right there on the spot. "Daddy, I—I'm scared." Her voice trembled and she sounded like she was about to cry, which was the last thing I wanted to hear right then, the very last.

"No, baby, it's okay," I said, feeling like the liar I was every time she cried out in the middle of the night and I went to her room, comforted her and told her everything would be all right —and then instead of going back to bed would go down to the den and log onto the Internet, watch some naked women do some naked things.

It sounded like Casey was going to say something else, but the phone was taken away and it was Simon's voice I heard, Simon's goddamned happy voice.

"Better?"

I was silent for a very long time. A pickup had pulled into the gas station, parked right beside me. Its driver, who looked like a farmer but who may have been a teacher or plumber or the town's mayor, gave the Taurus a curious look, probably hesitant about the Nevada license plate, before heading inside.

"Much," I said finally. I could feel the tears beginning to creep past my eyes. I closed them, wanting to see only darkness, wanting my mind to show me a happy image of my wife and daughter in that void.

THIRTY

The Hickory View Retirement Home was a four-story brick building that sat near the southern end of town. On the outside it had a homey feel to it, the kind of place anyone might decide to settle down in when they reached their sixties and knew it was time to start collecting social security. A flagstone walkway leading up to the entrance, benches spread out around the leaf-strewn lawn, some hidden in the shade of hickory and white oak trees. An occasional bed of flowers against the building, what looked to be mostly withered mums, and shrubbery that would never lose its green, no matter how cold the weather.

I knew exactly what I would find when I stepped inside, leaving the chill of the oncoming autumn evening and entering the chill of oncoming death. Despite the building's welcoming exterior, inside the air had a stale smell to it, mixed with the bitter scent of disinfectant. Decorations had already been put up for Halloween: orange and black and purple paper ribbons drooped from the ceiling; a large ceramic jack-o'-lantern sat grinning in the corner; crudely made construction paper cutouts of friendly ghosts and witches and scarecrows hung taped to one wall, beneath a large hand-printed note saying courtesy of Miss Thompson's third grade class.

A sign just within the doors reminded guests that visiting hours were until six o'clock. By the grandfather clock in the corner beside the main desk, I had about an hour to get my visiting done.

The woman behind the desk looked as if she had another ten years or so before being shipped to a place like this, and she knew it. She seemed pleasant though, smiling up at me from her spot behind the desk. A bowl, filled with silver-wrapped Hershey's Kisses, was on the desktop next to an upright calendar that presented small Norman Rockwell prints.

She asked, "May I help you?" She wore bifocals and slipped them off her face, let them hang down in front of her by the thin chain around her neck.

"I'm here to see my uncle," I said, giving her my best smile. I'd changed my clothes at the gas station, was now wearing the khakis and shirt and tie, all of which were wrinkled but I had on my baggy winter coat so nobody could really tell. I needed the business look to pull off the reason I was carrying the brief-case—a reason that I wasn't even yet sure about. "Phillip Fagerstrom?"

"Ah yes, Mr. Fagerstrom. He's one of our favorite residents." She smiled, waiting a moment to let that sink in, as if she didn't say the same thing about all the residents. Then she tilted her head just slightly and said, "But I don't think I …"

"I know—you've never seen me before. That's because I'm a bad nephew." I shrugged, forced a smile. "I live near Philadelphia and hardly ever come out this way. But this week I've got meetings in Peoria and decided to make the drive down." I paused again, watched two nurses as they headed down the corridor, talking quietly to each other. "Look, I completely understand if you want to call him and confirm. I'm Tom Scheffler. Uncle Phillip's my mom's brother."

The woman continued smiling, clearly sympathetic with my story. She probably never got any visitors who came from all the way out east to see their uncle they hadn't talked to in years, and it broke her heart. Besides, if she was sincere about Phillip Fagerstrom being one of their favorite residents, then she'd no doubt be more than happy to assist in the long overdue meeting of uncle and nephew.

"He's on the second floor," she said, still smiling, but then her eyes shifted away from mine for a moment, giving her the look of someone who has bad news. I asked her what it was. She sighed, looked so miserable for a second, and asked in a low voice, "When was the last time you saw Phillip?"

I paused a moment. Shrugged. "At least two years," I said, hoping that he hadn't been dropped off here a year ago.

The woman looked relieved at once. "So then you know about his … condition."

"Oh, yeah," I said, giving another nod, this one much more sympathetic.

"Good. Because … well, it's gotten worse. I mean, he's not completely incapable of moving, but he can't really talk anymore. He can listen—believe me, he can listen—and he'll be happy to see you."

She told me his room number. I thanked her. She smiled and waved, told me to give Phillip her best, no doubt hoping that when she was eventually stuck in a place like this, one of her long lost relatives would be kind enough to stop by while passing through, to at least show some concern and love for someone who had been put here and forgotten by everyone else.

I stepped into one of the two elevators, pressed the button for the second floor, waited the forty seconds or so before the doors opened again and I stepped out. I'd been holding my breath the entire time—it smelled like someone had shit them- selves and used it to paint the walls—and I let it out slowly as I started down the corridor. I passed opened doors where Hickory View's residents either lay confined to their beds, watching Dr. Phil or Dr. Oz or whatever other celebrity doctor was on at this time of day, or else asleep. The smell was even worse up here, that constant scent that precedes death and decay through living tissue.

A desk was at the middle of the corridor, just where the one had been downstairs, and behind this a younger woman sat. She looked to be in her thirties, had red hair tied up in a bun, and was typing something on the computer when I passed. Monitors were stacked against the wall, close to the desk, keeping whoever was positioned there an instant update in case one of the residents needed something important, like some pudding or help taking a piss. Other monitors were there too, smaller ones with green moving lines that showed heartbeats and whatever else.

"Phillip Fagerstrom?" I said, pointing down the corridor as if I wasn't sure where I was going, and she smiled, told me which room number, and I thanked her and continued on. Next thing I knew I was standing in front of his room, this man I had never seen a day before in my life. His door was open and he was somewhere inside. It was dark in there, like he had all the lights off, and I wondered what would happen if it turned out he was dead. If his heart had just decided to give out in the last couple of minutes and nobody was aware of it, not even the redhead at the desk, and I would be the one who found him. Would I even say anything? Or would I just leave, let them figure it out on their own?

I waited a very long time before stepping inside. I saw immediately that no, he wasn't dead, and that no, all the lights weren't off. His TV was on, but it was muted. Dim light bounced off where he lay in his bed as I approached him. Simon had told me to come here, to ask for this man, to come to his room, but that was it.

I could barely see him from where he lay underneath his sheet. The urge to turn on the lamp beside the bed was strong, but I didn't want to touch it. I didn't want to touch anything. Not the two framed pictures of what looked like grandchildren —three of them, two boys and a girl—or the American Legion clock. So far there was no physical evidence of my presence here and I wanted to keep it that way.

Phillip Fagerstrom finally acknowledged me. His eyes moved slowly from the television to search my face. He'd probably thought I was one of the nurses, or else someone else on staff, and the fact that he couldn't recognize me must have startled him. But he made no movement, no sound at all, and just lay there staring back at me. The majority of his body was covered by sheets so all I saw was his neck and his face, both wrinkled and gray in the dimness.

The cell phone vibrated in my pocket. I let it go on, for some reason thinking it wrong to answer in front of this man. I began to worry what would happen if the woman downstairs decided to make a surprise visit to see how things were going between nephew and uncle.

The phone vibrated a fifth time and I pulled it out of my pocket.

"Why am I here?"

"Well," Simon said, "that's up to you. This is where the true reality part comes into play. I'm not forcing you to do anything, not like before. This time I'm giving you the choice. One of the choices is easy, the other is hard. I'm not going to tell you which is what."

I just stood there, waiting. The light from the TV continued to bounce around the room. Out in the corridor, in another room, one of the residents began coughing violently, as if hacking up a vital body part.

When I realized Simon was waiting on me, I said, "What

are my choices?" My hushed voice sounded strange in the room. Phillip Fagerstrom continued to stare back at me.

"First tell me what you think of the old man."

Across the hall, the cougher continued coughing.

I whispered, "He looks like he's almost dead."

"Is that your professional opinion, doctor?" Simon chuckled. "Yes, Ben, he does look that way. He's had three strokes in the past two years. The last was just two months ago. It's surprising he's lasted this long."

"Why am I here?" I asked for a second time. The weight of the briefcase started to become evident again. I wanted to set it down but kept holding it, my sweaty hand gripping the handle tightly.

"Remember, Ben, two choices. Either you can place that briefcase you brought with you underneath his bed, or …"

Something told me he had drifted off on purpose, that this was all part of the suspense, all supposed to keep the audience on the edge of their seats. As much as I didn't want to go along with his stupid tricks, I knew I had no choice, so I said the word he was waiting for.

"Or?"

"Or else," Simon said, "you can kill him."

THIRTY-ONE

The coughing out somewhere in the corridor had died down. There had been no echoing sound of footsteps, so it was clear the redhead hadn't come in any hurry to see what was wrong.

"If I kill him," I whispered, keeping my gaze level with his, "then what happens?"

"Then you take the briefcase and go on your merry way, off to the next part of the game."

"If I kill him I want either Jen or Casey released. I want them let go."

"I'm sorry, Ben, but where do you keep getting this crazy idea you're free to negotiate? Didn't I already tell you negotiating wasn't an option?"

Yes, he had told me that, but I had pulled over and refused to go any farther and he had let me speak to Casey, I had been given the chance to hear her voice for less than a minute.

"Well?" Simon said, the grin no longer in his voice.

"What's in the briefcase?"

"What do you think?"

I paused, as if trying to come up with something, when in

reality I'd been trying to guess ever since I placed it on the Taurus's passenger seat back in Creston.

"I … I don't know."

"Well, I can definitely tell you that's not in there. Any other brilliant guesses?"

I was silent again. Out in the corridor, that sound came once more, that coughing sound, only now it was very weak, hardly even there. Phillip continued staring back at me. He blinked, which seemed to cause him more trouble than it should have, and blinked again.

Simon said, "What if I told you he was a bad person? What if I told you he used to molest children? The police had never been able to figure out who was doing it, the kids refused to tell, and so he got away with it. Would it make it easier then? Could you find it in your heart to rid the world of one more child molester?"

"He's an old man now. It's not like he's going to"—I paused, couldn't bring myself to say the words—"do that anymore."

"No, that's true. But shouldn't he suffer for his sins? Isn't that only fair? Or are you just going to stand by like you did with Michelle Delaney? Just stand by and watch while there's still the chance to do some good?"

"What's in the briefcase?"

"Does it really matter? Does it matter if it's stocked full of candy canes or if it's loaded with sand? Maybe there's nothing in there, Ben. Have you thought of that? Maybe there's nothing in there at all, maybe the briefcase is just naturally this heavy, and the entire purpose has been to mess with your head from the start."

Actually this last had crossed my mind a time or two during my four hours of driving, but I knew that wasn't the case. It just wasn't Simon's style.

"So what's it going to be, Ben? You don't want to drag this

out too long. Audiences hate it when things go on too long. The world has ADD, didn't you know? Blame it on MTV if you want. The fact is the average cut in today's movies is three seconds. The same goes with TV. Books with shorter chapters are bestsellers. Is it all a coincidence?"

This wasn't the first time Simon had gone off on a tangent and something told me this wouldn't be the last. He liked hearing his own voice as much as he liked hearing my silence when he asked his unnerving questions, but I didn't mind letting him ramble now. Because now I had a difficult decision to make, though in the back of my head I wondered just how difficult it really was.

"What you said this man did," I said, choosing my words carefully, "it's all a lie, isn't it."

"Well of course it is. But just because I made it up doesn't mean it didn't happen. For all either of us knows—for all anybody knows—this man has molested children before. Maybe even worse. Why don't you ask him? Maybe he'll want to confess before he dies."

Without wasting another moment I stepped forward. Phillip Fagerstrom's eyes widened just a bit as I approached, but I stopped only a few feet away and set the briefcase down. I mouthed *sorry* to him, not quite sure why I'd done so (even now I'm not sure), then turned and headed out of the room. In my ear Simon was chuckling.

"I see," he said. "Are you sure you want to do that, Ben? Now's the time to take it back."

I disconnected the phone and shoved it in my pocket, never breaking my stride as I headed back down the corridor. Behind me, the resident had started coughing again, and I wished I'd been told to visit that person instead. At least then I would have felt pity, I would have felt some compassion, unlike standing there with Phillip Fagerstrom and feeling nothing.

The redhead at the desk was still typing at her computer

and smiled up at me as I passed. I wanted to stop and ask her why she didn't check on the resident down the hall, the one I could almost see spitting up blood right this instant, but I just kept walking.

Downstairs, as I passed the welcome desk, the woman there asked how everything had gone.

"You weren't up there long," she said, concern obvious in her voice. "Everything okay?"

"He was sleeping," I said, and told her I'd try back tomorrow. By then I figured I'd be at least another state away.

Then I wished her a good evening and headed for the exit. The sensors activated the doors and cold wind whipped at my face. I thought I heard the woman say something behind me but it was lost in the harsh October breeze and I continued toward my car, never once looking back.

THIRTY-TWO

I went back through town, heading north, until I reached 80 again. Then I headed east. I drove for close to two and a half hours before I decided to stop for the night at a Ramada. I checked in, went up to my room and fell into bed. I was still wearing the khakis and shirt, though I'd taken the tie off once I left Hickory View. I'd smoked most of the drive too, and my mouth felt raw.

The cell phone vibrated.

Lying with my face down, my eyes closed, I huffed. I rolled over, pulled the phone from my pocket, answered it.

Simon said, "Turn on the TV. The local news just started and there's something you might be interested in seeing."

He disconnected and I just lay there, the dead phone to my ear, wondering what the hell he wanted me to watch now. I remembered the last time he'd told me to turn on the television, how it had broadcasted the murder-suicide of Gerald and Juliet.

I thought of the briefcase. I remembered how heavy it had been.

I closed my eyes, murmured, "No, God, please no," and quickly turned on the television facing the bed.

The local news had already begun. The newscaster looked very serious and somber as he stared back into the camera and reported tonight's top story. Over his right shoulder there was live footage of a building on fire, a four-story brick building, with police cars and fire trucks surrounding it. At the bottom of the screen was the heading UNEXPLAINED EXPLOSION and the newscaster was saying something about the town of Ryder, Illinois, about Hickory View, about close to thirty people confirmed dead, nearly fifty wounded, possibly even more.

With a shaking hand I raised the remote and turned off the TV. Sat in mind-numbing silence for a very long time. Eventually the cell phone began vibrating and I picked it up, not really sure why I was doing it just as I wasn't sure what I was going to say. Then, almost at once, everything came together and I gritted my teeth.

"You fucking son of a bitch, I can't believe you—"

"No, no, watch it there, Ben. I didn't do anything. Remember, it was your choice. You could have killed that old man and taken the briefcase with you. *You*, Ben. Not me."

I said nothing and just sat there, shaking, listening to the silence and the blood pounding in my ears. I continued staring at the blank television screen ... yet even though it was blank I was still seeing the live footage, and I remembered everything about the retirement home: the dry and bitter scent of disinfectant, the old woman behind the desk, the bowl of Hershey's Kisses by the calendar, the redhead upstairs, and the resident who had been coughing and coughing and coughing. And of course the rest of them, all the others who'd been confined to their beds watching TV or sleeping, the ones put there to be forgotten by their families, by their children and grandchildren.

Staring at the blank television screen, thinking about all

those innocent lives lost, I slowly shook my head. "No," I whispered.

"No? No what?"

"I can't … I can't do this anymore."

Something changed in Simon's voice. "What do you mean you can't do this anymore? Don't you love your wife and daughter? Don't you want to save them?"

"Of course I do," I said, almost snapped, "but those innocent people"—I was still shaking my head, still staring at the blank television screen and seeing it all—"they had nothing to do with anything."

"So what are you saying? You're quitting?" Simon chuckled. "You can't quit now. You're having so much fun."

"Fuck you!" I shouted, my body still trembling, something churning in the pit of my stomach. "Fuck you and your fucking viewers. I'm done with this. I'm going to the police. I'm turning myself in. I'm going to tell them all about your—"

"Okay, Ben," Simon said, his voice calm and neutral, "go ahead and quit. But Casey's preschool? We'll bomb it. And believe me, it'll be a whole lot worse than Hickory View."

I went silent. Just sitting there, my shoulders slouched, my body continuously shaking. Still staring at that blank screen, not seeing the footage of the retirement home anymore but imagining what the footage would look like of Casey's preschool, that stucco-sided block of a building, the swings and slides outside, all as they burned to the ground.

"We'll do it in the middle of the day. Right when the kids are napping. Or maybe we should do it earlier, during reading time? How many kids are there on a daily basis, Ben? Thirty? Forty? How much staff?"

Still I said nothing. My stomach was churning even more.

"I suggest you do yourself a favor and get some sleep."

I closed my eyes. Saw all the kids inside that preschool,

Casey there among them. I heard myself say, "I want to see my family."

"Sorry, Ben. Can't help you there."

"Let me at least speak to them."

"Um, no, I don't think so."

"Goddamn it!" I shot up and started toward the TV, caught myself an instant before I threw the phone right at the screen. In my ear, Simon was chuckling.

"You need sleep, my friend. It's been a long day. Tomorrow is going to be even longer."

Then he was gone and I was left standing there, tears in my eyes, shaking. The room began to spin. I took one step, another, my legs wobbly and unsure of themselves, and before I realized it I was rushing toward the bathroom, slamming into the door, falling on my knees before the toilet. And there I spent the next half hour, kneeling on those cold tiles as I sobbed, dry-heaving so much I thought I would never stop, dry-heaving to the point I was certain that any moment I would bring up what was left of my withered and despair-ridden soul.

THIRTY-THREE

I'd already been driving for close to an hour, headed down 80 and then up 55, getting closer and closer to Chicago, when the van came out of nowhere and struck the Taurus from behind.

It was close to ten o'clock—Simon had let me sleep in, giving me close to ten hours of much needed rest—and traffic wasn't too heavy. Even though I couldn't see the Chicago skyline yet, I could sense it, which made me think more and more about Jen, which made me think more and more about Casey, which made me realize just how much I hated Simon and whoever was watching me right now.

I'd just passed Bolingbrook and the 355 interchange when the van struck and the Taurus lurched forward and my head snapped back. I'd already been doing over sixty and the steering wheel jerked and I had to hold on tight to keep it steady, to keep the car from skidding off the highway. I checked my rearview mirror and saw a black utility van. It swung over into the left lane, passed me, swung back into my lane, and immediately hit its brakes.

I didn't have time to think—I just stomped on the brake

and swerved the wheel and closed my eyes and braced myself for the impact.

None came.

The phone in my pocket vibrated right as I opened my eyes. The utility van was stopped just a few feet ahead of me. We were in the right lane, the Taurus a little closer to the side of the highway as I'd swerved, and traffic was speeding by on the left, some people honking.

I answered the phone just as I put the car in park and undid my seatbelt. Simon was already shouting—"Don't get out of the car! Keep driving!"—but by then I had the door open and my left foot was on the macadam, followed by my right foot, and I was standing, turning, listening to the traffic as it flew by on the highway, listening to the honking, wondering just what the hell had happened and not really even sure why I was getting out of the car in the first place. Simon continued shouting at me to get back in the car and I was listening but at the same time I was looking up at the two men approaching. One was black and one was white and at first I couldn't place them—they looked familiar but at the same time they didn't— and then before I knew it they were on me, grabbing my arms, one of them tearing the glasses off my face and throwing them aside, the black one taking the phone out of my hand and placing it to his ear and saying, "Game over, Simon," before he disconnected the call.

"Hey," I said, trying to fight the men as they dragged me toward the van and the side door which was open, "stop, don't do this," but the men ignored me and threw me into the van and climbed in after me and the black one said, "How long?" and the driver said, "Less than sixty seconds," and the white one slid the door shut and shouted, "Go!"

The driver punched the gas, the van jerked forward, and an instant later we were speeding down the highway and I was in the back of the van with my two assailants, the same two assailants, I realized, who had attacked me back in Reno.

"What's happening?" I asked, squinting at the two men, my back against the rear doors. "Who are you people?"

The black man tossed the phone to the other man now in the passenger seat. "Check it," he said, then turned back to me. "You have a prescription, don't you?"

I just stared back at him.

"We'll get you a new pair of glasses at some point." He nodded at the rear windows. "In the meantime if you're interested, the show's about to begin."

"Who are you? What are you talking about? Why are you *doing* this?"

I was babbling, almost incoherently, afraid that what these men had just done would cost Jen and Casey their lives, that it would cost Casey's fellow preschoolers their lives.

"My name's Carver, Ben. My men and I are here to help you. And like I said, the show's about to begin."

At the sound of my name I paused. "How … how do you know my name?"

The man in the passenger seat called back, "It's clean."

"Good," Carver said. "Take out the battery and we'll get it to the Kid later." He looked at me again and said, "And to answer your question, Ben, it's because my men and I have been watching you for the past five days."

"The past five …" I shook my head, trying to wrap my mind around everything this man was telling me. "My family—"

"Is dead," Carver said, his voice suddenly somber. "I'm sorry to be the one to tell you that, but they've been dead from the beginning."

I started shaking my head. "No. No, that can't be."

"Carver!" This was shouted from the driver. "Here they come."

Still shaking my head, still trying to accept everything this man had just told me, I said, "Here who come?"

"Your escorts."

"My … what?"

"Just watch."

He moved up beside me and peered out the left rear window. I squinted back at him, not sure what to say or do or even think, my entire body trembling at the idea that Jen and Casey might already be dead, but then curiosity got the better of me and I glanced out the right rear window.

The utility van was going fast—maybe eighty, ninety miles per hour—leaving most of the traffic in the dust. Except for one car, swerving in and out of all the rest, gaining on us.

"See them?" Carver asked. "They've been following you from the start of the game. They were the ones that stopped us back in Reno."

I looked at him, remembering his words—*This is for your own good*—and then looked back out the window at the car. Without my glasses I could only see the car as a dark shape, but I could tell it was getting even closer, now less than one hundred yards away.

"Carver," the driver warned, and Carver said, "I see him," and I squinted even more to just make out the car's passenger side window coming down and someone leaning out pointing a gun at us.

A hand touched my arm, pulling me away, and Carver said, "You might want to get down," and immediately the window I'd been staring out spiderwebbed.

Carver said, "Larry, hurry the fuck up, we're taking on fire."

I wasn't sure who he was taking to, the driver or the passenger, but then I realized he wore an earpiece. I squinted to see him listening and then he said, "I don't care, make it happen," and then I ducked down even lower on the floor as more bullets tore into the van.

"Bronson, do something!" Carver shouted, and the driver said, "I'm trying, I'm trying," the van swerving now from lane to lane, the car behind us firing even more, the window that had been spiderwebbed now shattering completely, the glass raining down everywhere.

Carver pulled out a gun and stood up and fired out the window, the sound of his gun deafening in the van. I clamped my hands over my ears, jumping with each gunshot. Then Carver stopped and said, "Okay, here they come," and I opened my eyes and squinted up at him.

"About fucking time," said the passenger.

"We'll bust their balls later," Carver said. "Right now let's just make sure they make it work." Carver glanced at me. "Do you want to see?"

No, I didn't want to see, but I found myself getting up anyway and looking out the window. The car was back there—my escort, whatever that meant—and behind it, coming on strong, was another car. I squinted enough to see that the passenger side window of that car was coming down just as the car came parallel with my escort. A hand reached out holding something, threw that something at the highway right in front of my escort, and then suddenly there was a brilliant flash and the next thing I knew the escort's car was flying, flipping up through the smoky air and coming down on the roof.

The two guys in the front laughed and whooped. Carver said, "Good job, guys," and listened to his earpiece for a second, nodded and said, "Yeah, we're going to need to ditch this one as soon as possible too." He shouted up front, "Bronson, take the next exit. We're going to need new wheels ASAP." Then he sat down, leaned back against the side of the van, and looked at me.

I said, "What … what just happened?"

"Some powerful C-4 is what just happened."

"Who are you people?"

"Us?" Carver smiled. "We were just like you once upon a time. We had families, jobs, a mortgage. Now all of that's behind us."

"I don't"—I shook my head, my body still shaking—"I don't understand."

"I don't expect you to. Not at first. But we have some time, so I might as well get it out of the way."

"Get what out of the way?"

"There's no short or long version, just one, and here's what I can tell you. What seems like one hundred years ago I worked for the FBI."

THIRTY-FOUR

It had been simple bad luck that Carver Ellison stumbled across the thing that would eventually change and ruin his life.

He was thirty-five, had a wife and newborn baby at home. He'd been with the FBI for almost ten years, climbing his way up the bureaucratic ladder, and now worked in a vital section of the organization. His job was mainly to scour the Internet and keep tabs on certain terrorist cells. Ever since its conception the Internet had been a major threat not only to the security of the United States but to the entire world. Anybody was free to post whatever they wished, just as anybody was free to access it. It was then Carver's job to ensure that when something was posted that sent up red flags, they not only kept an eye on it and whoever was accessing the material, but found out who those people were and shut it down.

His bad luck started one night as he sat in front of a half dozen computers programmed to access any number of URLs at any given time. Something strange had popped up on Carver's screen. The computer he was using ran through a series of letters and numbers to see if anything came up, as sometimes terrorists will use addresses that are complete gibberish but which their contacts will know and link to and then read whatever message is posted before that message is deleted.

What he was looking at now was mostly a black screen with a box in the middle. In that box—it couldn't have been more than four inches wide and four inches high—was the inside of a car as it would look like from a driver's perspective. There was the steering wheel, the dash, the windshield and hood and the road in front. There were even hands on the steering wheel, and for a moment Carver, staring at the screen, had the vertiginous feeling that he was actually driving. The highway itself was moderately busy, traffic passing by trees and fields and buildings. Nothing was really happening at all except this person driving.

Carver ended up watching it for close to an hour—the driver doing nothing more than driving—until suddenly the screen went blank. He typed in a few commands and tried to bring it back up but whatever he'd seen was now gone.

Days passed and he started to forget about the driver. He had mentioned it on his nightly report, but besides that it had no real meaning. Then he was called in to see his supervisor, who had just come across his report and wanted a full and detailed account. Carver tried explaining the best he knew how, though the fact that nothing had really been happening on screen made it difficult. Yet despite this his supervisor seemed very interested. Finally he was dismissed and went back to work, sitting in front of the computers as they scrolled through the millions of possible addresses. As usual he sat there and thought about his wife and baby at home. Leon Michael Ellison, his four month baby boy, named after Carver's own father. He had Carver's eyes and nose, and always smiled every time Carver held him up and kissed him on the forehead. He couldn't wait until his boy got old enough to play baseball and basketball, to take fishing.

But one night, about three weeks later, he came across the

same website again. Only this time it was different. The screen was again black except for the box in the middle, the box which now showed one man killing another man. The man in question—the killer—was using an ax. Sound was provided this time, letting Carver hear the hard splat each blow of the ax made as it sank into the victim's body, while the other man, the killer, cried.

Carver sat up, began saving this data at once. He called in another one of the techs and they started playing with the site, trying to analyze it to see if they could come up with an origin. What they found instead was a link, which took them to another black screen with a box in the middle. Inside this box was the same thing: a man killing another man with an ax, only now Carver and the tech were viewing it from the killer's point of view. Just like before, when he'd been watching the highway in front of him—those two hands holding onto the steering wheel—it was like he was actually there, actually the one driving. Now it was like Carver was the one killing this other man—this other man who was no longer crying out, who was no longer even moving.

His report came to his supervisor's attention the next day, and he was called into his office, made to explain everything he'd seen. Carver described it the best he could—it had haunted him, so much so that he hadn't gotten much sleep the night before, and when his wife Sandra asked him what was wrong he just shook her off. His supervisor listened without a word, nodding at certain parts, jotting notes down in a note-book at other parts. Finally he told Carver that this case would be reassigned to somebody else, so Carver could continue his normal work.

"I beg your pardon, sir," he told his supervisor, "but I would like to further investigate."

He was thinking of all the things he'd seen in his time at the FBI, images so terrible he never once told Sandra about them, never once even hinted about them. Websites that provided its customers with naked pictures of children. Videos of children being forced to do obscene things with each other and sometimes even animals. It had been enough to make his stomach turn but Carver had conditioned himself to acknowledge there was evil in the world, and that the only way for evil to succeed was for good men to do nothing (a paraphrase of a quote he'd heard in high school and which had stayed with him ever since). He had made it his mission to stop these sick people—those who provided this egregious content and those who purchased it—and every time one of these websites was shut down and someone placed in jail, he felt a little better about himself and the world in general.

Regardless, Carver was reassigned to work strictly on al-Qaeda-related issues. Yet what he'd seen—the man using an ax to kill another man, the killer crying the entire time—stayed with him.

He contacted a young man whom he'd busted years ago, a computer hacker who once infiltrated the Pentagon's main server and sent out a mass email to every mailbox saying they were going to have Secret Santas this year, no matter what creed or faith each person followed. When Carver went with the agents to the boy's house, he found just a seventeen-year-old kid, a good-looking kid with a clean completion and smart eyes and trendy clothes. As the kid was taken out in handcuffs, Carver said, "You don't look like a hacker," to which the kid said, "You don't look like a nigger." The kid spent a few years in prison, as well as being forced to pay an exorbitant amount in fines. Carver had managed to speak with him once again, right before he'd been arraigned. When Carver asked him why he'd gone ahead and done it even though he knew he would most likely get caught, the kid said, "Actually, I didn't think I would get caught. Guess you got lucky. And why'd I do it? Shit, I thought it was funny."

This was the person Carver now contacted. Ever since the young man was released they had created a close relationship when it came to matters such as these. Carver explained what he'd seen and asked for some insight if there was any. The Kid —this was how Carver always referred to him, wanting to keep his identity secret—said he would look into it and call him back.

Carver didn't wait long. The Kid called the next day.

"Did you find anything?"

"Did I find anything?" the Kid said. "Shit, Carver, you wouldn't fucking believe what I found."

The Kid, always up for a challenge, had spent all night doing the same thing Carver had been doing for the past few years. The only difference was the Kid knew exactly what he was looking for, just where to look, and had no problems (well, no major problems) uncovering it.

"It's like a webcam," the Kid told Carver a couple hours later, in a coffee shop thirty miles outside of D.C. "You know, how men will pay these girls all this money just to watch them traipse around in their underwear. Sometimes they can even request the girls to do things, like touch themselves and shit. This usually costs more, though, depending on what they want the girls to do."

The Kid explained what Carver had come across was a few steps up from a simple webcam. Whoever was coordinating this knew their shit and had the money to think big. Cameras were sometimes placed in certain locations, like in the car Carver had seen being driven earlier, or in a place where something was to occur, like the man being murdered with an ax. Had Carver known of a different link the first time around, he could have gotten a view of the driver himself. Mostly though the camera that was used was the one positioned in the glasses the subject always wore. Even if they normally didn't wear glasses they were forced to wear them. Inside was a micro camera, so small and yet so powerful that it wasn't like the webcams, which updated themselves every couple of seconds, but was a live feed. So that whoever was watching could see in real time the events as they unfolded.

"So what does this mean?" Carver asked the Kid, who was drinking hot chocolate because he hated the taste of coffee. The place was mostly deserted, it of course being the middle of the night, and anybody who would have cared might have found it odd that a well-dressed black man was talking to a kid who looked like he could have stepped out of the pages of an Abercrombie & Fitch catalog.

"It means," the Kid said, looking more solemn than he ever had before, even when he was in court, "this is some serious shit."

Carver told the Kid to keep working on it and they parted ways. The entire thing consumed his thoughts for the next week. At home, Sandra asked him what was wrong, but he merely smiled at her, went to play with his son or check on him in his crib. At work, nobody asked him what was wrong. Then the Kid called and told him to come to his place immediately.

He said, "You're not going to fucking believe what I found."

Apparently this entire thing had consumed the Kid's thoughts as well, because he'd been working on it day and night. He was even starting to look like a zombie to Carver when he arrived at the Kid's house, the same place Carver had come to years before when he'd made the initial arrest. The Kid's face was pale, he had bags underneath his eyes, but when he shook Carver's hand there was a firmness there that said the Kid was never going to lose his strength. They went down to the basement where all the computers were set up—the Kid had about a dozen, always working on something different— and Carver pulled up a chair.

"What do you have?" Carver asked. It was his first time

down here in years and he glanced around at all the posters taped to the walls: *Monty Python and the Holy Grail*, *Brazil*, *The Fisher King*, *Fear and Loathing in Las Vegas*, *Twelve Monkeys*.

When the Kid noticed what had caught Carver's attention, he said, "What? Terry Gilliam is a fucking genius."

Carver pulled his chair closer to the computer they were sitting in front of. He said, "This better be good."

"Well," the Kid said, "I guess that depends on your point of view."

What the Kid had concluded was that the two things Carver had seen before were types of shows. Reality shows in a way—real people doing real things. Only instead of working for some multimillionaire business owner or attempting to lose a ton of weight, these shows had a much darker, sinister angle.

While the Kid was explaining this, he brought up part of a show he'd saved, what was basically the same thing Carver had seen the first time he stumbled across the website that was mostly a black screen with a box in the middle: the inside of a car, hands on the steering wheel, an open highway stretching toward the horizon.

"And now," the Kid said, doing his best John Cleese, "for something completely different."

He typed in a few commands and sat back in his chair as the picture inside the black screen changed. The perspective was still of whoever was wearing the special glasses, only there was no open highway in front of them anymore. Now Carver was seeing a woman lying naked in front of him. Everything behind and around her was fuzzy, but her face was clear, and he could see that her mouth was open just a bit, her eyes bulging. And around her neck were hands, hands which belonged to the person wearing the glasses.

"Holy shit," Carver said, leaning forward. "Is he—"

"Choking her? You bet he is. But that's not all. He's fucking her too. Fucking her and choking her at the same time."

The Kid explained how he'd come across this particular scene two days ago. After the woman was dead, the man—he was listed as The Joker—went to some motel room, where he threw up and then showered for three or four hours. The next morning he started out into the city (after a half hour the Kid narrowed it down to Tampa) and just began walking the streets.

"The Joker?" Carver asked.

The Kid nodded and typed a mile a minute and brought up another screen. On it was the picture of a man who looked to be in his thirties, pale and overweight, badly losing his hair. There were a few paragraphs about him, where he'd been born and where he went to school and his hobbies, his likes and dislikes, where he worked.

"They don't seem to list real names," the Kid said. "They always give codenames, though they identify each person to an extent. Like the guy you just saw choking that girl? In his bio it said he'd always wanted to be a comedian, had even done some of his material on open mic nights at clubs. Hence he's The Joker."

The Kid continued to show Carver what else he'd come across. A list of other people—what Carver and the Kid quickly assumed were contestants—that included names like The Writer, The Poet, The Singer, Woman of Gold, Man of Cars, and so on. No real names were ever given. Another page, linked to the bios, told about each person's families. Their husbands and wives, their children, sometimes even their parents. Evidently these family members were being held captive (something that was freely mentioned on the site to its users), which forced these people, these contestants, to do what was asked of them.

"They're given instructions," the Kid told Carver, when he took a break and they were in the kitchen. The microwave was humming, popping a bag of Orville Redenbacher. "From what

I can tell their only contact is someone named Simon. You know, Simon Says? This guy tells them what to do, how to do it, all that shit. Though, to be honest, I can't be one hundred percent sure it's the same guy every time. From what it looks like, the people who do this shit are very well connected, and there're a lot of them. Make good money, too."

"What do you mean?"

"From what I can tell those people who aren't as web savvy as someone like me—just normal people like you, for instance —pay a shitload to access these shows. Depending on what each person wants to see or witness or even experience, it all ranges from thousands of dollars up to tens and sometimes hundreds of thousands. I mean, these sick fucks are major high rollers."

"But how can we be certain it's even real?" Carver asked, trying his best to play devil's advocate.

The Kid said, "Dude, you've seen shit like this before, only a lot tamer. You just know when it's real and when it's not. Tell me I'm wrong."

No, as much as Carver wanted to, he couldn't tell the Kid he was wrong. It was a feeling Carver always got in his gut, the one that said this wasn't just some bullshit a bunch of kids were trying to play as a prank. And he'd seen his share of websites offering the promise of dark desires and pleasures, like those people who loved watching snuff films. He'd seen so many he could tell almost at once when one was real and when one wasn't.

Back in the basement, surrounded by Terry Gilliam movie posters, with the computers again, Carver asked why the websites had disappeared before. The Kid explained they all seemed to be timed to stay in one place for any given hour, sometimes half an hour, and then move to another spot. This made it difficult for hackers or anybody else who was interested to try to infiltrate the system. The Kid even admitted—a little abashedly—that there had been a few instances when he'd been having a hell of a time tracking down where the sites went to next. His thought was whoever paid to get the full show was sent constant links, so they never missed a minute of the action … though really, with the cameras on the contestant twenty-four-seven, the action was limited. Most of the time the person was either sleeping or riding in some form of transportation, that was all. But then the time came, no matter how brief, when something did happen. So far the Kid had witnessed two murders, a rape, and a man who sliced open a living donkey and began eating the intestines raw. And those were for the sites he'd managed to locate and track.

"I have to be careful myself, though," the Kid said. His bowl of popcorn was beside him and he ate it happily, shoving handfuls into his mouth. They were staring at the one monitor, again watching the man listed only as The Joker as he cleaned himself up after murdering the woman. He was in the bathroom, having just thrown up in the toilet, and was now washing off his face, crying.

Carver asked, "What do you mean?"

"Like I told you before, whoever's doing this stuff knows their shit. They can probably tell when an outside source has found any given site. They might try to move the site faster than planned, or they might try to put a trace on whoever's stumbled across their show. Or maybe both. All I can say is thank God I have up-to-date anti-tracking software. Fuck the stuff from last month."

Based on everything the Kid had shown him, Carver was certain he could bring this to his supervisor. He had yet to hear of any progress from the other team who'd been assigned to the case, and was beginning to suspect no team had actually been assigned. He had even looked into it himself and came up with nothing. He asked the Kid to copy some of the saved files and then took it to work with him on Monday and showed his supervisor.

His supervisor sat quietly for a long time behind his desk before sighing and leaning back in his chair. He asked Carver why he'd blatantly disregarded an order. Carver explained that he'd been troubled by what he'd seen, that he'd been working on this at home on his free time (he wasn't about to mention the Kid's assistance in this matter), and that from the evidence he'd collected it seemed a full out investigation should be conducted.

For a long time there was silence. Then his supervisor said, "Good work," stood up and extended his hand for Carver to shake. "I can't promise anything but I'll see if I can get a team together to work on this exclusively. I'll put you in charge."

At home that night, Carver decided not to tell Sandra about what had happened. He'd wait until his supervisor made everything official before telling her anything. Besides, even if things did go through, he was leery of telling her about what he knew. She was a woman who spooked easily and the last thing he wanted to do was scare her.

Much later, while Sandra was sleeping, Leon started fussing in the next room. Carver got up and took him out of his crib, began rocking him back to sleep. He stared at the pictures stenciled on the walls of the nursery, the ones his wife was very slowly going about painting. Scenes from *Alice in Wonderland* and *Through the Looking-Glass*, Lewis Carroll being Sandra's favorite children's author. Carver sort of felt like Alice now, going down that rabbit hole, uncertain what he would find. Eventually he placed his son back in his crib, stared down at him for a very long time, and returned to bed.

When Carver woke that morning he was not in his bed. He was not in his bedroom. He was not even in his house.

He was in what appeared to be a rundown motel room, the kind with stains on the ceilings and cigarette burns on the carpet. What had woken him was the phone ringing beside the bed. He answered it and listened to a dark voice introduce itself as Simon.

"It seems you've gotten a little too close to what we do, Carver, so we thought we'd include you in on the fun. You're going to play a game. As long as you do everything I say you'll see your wife Sandra again. If not, she dies."

"Fuck you," Carver said. He scrambled up from the bed, looking around, trying to spot the cameras in the corners, hidden in the vent, wherever. A pair of glasses sat on the bedside table beside the phone.

Simon said, "That's not very nice, Carver. Either you'll play nice or you won't play at all. Now are you ready for the first part of the game? It's easy. Go take a piss."

Even though everything in Carver's mind told him not to, he started toward the bathroom. It was dark inside and he expected someone to be waiting in there, someone who might be his supervisor though he doubted his supervisor would be stupid enough to place himself at the scene. Then again maybe his supervisor had nothing to do with this. But someone sure as hell did. Someone had sold him out, and now Carver was certain he was very close to finding out who.

But then he went into the bathroom, turned on the light, and stepped toward the toilet.

Lying in the water, facedown, was his son.

THIRTY-FIVE

Carver's story wasn't told uninterrupted. Not with the utility van shot up the way it was. Simon would take care of his own people, Carver explained, make sure the police didn't get involved right away in case any of the escorts were still alive, but that didn't mean an APB hadn't already been put out on the van. One hadn't come across on their own radar yet, but the fact was they needed new wheels and they needed them fast.

At that point I was just along for the ride, listening to Carver tell his story while first they checked me for any tracking devices (in my clothes and shoes) then while we got off at the first exit and searched for a new van to steal. That came pretty quickly, the driver and passenger jumping out and breaking into a new van and then we were in there too, Carver and myself, leaving the old van behind.

"What about the others?" I asked at one point, and Carver said, "They know what to do and will meet up with us later," and before I knew it I broke down and started crying. This man claimed my wife and daughter were dead, that they'd been dead from the start, but I refused to believe it. I couldn't give up that hope. All I had left was the promise of seeing them again, of hearing their voices, of hugging them and never letting go, and the only way to do that was to understand what exactly was going on.

So I stopped crying, wiped my tears, and asked, "Then what did you do? After you found your ..." But I couldn't say it, because it made me think of Casey.

Carver didn't answer me for the longest time. He just stared off into space, shaking his head almost imperceptibly, and sighed. "I took him out and ... he was bloated, so bad I could hardly even recognize him. I laid him down on the bed, wrapped him in a sheet, said a prayer, and left." He paused and looked at me. "I just walked away."

"But your wife," I said. "You let her ..." Again I couldn't say it.

Carver's dark face continued staring back at me. "I knew there was no outlet. I'd seen the game played before. Nobody ever wins. They're forced to do whatever Simon tells them to do with the hope they'll win and get their family back. But they never do. My wife was already dead, just like my son, and I refused to play Simon's game."

He'd left, finding himself in a mountainous region of the country, coniferous trees everywhere. He stripped off his clothes, thinking there might be some kind of tracking device in them, and continued through the woods. Eventually he came to a nearby town. Managed to steal some clothes at night while nobody was around and then hitchhiked to the next town, where he learned he was in Maine, in the county of Wytopitlock. There he contacted the Kid, explained what had happened, to which the Kid had said, "I know, dude. I watched you wake up."

Apparently Carver's show had been listed as the Man of Honor.

"Your show's listed as the Man of Wax," Carver said. Something was different about his voice, it didn't sound completely there, and I wondered just how often he thought about that moment in the motel room in Maine, the moment he woke up and realized his world had changed forever. "The only reason I know your real name's Benjamin Anderson is when that delivery girl dropped off that package to you the first day."

I only nodded. I was hoping this man wouldn't get into the reason for why my "show" had been listed as it had. I remembered what Simon had told me, how that grin had been so clear in his voice.

"So then what?" I asked finally. We were driving through the streets of Chicago now, an entire other world outside the windows that I could barely see, nor see myself ever living in again.

"That was three years ago," Carver said. "I've made it my mission to stop these people any way I can ever since. For the past five years or so the Kid's been working as a white hat hacker for major businesses. In his spare time he monitors the web for when a new show's posted, then tries to determine the location, and I go there with my people to try to stop it. Just like back in Reno."

"Your people."

Carver nodded toward the front. "That's Bronson driving and that's David in the passenger seat. There are three others I've saved in the past three years. There was one other but she"—he shook his head—"she wanted to continue playing the game. Suffice it to say she's no longer alive."

I closed my eyes, took a breath. "This is just so … unbelievable." Except it wasn't, not after everything I'd done in the past five days, but it was something that needed to be said, if not to maintain my own peace of mind. "You said you were FBI. Why didn't you go back?"

"Are you kidding me? Either my supervisor or one of the higher-ups was involved in this. You have to understand these people are very powerful. They have resources like you'd never believe. What I did do was contact someone I knew at the *New York Times*. He looked into things, was going to blow the story wide open. Then I found out he killed himself. A forty-three-year-old Harvard grad hanging himself by a noose in his high-rise condo in Manhattan. Don't you get it? When you start fucking with them, they make sure to fuck you first."

"So now what?" I asked.

"Now we lay low for a day or two. Simon's people are going to be looking for us. Especially you."

"Why me?"

"Because they want you to keep playing the game."

I shook my head. "That ... that's insane."

"Maybe. But it's happened before. Simon can be very persuasive when he wants to be."

Carver touched his earpiece, listened for a moment, and said, "Shit."

"What is it?" I asked.

He ignored me and called up front, "Bronson, did you hear that?"

Bronson was nodding, already turning off onto a side street.

"What is it?" I asked again.

"This van was just reported stolen. We're going to need to go without wheels for a while."

David called back, "There's an L station coming up."

"Let's do it," Carver said. "Call Larry and let them know."

Seconds later the van was parked and the doors opened and we all piled out. I stepped onto the pavement, for the first time actually feeling the presence of the city around me. Traffic loud on the street, people walking the sidewalks, that ubiquitous stink of exhaust. I had to squint to see the tall buildings around us and then my arm was gripped and I was being pulled forward.

"We need to take you someplace and get you new clothes, new shoes, everything." Carver was talking while we hurried down the sidewalk. Bronson and David were behind us, bags over their shoulders. "Do you know your prescription off the top of your head? If not, we'll figure it out and get you new glasses so you can actually see."

We headed up the steps toward the train.

"What about the cameras?" I asked.

"Keep your head down. They can hack into practically any security system."

I kept my head down as we reached the platform and whispered, "But what—what if they come after us on the train with guns and stuff?"

"This isn't the movies," Carver said. "What happened back on the highway was a fluke, since they thought they could contain us quickly. They're not going to chase and shoot at us through a crowd of people. Too many witnesses. Besides, that's not the way they work."

"How do they work?"

Carver shook his head, shrugging off the question, and stepped forward as a train came screeching to a halt in front of us.

THIRTY-SIX

At the same time the three of us were getting on the Brown Line train at Sedgwick, a young cop named James Henley was working his shift less than three miles away by Navy Pier. He was twenty-five and had wanted to be a cop ever since he was a kid. His life's ambition was to become a detective. But before he could do that he had to work the street, and today he was working bicycle patrol. Unlike some of the other men, he preferred the bike to the patrol car. In the car it could become cramped, stuffy, while with the bike he had the freedom to take a break and stretch his legs, to not have to roll down his window if he wanted some fresh air. Of course he wasn't fond of wearing the helmet constantly, but regulations were regulations.

He had been married for just two years. He and his wife had found out they were pregnant four months ago. The ultrasound said they were having twins.

I like to think he was thinking of this in the final moments of his life. Pedaling his Trek around the plaza, the wind coming in off Lake Michigan, taxis and cars and buses making their deposits and pickups. Coasting over the sidewalk, watching the people but also thinking about his wife, about the twins he would be raising in the next couple years.

It was almost one o'clock and people were everywhere, tourists mostly carrying cameras and backpacks and shopping bags. They were headed toward any number of places—Bubba Gump or Capi's Italian Kitchen, the IMAX theater, the Children's Museum, the Crystal Gardens—or else they had set out early and were finished for the day, heading away from the mall with souvenirs and snacks. Maybe James was watching them and didn't notice the man approaching from behind. Or maybe James had been watching the man the entire time, had even begun to suspect that something was wrong. It's impossible to say, just as it's impossible to know if the man said something to James before taking out his gun and shooting the cop three times in the chest. What is possible to know is that he was thrown a couple feet from the bike, the helmet doing little to protect an already dead James Henley. What is also possible to know is that there were witnesses who claimed they'd seen everything. There was even one witness who said he managed to snap off a picture of the cop killer's face before the killer hurried away.

As the news would tell us an hour later, not surprisingly, that face belonged to me.

THIRTY-SEVEN

We eventually ended up in a motel in Evanston, not too far away from Lake Michigan. It was a small room with two narrow beds and a chair and a TV and a closet that squeezed in a shower and sink and toilet. When I went to take a piss I couldn't help but remember Carver's story and imagined Casey floating there.

Carver's other team would meet up with us later; right now they were searching the city for new transportation. It was important, Carver explained, that they stay split up at all times in case something happened to either team.

When I came out of the bathroom Carver was sitting in the single chair in the corner using the cell phone to talk to the Kid. Bronson and David were both lying on a different bed, their eyes closed.

Carver said, "Well when you do, call me on my cell," and disconnected the call. He took the battery out of the phone and tossed them on the bed by Bronson's feet. He said to me, "I wanted the Kid to know the number, see if he can trace it."

"You really think somebody set this up?"

"Yes," he said. "Based on your wife's job and your own job

and your social standing in the community, it doesn't make sense—if you all went missing, too many people would notice. Normally the people they use are … well, trash. People with no real job, no real life, who could go missing and nobody would ever notice. The fact that your wife is a lawyer"—he shook his head—"something just doesn't feel right."

Silence fell between us. On one of the beds, David began to snore.

I asked, "Why are you doing this?"

Carver was staring down at his hands in front of him, lost in his thoughts. He blinked and turned his head in my direction.

"I told you that quote before, the one by Edward Burke? About how all that's necessary for the triumph of evil is that good men do nothing? I'm just doing my part to keep the evil at bay as much as possible."

"But … how is it evil?"

A second later my question really hit me and I wanted to take it back, but by then Carver was speaking.

"Your bio said you're addicted to pornography. Have been ever since you were in high school. Do you consider that evil?"

I looked away and then looked back. Didn't really feel like saying anything.

"Okay, how about this—do you consider it good?"

Even though I couldn't really see him, I just stared back.

"The world's full of sick things, Ben. Pornography's just the tip of the iceberg. It's a gateway into the other stuff."

"The other stuff."

"Yeah. I don't want to pry, but can I ask what you started looking at in the beginning? Was it just naked women? Almost tasteful?"

Again I said nothing.

"It gets deeper and deeper," Carver said, "believe me. I've worked scouring the Internet for a long time. People get sucked in and eventually get bored. They want to try something new. So they go from softcore to hardcore. Then do you know what's after hardcore?"

I just stood there. Again had no will to answer him.

"There's an underground to the Internet," Carver said, sinking down even further into his chair. "Then below that underground is another underground. A place where the people who can afford it can see whatever the hell they please. Sometimes, if they have enough money, they can even direct what happens. That's what this entire thing's about. These powerful people who try to get off on whatever they can. They have the money and so bad things happen and people die. It's that simple."

There was another beat of silence.

Carver said, "Remember a while back when President Bush put a task force together against pornography? Most of the nation was like, What, are you giving up on terrorists all of a sudden? They were too hung-up on that question—not to mention their own privacy—to catch the economical purpose in what was happening."

"Economical."

"That's right," Carver said, nodding, but when he noticed my expression he decided to switch gears. "Ben, do you realize that pornography is nearly a one hundred *billion* dollar enterprise worldwide? All politicians are puppets, and Bush was no exception. The world is run by those who have the most money, hence the most power. When the U.S. government said they wanted to crack down on Internet pornography, it was a case of simple economics: supply and demand. The fewer websites out there, the more the other websites can charge. Sure people will balk at first, telling themselves they don't need it. But they do the same when gas prices go up. In the end they fold, because they need it. Just like you need it."

"I don't need it," I said, but the words were hollow, fake

even to my own ears. I stood there for a moment, my arms crossed, thinking. "So let me get this straight. This is like an organization or something. A kind of … club?"

Carver shook his head. "Far from it. These are just people, Ben, people like you and me. It's not some conspiracy. The way the world's set up today, we're content with the entertainment provided to us. The others who can afford it, who get off watching children raped and killed and all that shit, they create their own form. I will say, though, that they are getting bolder. The bombing at the retirement home yesterday isn't their usual M.O. It raises too many questions, too many possibilities of exposure."

There was silence again. Now Bronson was snoring too.

Carver said, "Sorry about those two. They've been up for the past twenty hours trying to get to you."

"How long have you been up?"

"Much longer."

"I don't believe you about my family." Even though I couldn't really see his face without squinting I looked back at him evenly. "They're still alive. I … I can't give up that hope."

"So what do you want to do? You want to go back into the game? I've told you already there's no outlet. The only way I survived—the only way David and Bronson and the rest survived—is they made their own way out. They walked away. Unless you do the same, you're as good as dead."

I shook my head, started to say something else (what, I realized a few moments later, was just more self-denial), when Carver's cell phone vibrated. He pulled it out of his pocket, put it to his ear, listened for about thirty seconds. Finally he said thanks and disconnected the call, slipped the phone back into his pocket.

"Shit," he said, rising to his feet.

"What is it?"

"Remember how I told you these people work a certain

way? According to the Kid, we're royally fucked." He said force-fully, "Bronson, David, wake up," and hurried past me to the TV.

Both men stopped snoring and opened their eyes and asked what was wrong. By then Carver had the TV on and was scanning through the channels until he came to the channel the Kid had apparently told him to see, what appeared to be a news break. On the screen the newscaster, a deeply tanned man, reported that just an hour ago a Chicago police officer was gunned down while on duty at Navy Pier. One witness even provided police with a picture taken with the use of his cell phone. On the screen a blurry picture of the perpetrator in question popped up—and the moment it flashed on my heart dropped.

"Oh my God," I whispered. Both David and Bronson sat up in bed, cursing under their breath.

Carver was shaking his head. "This is just great. Now every police officer in Chicago is going to be looking for you." He went back to his chair, sank down into it, and just continued shaking his head. "Someone must really be pulling strings to keep you in the game."

I managed to look away from the TV and said to Carver, "What do we do now?"

"That," he said, staring back at me, "is a very good question."

THIRTY-EIGHT

A little while later Bronson and David went out and brought back Chinese food. We all ate in silence. Neither man hardly looked at me, and I wondered just what kind of game they'd been put through, and how far they'd listened to Simon before walking away. They were just ordinary people, seemingly picked at random because they wouldn't have gone missing, and Carver intervened and helped them understand there was no outlet. He had them trained in firearms, in hand-to-hand combat, and constantly moved them around the country, supported on the extra money the Kid earned legitimately.

When we were done eating, Carver checked in with his other team and found they were still searching for transportation. It wasn't easy, especially in a major city, Carver said, trying to secure a quick vehicle without stealing it. Then he asked Bronson to set up the laptop.

Bronson pulled a MacBook out of his bag, powered it up, and inserted a wireless card. He typed in some commands, said, "I'm downloading them now," and turned the laptop around so the screen faced us.

Carver motioned me toward the laptop. "I asked the Kid to

email everything he'd saved so far regarding the Man of Wax. It should be ready soon."

The download only took a few minutes, but it seemed to take an hour. The little Chinese food I'd had—pork fried rice and an egg roll—hadn't settled well in my stomach and I felt like I might vomit at any moment.

"Finally," Carver said when the download was finished, "here we go."

I had to squint to see anything. The majority of the screen was black, except for the small box inside. And in that box was a bare motel room. The position of the camera was in one of the corners, looking down at someone lying on a bed. That someone was me.

Carver said, "It starts with you just sleeping for about an hour." He clicked the trackpad and the screen cut to me slowly sitting up, reaching for the ringing phone. "Once you put the glasses on the option comes to see that view too." He glanced at me. "Was that really blood on the bathroom door?"

"I … I don't know." I squinted down and watched myself as I tentatively answered the phone. I could almost hear Kevin's exasperated voice telling me this was my nine o'clock wake-up call.

Carver clicked the trackpad again and at once the screen changed, this time from my perspective—which felt completely vertiginous because it was just like déjà vu. At the moment I was strolling across the Paradise Motel's parking lot, glancing at the three vehicles parked there. Soon I would be entering the office where Kevin would be waiting to explain to me that this was California, that yes I had checked in last night, did I wish to see my credit card receipt?

I stared at the screen, completely entranced. "How … how did they get me there in the first place? I still don't understand that part."

"Most likely broke into your house in the middle of the

night and used chloroform to knock you and your family out. Our theory is that they then give you a sedative to make sure you won't wake up. Like I told you, these people somehow have an unlimited supply of resources. They can pretty much do whatever they want. Don't you remember what was just on the news?"

Sunday, the very last day I was together with my family, felt like forever ago. Sitting at home, watching football. Debating with Jen whether she should cook or just order a pizza. Casey drawing one of her pictures and bringing it to me, so proud of her work, and me smiling at her and telling her, "That's a hat," and her giggling, saying "*Da*-dee." Except the worst part was, I realized standing in that motel room in Chicago, with Carver hunched over the laptop and Bronson and David standing behind me watching, I couldn't even remember what it was she'd drawn.

I said, "I don't want to watch anymore." On the screen I'd parted ways with Kevin and went back to my room, was now approaching the bathroom door. "Just turn it off."

Carver clicked the trackpad once more. For a moment the screen was still there, and I was approaching the bathroom door, telling myself this was just some kind of dream and there was nothing on the other side. Then it went blank and it was the present again, yet somehow nothing had changed.

THIRTY-NINE

I woke in the middle of the night to a cold sweat. The room was silent except for David's and Bronson's snoring. They'd let me take one of the beds, Bronson taking the other bed, David asleep in the chair. Carver had said he would sleep on the floor, but when I squinted around the dark room I couldn't see him. Then I noticed that the door was open just a bit and got slowly out of bed.

We were on the second floor of the motel, and Carver was standing outside against the paint-flaked railing, looking down at the parking lot as he smoked. He heard me and turned slightly, saw it was me, turned back. Took his pack of Winston's out of his pocket and offered me one.

Neither of us spoke for the longest time. The only noise was the sporadic traffic on the street, the sound of the wind as it rustled the trees by the motel. A few scraps of trash and leaves skittered across the parking lot. The sky was filled with stars. A distant plane was making its approach to O'Hare. It was a sad realization: my life was fucked and still things ran as scheduled.

Finally Carver said, "Couldn't sleep?"

I finished the cigarette, flicked it over the edge and shook my head. "I had a nightmare."

Carver said nothing, didn't even nod. He just gripped the railing and leaned forward, stared down at the ground a floor below us.

I don't know why, but I told Carver about my dream. He'd asked why I was listed as the Man of Wax and maybe I figured this was the best way to explain it. But even though I told myself that, I knew it was a lie. I was simply doing the same thing I did every time I had the nightmare. I told Jen because just as I helped her out of her nightmares, she helped me out of mine. She held me and told me it was all right, that there was nothing I could have done about it, and I believed her. Of course I didn't expect Carver to comfort me in the same way, but I'd just had the nightmare again, the same nightmare twice in a week's time.

Carver listened without a word. He lit another cigarette, offered me a second. I shook my head, though I did want it.

"You think it's your fault, don't you."

I said, "No," shaking my head. Paused and said, "Yes." Then said, "I don't know."

"I think you do know. It's what made you drop out of school, right?"

I hesitated, glancing at Carver from the corner of my eye. "Actually, I was failing school. I mean, my grades weren't that bad, but I knew if I continued I'd never become a lawyer, no matter how hard I tried."

"Why did you want to become a lawyer in the first place?"

"To be honest," I said, "I have no idea. It's just ... all my life I'd been poor. Every month growing up I saw how my parents agonized over paying the bills on time. More than once our electricity had been turned off. Around Christmas both my parents got part-time jobs at the mall, and even that money went to help pay the bills. And I ... I didn't want that for my life. I didn't want to be a failure like my parents."

I took a deep breath.

"But you know something? It wasn't until I met my wife that I understood my parents weren't failures. That while you can fail in work, in school, life is something that doesn't take money. Neither does love. And my parents ... they loved each other. It sounds trite, but even if they were the poorest people in the world, as long as they had each other they would have been okay. They would have been happy. And I didn't understand that until I met Jen. Until we had Casey. That with them I finally had purpose."

I shook my head.

"But that night, with that girl ... that's when I really felt like a failure. That's when I felt like none of it mattered. Like I'd failed life. I wanted to do something. I tried shouting and couldn't, but even that would have been enough. Even if I didn't actually try to help her, at least I could have said something. That ... that might have made a difference."

"It wouldn't have," Carver said, tilting his head slightly to look at me, "and you know it."

I thought about it for a second. "Maybe. But I ... I just keep telling myself things would be different had I done something. Maybe I would have stayed in college, become a lawyer like I wanted. Or ... I don't know. But I wanted to do something, I wanted to help. Even in my nightmare I want to help. I keep telling myself if I move, if I take just one step forward, everything will change. Everything will ... it will be better."

I didn't want to get into the fact that, had I never dropped out of college, I probably never would have taken Clive up on his offer and gone out to Chicago, and I never would have met Jen—all factors leading up to the fact that Casey never would have been born. And while this crossed my mind many times before—my mind's way of finding good in my not acting when

I had the chance, to letting that poor girl be beaten into a coma —I had begun to believe it wouldn't have mattered. Like Jen said, she was my other half, I was hers, and eventually we would have found each other. What good was it having another half out there in the world and never getting the chance to bump into them, to never becoming complete? The world wasn't that unfair. It couldn't be.

Carver had smoked his Winston down to the filter and now flicked it over the edge. He gripped the railing, leaned forward, leaned back.

He said, "If I've learned one thing over the past three years, it's this: the world was evil at the beginning, and it'll be evil at the end. It's up to us to make sure we don't get sucked into all that evilness in the meantime."

I looked at him. The light was bad and because I had to squint I could hardly see his face. "What do you mean?"

He looked at me, stared for a long moment, and shook his head.

"If you haven't figured that out by now, Ben, then maybe I can't help you after all."

He went inside, shutting the door quietly behind him. I waited for another couple minutes. The wind picked up, blowing more scraps of trash and leaves across the parking lot. Finally I glanced up at the sky, stared at the stars.

I whispered, "Has the sheep eaten the flower or not?"

I listened as closely as I could, but the stars were silent.

FORTY

In the morning the Kid called. Carver listened carefully for about a minute, nodded once, said thank you, and disconnected. Then he said to me, "Sit down."

"What is it?"

"Sit down."

I sat down on the edge of the bed.

Carver stepped forward, crouched down so we were at eye level, and said, "Simon broadcasted a message across the Internet not too long ago, a message that only someone like the Kid could find. It basically said that there's still a chance to save your family if you're willing to go back into the game."

I stared at him, shaking my head slowly. "But you ... you said they were already dead."

"And I still believe they're dead. My advice is to ignore the message completely. But it's your life, so the decision is up to you."

I glanced up at Bronson and David, both who were staring back at me.

I said, "But what if they are still alive?"

Carver shook his head. "Then they're still alive. But they won't be for long. Neither will you."

I looked away, swallowed, took a breath. "If I … if I wanted to continue, how?"

"The message said to just turn on your phone. And that if you no longer had your phone, to—"

I was already moving, standing up and walking to the bedside table where the cell phone and battery lay. I picked them up, inserted the battery and then turned on the phone, ignoring Carver telling me to stop.

The phone vibrated less than thirty seconds after finding a signal.

Carver said, "They're going to lock onto that signal as soon as you answer, so make it quick."

I nodded, took another deep breath, and answered the phone.

"About time," Simon said. "I've been calling every sixty seconds. Was worried my little distress message would be ignored. I was also beginning to get bored and figured we'd have to go blow up that preschool just to teach you a lesson."

I didn't say anything.

"Are you enjoying yourself, Ben? Because I wanted to let you know your wife and daughter certainly aren't enjoying themselves."

I sank down onto the bed, my shoulders slouched. I closed my eyes. "Let me … let me talk to them."

"No."

"*Yes*," I said, my voice rising. "If you think I'm even going to consider stepping one foot back into the game, I won't do it until I hear their voices."

There was a long silence and for an instant I worried that Simon had disconnected. Then he said, "Mr. Ellison has been telling you stories about me now, hasn't he? He's probably told you that your family is already dead. That's how you suddenly grew a pair of balls."

"I just want to make sure they're still alive."

"Oh they're alive, Ben. Trust me."

"Then let me speak to them."

"Not yet. First, let me speak to Mr. Ellison. I want to say hello."

I glanced up at Carver. Held out the phone. Carver only stared at it, didn't look like he was going to take it, but then he reached out and took the phone. Placed it to his ear and said, "What?" Listened for thirty seconds or so, then handed it back to me.

"Thank you," Simon said. I could hear the grin back in his voice. "It's been a while since Carver and I really talked, you know? It seems everything always gets in the way."

Carver's eyes had shifted away from me, were now centered on the floor. Whatever Simon had said to him would not be repeated to me, or to Bronson or David, or even to the Kid. It was something between Carver and Simon, something that kept them connected in a way I hoped to never know.

I said, "Now let me speak to my family."

"Of course," Simon said. "Who would you like to speak to first, your wife or daughter?"

I said nothing, knowing what Simon was trying to get at— after all, he had been asking me all this week which one, Jen or Casey, I loved more.

Simon chuckled. "Fine then, be that way. Hold on a moment."

The moment lasted nearly a minute. Then a new sound entered the silence. A small and soft voice uttering just one word.

"Daddy?"

"Casey," I said, jumping up from the bed. "Baby, are you okay?"

"Daddy, they—they hurt me."

"No, Casey, no," I said, starting to sob, already feeling the tears on my face. I went to say more but Casey was no longer there.

Simon asked, "Satisfied?"

"What about my wife?"

"What about her?"

"I want to speak to her."

"And I want a blowjob from the Queen of England. But just like the Stones taught us, we can't always get what we want."

I gritted my teeth. "Let me talk to my wife, you son of a bitch!"

"Whoa, watch it, Ben. What did I tell you before about name-calling? Now you've forced me to do this."

There was a pause, followed immediately by a high-pitched shriek. I'd heard it many times before, running from my bedroom to Casey's to wake her out of her nightmares, but never like this.

"Don't!" I shouted. "Please"—my voice was starting to crack, to tremble—"please don't."

"Then don't be mean. Next time it will be worse. I'll let you listen to the bone snap."

I fell back on the bed, closed my eyes.

"Now if you want even the half-hope of seeing your family again, here's what I want you to do. Listen carefully, because I'm only going to say this once."

When he was done he disconnected. I set the phone aside, lay there for a very long time, slowly sat up. Opened my eyes to find Carver and Bronson and David watching. Carver seemed to already know what Simon had told me. He was shaking his head.

"Don't," he said, almost simply, though by now he must have realized his attempts had become wasted.

I looked up at him. I could feel tears threatening to press their way forward again. I didn't say anything.

Yet, somehow, my silence said it all.

FORTY-ONE

A cab took me all the way to Navy Pier, about a half hour's drive. Either the driver hadn't seen the news in the past twelve hours or else he wasn't very observant, because I'd caught him glancing at me a few times in his rearview mirror but nothing ever came of it. I wanted him to drop me off a few blocks away from the place and he gave me a curious look, said it was no trouble dropping me right off in front of the plaza. "I want to walk," I told him, and minutes later I was dropped off at the corner of North Peshtigo and East Illinois. I paid him and got out, then started walking, heading beneath the highway overpass, squinting at the large building and the red archway and the boats out on the water. From my angle I could just see the top of the slowly revolving Ferris wheel.

For a Saturday afternoon around twelve o'clock you'd think this area of the city would be a little busier. A number of taxis and buses and cars drove around the loop of North Streeter Drive like normal, their taillights glowing red as they made their stops, but the number of pedestrians walking the sidewalks was limited, as if there was something wrong.

Of course something's wrong, I thought. *Yesterday someone just got murdered here.*

I had to squint to make sure I was headed in the right direction. I would have let the driver drop me off right in front of the plaza (presumably where the cop was shot), but I wanted to put off the inevitable as long as possible—whatever that may be. All Simon had said was to come down here, to where James Henley was killed, and to not talk to anybody. Not a word.

So when ten minutes passed and I was just standing there on the sidewalk, right near where the incident tape had been strung up, and the first police car arrived, its lights flashing, followed by another car, then another, then another, and the cops all got out, their weapons aimed, shouting at me to get down on the ground, shouting at me to put my hands on the back of my head, I did so silently.

Next they rushed forward, their guns still drawn, approaching me like I was strapped with explosives. They worked quickly and efficiently, keeping their desires to beat the shit out of me temporarily at bay. Hands fell on me, pushing me into the ground, and my arms were jerked up so they could place the cuffs around my wrists.

And still I was silent.

I just lay there, my body pressed against the cold cement, and glanced out at the people heading toward the plaza, even the people who'd gotten stuck in traffic because of the commotion. They had all stopped moving, were now standing still. They were all watching the action intently.

Something told me they couldn't look away.

FORTY-TWO

The interview room was bright, its fluorescents humming in the ceiling, and the walls were bare, not a thing marking any space except for where the door stood and the long mirror stretched to my right, which all the movies and TV shows in the world told me was one-way and which a number of policemen stood behind watching at this moment. The room had no distinguishing smells, except for what may have been the lingering ghosts of sweat and body odor. When I'd first come in the temperature had been moderate, but now it was cold, a biting chill that reminded me of waking up in room six of the Paradise Motel.

The only things in the room were a metal table and two chairs, one of which I'd been sitting in for the past five or ten hours. My sense of time had quickly dissipated the longer I'd been stuck in here. There was no noise except for the humming of the fluorescents, no noise except for the blood which some-times pounded away in my ears. No noise except for the few times the detective had come into the room, had sat down at the other side of the table and just stared at me.

He hadn't given me his name, and for all I knew he wasn't

even a detective. Maybe not even a cop. He was a tall menacing man with a buzz cut and eyes that had clearly seen more darkness than they had been promised. He was dressed in slacks and a shirt and tie. The first time he came in he just stared at me with his dark eyes, didn't say a word for at least ten minutes. I stared back at him (squinted really, because I was still without my glasses), not saying a word, and he left. He came back later and this time spoke, his voice a heavy and meaty bass, asking me if I knew what kind of trouble I was in. Explaining what happened to people who killed cops. Telling me about all the different things that were going to happen to me in prison—how the guards were going to treat me, then the prisoners, and then the guards again. Still I said nothing, not a word, and he stood up from his chair, cracked his knuckles and slowly started walking around the table. I was certain he was going to hit me but instead he just leaned in close, placing one hand on the table, his other hand on the back of my chair.

"You know," he whispered, "silence always confirms guilt. Don't think by not saying a goddamned thing it proves you're innocent."

I forgot if it was on TV or in some movie, but I remembered seeing a detective once chewing or eating something to make his breath smell rank before coming in and talking to whoever was trapped in one of these rooms. An onion, mustard, jalapeños—any number of things that would cause halitosis. I didn't know what this detective had done today, but there was definitely something foul coming from inside his mouth. It almost smelled like he had a decayed tooth that he'd never taken care of and which he'd purposely kept for situations like these. I noticed the wedding band on his finger and almost felt sorry for his wife.

But still I said nothing. I didn't even turn away. I just sat there and stared forward. This detective thought I was playing tough but that wasn't it at all. My reticence had nothing to do with the fact I'd been caught and didn't want to say anything that might later bite me in the ass. I didn't know what he wanted, exactly—I hadn't been read my rights, which meant I wasn't under arrest, which meant I was here for questioning purposes until they either found the murder weapon or some other thing to nail me with—but I knew what Simon wanted, what Simon had pretty much demanded, and that was to not say a word to anybody, no matter what happened.

"And I'll know if you do," he told me, right before disconnecting, "which means that Jennifer and Casey will know too."

I didn't doubt him for an instant. I knew he'd know, and that was why I hadn't said a word, not even one syllable, this entire time.

On Detective Rotten Tooth's third visit he brought a stack of photographs. Many were four-by-sevens of James Henley and his wife, who, the detective made a point of constantly noting, was pregnant with twins. Most of the pictures showed what were no doubt James Henley and his wife in the early years of their relationship, their arms around each other, both smiling widely for the camera. A few others showed them both on their wedding day, in what looked to have taken place in a small and dimly lit chapel. Another at the reception, with James and his wife posing as they together cut the cake. A final picture showed James in uniform, standing tall and proud, and the detective talked just about him for a while, how the man's ambition had been to become a detective ever since he was a kid, how James actually liked working bike patrol, how ever since he found out he and his wife were having twins it was all he ever talked about.

Detective Rotten Tooth asked, "Why you squinting? You need glasses or something?"

I didn't say anything.

"Well?" he said, but I kept my attention forward, didn't nod or shake my head. I'd had no ID on me when they brought me in, so they didn't know who I was. They had taken my picture and scanned my fingerprints, but I knew nothing would come up. Like Simon had said, I had never once been arrested, so I wouldn't be on some database, and even if I was I was pretty confident Simon would take care of that on his end. The only thing on me was the cell phone, which Simon had told me to bring (he'd told me to ditch everything else) and which was probably stored away as evidence somewhere. I didn't even have Jen's wedding ring anymore, or the black and white photograph of my wife and daughter gagged and crying —I'd left them behind because they were just another part of Simon's instructions, and another way I felt like less of a man.

"To hell with you," the detective said finally, and left the room, leaving me sitting there and staring down at the table.

I didn't touch any of the pictures. The detective had laid them out for me, facing up so I had no choice but to look. And I did look. I couldn't help myself. James Henley was a young guy, not much younger than myself, and while his wife was blonde and looked nothing like Jen, I began to see the both of us replaced in those pictures. The years we'd dated, then our wedding day; the ritual of cutting the wedding cake and feeding each other a piece.

I wondered what would have happened had I been used just as James Henley had been used, a simple pawn in a game constructed by those who wished to entertain only a select few. Except James hadn't even been a pawn; no, he'd been so much less. He'd been a throwaway, just a man unlucky enough to be in the wrong place at the wrong time. It could have happened to anybody, and thinking this, I wondered about all the other people gunned down in the streets, the fatal accidents on the highways, the women raped by men. How many of those had been true accounted incidents of a world gone mad, and how many had been simply designed to fulfill the dark desires of only a few?

Around what may have been the fifth or sixth hour—again, I'd lost my sense of time, and when Detective Rotten Tooth came in he wasn't wearing a watch—the need to move my bowels became very strong. So strong, in fact, I felt that any moment my body might start pissing without the express written consent of my mind. But that was probably what they wanted anyway, the cops and Simon. To see me wet myself, to force me to soak in the stink of my own piss.

But what if Simon was gone?

It was a question that had been in the back of my mind this entire time, even while I was taking my cab ride to Navy Pier. What if Jen and Casey were really dead and Simon had no use for me anymore, wanted me to just take the fall for the murder one of his own people had committed? This would be the perfect ending in a way, wouldn't it?

Except I refused to believe that. I thought of what the fox had told the little prince, his secret—"One sees clearly only with the heart"—and I knew Jen and Casey were still alive. I knew it in my heart, in my soul, and I wasn't going to give up the slightest bit of hope that Carver was wrong. I wanted to believe Jen would do the same in my position. Besides, it had been my job to save her and Casey from their nightmares, from those monsters chasing them. Now that I'd failed them I needed to make up for it, I needed to prove that even though those monsters had turned out to be real, they could still be defeated. Wasn't that the reason for all the fairy tales told throughout time—to remind children that not only do monsters exist, but they can also be beaten? Wasn't that the real reason Casey loved the *Shrek* movies so much, that in the end love conquers all?

Time worked overtime to stretch itself out. I was hungry, cold, and I needed to take a piss. I'd even begun nodding off but managed to stay awake. I kept referring to the pictures set before me, sometimes leaning close and squinting so I could make out every detail, and I wondered how Detective Rotten Tooth had gone about getting them. He'd no doubt had to contact James Henley's widow, explain the situation. Had she been hesitant about providing pictures from her beloved albums? Had she really wanted the man who'd killed her husband to witness snapshots of the two of them when they were happy? Wouldn't that have just sunk the nail in deeper to the fact that all those happy times were what I'd viciously taken away?

Maybe she was standing on the other side of the one-way mirror right now. I'd barely even acknowledged it since I was brought in here, made to sit down at the table. I hadn't even stood up. I'd just been sitting in my chair, staring forward, hoping that Simon would take care of things on his end. Otherwise I didn't know what I was going to do. Could I really try explaining my story to Detective Rotten Tooth? It was almost too unbelievable to believe myself, and I'd been playing the game for close to a week now.

But it wouldn't matter what I said, and I knew it. To all these people I was just a cop killer. In their minds I'd taken away one of their own, a man everyone seemed to have liked, even if they'd never met him before, and they wanted to make sure I got what was coming to me. They all wanted me dead, and I couldn't say I blamed them.

At what may have been six days later—but was in reality only nine hours—Detective Rotten Tooth made his fourth visit.

While he'd looked angry before, now he looked livid. So much so I could see the red in his face, could almost feel the heat radiating off him. He came and leaned down beside me, his shirtsleeves now rolled up, and stuck his mouth only an inch away from my ear.

"Looks like you're more than just a cop killer," he whispered, his putrid breath warming my neck. "The FBI contacted us hours ago. Seems they suspect you were involved in that explosion down in Ryder. They say now it was a bombing. Is that right, you piece of shit? You get off killing old people too?"

He leaned back and slammed his fist down on the tabletop. A few of the pictures jumped.

"You want me to bring in pictures of them old people too?" he shouted. "You want me to bring in pictures of all of them?"

I remained silent. I was waiting for him to hit me, to slap me across the face. He'd probably told those people behind the one-way mirror to take a walk, go get themselves coffee. Maybe he'd asked James Henley's widow to stay behind. If they had a camera set up, he'd no doubt had it turned off. He could just say I'd fallen off my chair, broke my arms and nose that way. Nobody would ever call him on it, even if I did suddenly start talking and accused him.

But Detective Rotten Tooth didn't hit me. He just leaned over me a few seconds more, staring down at the pictures.

"You've been looking at these? You see what you took away from those unborn twins? Now they're going to grow up without their daddy around. He won't be there to hear their first words. He won't be there to rock them to sleep. He won't be there to see their first steps. He won't be there to pick them back up when they fall. I hope you can live with that, you sick fuck. I hope you can sleep at night with what you've done."

A part of me wanted to break down right there. It had nothing to do with what he was telling me, but from the simple fact I was tired. Tired of this entire game I'd been forced into, tired of everything these people had done to me and my family and everyone else. I wanted to tell him I had nothing to do with James Henley, that I had never killed and would never kill a person a day in my life.

Except Simon, I thought. If it came down to it, I could probably bring myself to kill him.

"When the FBI gets this all straightened out," Detective Rotten Tooth whispered, his breath still warm on my neck, "you'll be coming back here. I can't wait to see you again. I can't wait to show you more pictures. You're going to get what's coming to you, believe me. I'll get you to talk."

He leaned back and slammed his fist down on the table again. This time more of the pictures jumped.

"You understand that?" Detective Rotten Tooth said. "I'll get you to talk. That's a promise."

FORTY-THREE

There were two FBI agents, a man and a woman. They both wore suits and had long stolid faces. They looked at me, a supposed cop killer, just as they would have looked at a five-year-old child with a lollipop in her hand and ribbons in her hair. They gave nothing away with their eyes, with their faces, and when they took me into custody it was with professionalism and grace not many people have the patience to learn.

My arms and legs were shackled. I was still wearing the clothes I'd put on that morning. I still had no glasses and couldn't see much as I was led through the police station, got in an elevator with the two agents who hadn't even said a single word to me yet. I watched the numbers glow as we descended. For some reason I expected us to stop on the first floor but we kept going down.

Then the doors opened and we entered the basement garage, a cold and murky place that smelled of rubber and oil. I was loaded in the back of a black sedan. A few police officers waited by the cars, their arms crossed, watching us. Some had cigarettes in their mouths, making me crave one. They looked angry, pissed off, disgusted. I glanced at them briefly before the car started moving and then I stared down at my lap, my wrists bound in tight metal. This was the second time in less than twenty-four hours I'd been handcuffed. I'd never thought it could feel this humiliating.

The agents in the front continued their silent treatment. The driver brought the car up out of the garage and into the city street. It was close to eleven o'clock and the streetlights were lit up.

The sedan moved through the streets for another minute or two before it slowed and stopped and the back door opened and someone slid in beside me.

"How's it hanging, Ben?"

The voice was familiar but the face was not. This was because half of the face was covered in bandages.

"I've got to hand it to Carver," the man said. "He's building himself quite an army and it's starting to really piss us off."

The eye not covered by the bandage glowered back at me.

"As you can see," the man said, "I managed to survive that little incident back on the highway. The other two with me were not so fortunate."

This man was my one escort from Reno. He had been the one who initially "saved" me from Carver and his people and cleaned me up and dropped me back at the Sundown Saloon. He was the one who had been waiting for me on the other side of the door at Juliet's place when I tried to walk out. Shit, he had been the cop who had pulled up behind me on that highway after I'd thrown up because I thought my daughter's remains were inside the trunk.

The man said, "You can talk now, by the way. Really, Ben, you've fulfilled your task. Feel free to talk. Say whatever you want."

The sedan had started moving again, driving us through the city streets. I stared back at the man for a long time, then glanced at the two agents up front.

"Are they really with the FBI?"

"They are," the man said. "Does that really surprise you by now?"

It didn't. And I didn't know what scared me more at that moment—the fact that these were corrupt federal agents who had managed to get me out of police custody, or the fact that this was all being done for the sake of entertainment. And not just normal entertainment, where anybody's free to enjoy the fun, but only a handful, maybe fifty, one hundred, two hundred viewers who had the money and the resources. Carver had said whoever was doing this was well connected and this just proved it. Because the Chicago Police Department would not have given up their only suspect in a murder involving one of their own, even if it was for questioning. They'd probably refused at first, had kicked and screamed, but when it became clear they had no choice there was nothing left to do. No wonder Detective Rotten Tooth was in such a state the last time he came in to see me.

We left the city streets and got onto the expressway. I squinted at the signs as we passed them. As much as I didn't want to speak—it was my only form of defiance—I finally found I could no longer help myself.

"Where are we going?"

The man beside me simply said, "You'll see."

Twenty minutes later we stopped just outside of O'Hare, in what looked to be a deserted parking lot. The driver parked between two long rows of cars. The man in the back turned toward me, a thin key suddenly in his bandaged right hand, and started undoing my shackles. Once the cuffs loosened I released a breath, began massaging my wrists.

"Now what?"

"Now you continue the game." The thin key had disappeared and he was now holding another one. He motioned to a car parked just outside my door, a white Chevy Impala. "And no more fucking around, Ben. Got it?"

"You don't seriously expect me to drive without my glasses, do you? I can barely see anything as it is."

"Don't worry. You will soon."

"What does that mean?"

Neither the man nor the woman in the front had said anything this entire time. Now the woman cleared her throat. She was holding something that I couldn't quite make out in the dark. When the man beside me grabbed it, the thing passed in the little light provided by the lamps posted around the parking lot and I recognized it immediately. It was the cell phone the police had been keeping, the only thing of mine I'd had on me when I was taken in.

"This is yours too," the man said. He turned the phone on, handed me it and the key. "Make sure not to lose this one. It's always a pain in the ass shipping out new phones, and I can pretty much guarantee we won't bother sending you a third."

I sat there in the back seat and stared down at the phone and key in my hands. The shackles lay coiled between my feet. The sedan's engine continued to idle, the only sound in the car.

Finally I said, "What do I do now?" It wasn't the question I wanted to ask—though there were a thousand of them, so many I could hardly put them in order—but it sounded good once it was out of my mouth. I still couldn't see very well, I had to constantly keep squinting, which probably suited the one-eyed man beside me just fine.

"I can't tell you, Ben. Remember what I told you before, I'm not your Simon. Wish I was, though. This has turned out to be one hell of a game. Caesar said it might go down as an all-time classic."

"Who ... who's Caesar?"

The man produced a thin smile. "Don't worry about that.

Now it's time for you to get going. So scat, Ben. Get the fuck out of here."

I opened my door and started to get out but stopped when the man said my name again. He sounded irritated now, his voice not bringing across the grin that had been there seconds before. I turned, leaned down and poked my head in the sedan. He was glaring back at me.

"We save your ass when it's in a real fucking pickle and you don't even have the decency to thank us?"

"Thank you," I said, barely even hearing myself, and shut the door. Stood back and waited until the sedan pulled away. I watched it for a couple long moments until it had disappeared from the parking lot—though I knew it wouldn't go too far, that those three would continue on now as my escorts.

Up in the sky was the sound of an approaching plane. I looked up, spotted it there among the stars, and watched it for a while. At that moment it was better than doing anything else.

FORTY-FOUR

The cell phone vibrated the moment I started the Impala.

By then I'd already opened the driver's and rear-side passenger doors to conceal me from whoever might be driving past as I took a long and satisfying piss. When I was done I got inside. On the passenger seat was a large sport's bag containing underwear, jeans, T-shirts and a sweatshirt. Even a heavy jacket, much like the one I'd bought back in Wyoming, was stuffed inside the bag. I looked through it for only a few seconds before I realized just how cold it was in the car and turned it on to get the engine warming and the heat going.

When Simon called, I didn't answer right away. I kept thinking about Carver, about what he'd told me. The words NO OUTLET flashed through my mind again and again. Was it really true? Would this all lead to the same and inevitable conclusion? Were Jen and Casey already dead? Maybe it was true and all I had left was the chance to save myself. Simon and whoever else had ensured me some time away from the police. Why not just take full advantage and disappear?

On its tenth vibration I punched the green button and said, "I want to talk to my family."

"What, no hello?"

I was silent. I turned the knob for heat but all that came from the vents was cold air.

"Come on, Ben," Simon said, "you're not even going to thank me for bailing you out of that cramped interview room? It's a hell of a place to be for ten hours, especially when every man and woman in that building is convinced you're a cop killer."

"I already thanked my escort."

"That's great. Now thank me."

I bit my lip, clenched my other hand into a fist. It was no big deal to say the words, but at the same time it was. Because even uttering them acknowledged the fact that I owed Simon something, that he had power over me. I'd said it to my one-eyed escort but that was because I was convinced that, had I refused, he would have killed me on the spot.

"I'm waiting, Ben."

"Thank you," I said, almost spat. I crunched up my face, wanted to smack the steering wheel.

"You're welcome. We always look after our own. I understand that business with Carver Ellison wasn't something you had any control over. I'm sure he told you one hell of a story though, didn't he?"

Again I didn't say anything. I'd spent close to ten hours in silence, and while that might have been no large feat, it sure as hell feels it while a cop is pressuring you to make the slightest sound.

"Well?" Simon said. "Didn't he?"

I closed my eyes, took a deep breath. I was tired and hungry, and playing Simon's game was just going to piss me off even more.

"Yes," I said. "It was one hell of a story."

"What did he tell you?"

"That I'm being—"

I paused. Opened my eyes, squinted to look around the car a little more closely now, just like I'd done driving out of Doyle. At the dash, the radio, the glove compartment, the dome light.

"Where is it? Where's the camera?"

"Camera? You mean you think there's just one?" Simon chuckled. "If you haven't figured it out yet, Ben, there's always a camera on you. Always. There was even one in the interview room. I'll tell you, we got the most hits when you got in there. Word has certainly spread about the Man of Wax. Everyone wants to watch, and that's not including those in the Inner Circle. Here's a man that will very soon make national headlines, or at least your picture will, because that's all the press has been given at the moment. Granted, it is a little blurry, but that doesn't matter. They're only working on speculation. Hell, they don't even know your name. Nobody does. Did you know CNN is calling you the Anonymous Bomber? A little presumptuous, I'd say, but even Fox News and MSNBC are running with it. I only wonder what's going to happen tomorrow when people from your hometown see that picture in the papers. Do you think they'll recognize you? Do you think they'll be surprised?"

"If this is so big, how did I get out of the police station without any trouble? There weren't any news vans or anything waiting outside."

"Of course not. Our agents requested someone they had locked in a holding cell to be shackled and have a coat placed over his head. They took him out the front. It was crazy. Reporters scrambling asking him questions. He was a good boy though, kept his head down and just continued on his way. Misdirection, Ben, that's what it's all about. The public falls for it every time."

"Every time," I murmured. The air coming from the vents had warmed considerably, yet somehow I still felt cold.

Simon said, "That's right. Remember 9/11, what else happened that day? Of course you don't. See: misdirection."

I opened my mouth, started to repeat the word—I got as far as *mis*—but then fell silent. I didn't even want to start with Simon, because I knew he would never stop. He was more than just voluble when he needed to be; he was garrulous through and through, so much so that I sometimes wondered if he would ever shut up. If anything that was his weak point, the one thing I could exploit.

"Simon."

"Yes, Ben?"

"Who's Caesar?"

There was a long pause on Simon's end. "What are you talking about?"

"Caesar," I said. "You wanted to know what Carver told me. He told me something about Caesar. Who is he?"

The pause on Simon's end grew into a silence. I closed my eyes, took a breath. I was beginning to fear my bluff had backfired, that Simon had disconnected and was already approaching my wife and daughter with whatever tools he used to cut off body parts.

Then Simon chuckled and said, "Nice try, Ben. You had me going for a second, but someone else just brought it to my attention what Jerry said to you a few minutes ago. Fucking idiot. He'll be dealt with later, you can trust me on that."

Jerry, I thought, musing over that simple name. It reminded me that all these men and women had other identities, other lives. They probably had wives, husbands, girlfriends or boyfriends, children, a mortgage.

"Anyway," Simon said, "enough of that. Check the glove compartment."

I leaned forward, extending my hand ... but stopped.

"Go ahead, Ben," Simon near-whispered. "Look what's inside."

I knew I had no choice, so I opened it.

Another leather wallet, no doubt crammed with hundreds of dollars. A pair of the same glasses that had been in the bathroom of the Paradise Motel, the same glasses Carver had first tried to take away from me in Reno, and which he'd succeeded to take away from me here in Chicago. The frames were thick and cold and I put them on at once, relishing the simple fact that now I could actually see. I didn't even bother for a second to worry that others who wished to do so were linking over to another page so they could see things from my point of view. All I worried about was now, with my eyes adjusted to make out the slightest detail, I could see what else was in the glove compartment.

"No," I said. "I'm not killing anyone."

"It's a little too late to start saying that now. You've already killed close to thirty-some people. And as far as the country is concerned you've also killed a cop. A man who had a wife pregnant with twins. Such a pity. But this is the stuff primetime media loves. This is what keeps viewers checking in. And what do you think is going to happen when they find out you managed to escape?"

"I managed"—I swallowed, still staring down at the gun in the glove compartment, the revolver which I was pretty sure had once rested in the glove compartment of the Dodge—"to escape?"

"Well, officially not yet, but soon. It'll be embarrassing for the FBI, but embarrassing things have happened before. Now it's up to you to decide just how things will turn out in the news. Are you going to disappear into the night, never to be heard from again? Maybe go back to your hometown and bomb your daughter's preschool? Or is the FBI going to track you down? Is there going to be a shoot-out that's going to leave you dead? As always, the choice is up to you. But don't worry —the press conference won't be until tomorrow morning, so you have until then to decide. In the meantime, as far as everyone else in concerned, you're still in FBI custody."

I wanted to tell him to go fuck himself. I wanted to tell him to go to hell. I wanted to tell him to go eat shit. I wanted to break down and cry.

I asked, "Can I please speak to my family?"

"Hmm, I don't know. As much as I'd like to do you that favor, things have not been going well. You had originally been coming to Chicago for a completely different purpose than what transpired. We had even promised a few loyal viewers you'd do something special. Now it seems that's just not going to work out anymore. Your face is already plastered on every newspaper in the state. By tomorrow it will be in every newspaper in the country. Which makes your part in continuing the game much riskier than usual."

"I just want to hear their voices. I just … I want to know they're okay."

"They're okay, Ben. You're going to have to trust me on that. I mean, you and I have been through so much together already, haven't we? What kind of relationship would we have if we didn't have trust?"

"I'll refuse to continue," I said, and even when the words left my mouth I still wasn't sure what I was saying, or why. I knew the risks involved. I knew what they had already threatened to do to Casey's preschool. The Impala's engine had fully warmed and the heat had become so hot that I turned it down to its lowest setting.

"I'm sorry," Simon said, "but was that a threat?"

"From what I hear I'm making you guys lots of money. What did that one escort say to me? How Caesar said this game might turn out to be an all-time classic? Now all I'm asking is to speak to my wife and daughter, just once. You're going to deny me that?"

"Yes, Ben, I am going to deny you that. I don't let anybody

tell me what to do, especially piece of shit players. You might like to think you're in a position to negotiate, but what have I told you already? There's no negotiating. Yeah, so maybe this game has caught a lot of people's attention. That doesn't mean shit. We could end your life in a second and nobody would care. Don't you get that by now? They love watching people die. They love watching people tortured. If you want to fuck around and try to play hero then we'll kill you and we'll kill your wife and daughter. Probably rape them first a couple of times, put on a real good show, then kill them. After that it's on to the next show. There's always a new game, always a new player, so don't think yourself special, Ben. You're nobody. You're just a Man of Wax. You couldn't save Michelle Delaney in college, what makes you think you can save your family now?"

For the longest time I was silent. Even with the heat on low it was becoming too hot in the car. I stared out the windshield, wondering what was in the trunk. Knowing Simon, and from everything Carver had told me, there was no doubt in my mind that Jen and Casey were already dead. The little spark that had been keeping the flames of hope alive had just gone out. They were dead and they were probably in the trunk right now. If I were to get out and open it, I wouldn't find a mannequin in there like before, but a real dead body. Two real dead bodies. Just as real as the dried blood would be.

"What's wrong, Ben? Did I hurt your feelings? Do you want to cry?"

"Your viewers," I said. "They … they can't hear you, can they? They can hear me but not you."

Another slight pause on Simon's end. "What do you mean?"

"I'm just trying to figure out why you're constantly talking. I understand you need to give me directions, you need to do the whole Simon Says bullshit, but I don't really give a fuck

about what you have to say. I'm pretty sure whatever viewers
you have wouldn't give a fuck either. You just like hearing the
sound of your own voice. Come on; admit it. You're envious
that—"

"*Envious*? What the fuck do you think you're talking about,
Ben? Who the fuck do you think I'm envious of?"

"Me," I said. "I'm the star of the show and it pisses you off.
Because as far as anybody's concerned, you don't even exist.
That's why you keep me on the phone. The longer I'm talking
to you, the longer the viewers have to watch me, and they have
to wonder what's so goddamned interesting. Well do you know
what, *Simon*? Nothing you have to say is interesting. Not a
goddamned thing."

Silence on Simon's end, silence so deep and pregnant that I
was certain he'd disconnected. But I waited, and I listened, and
I could hear his breathing on the other end, a shallow sound
that was barely even there. I closed my eyes. Again thought
about Jen and Casey, and how if they weren't already dead they
soon would be. In the next couple minutes most likely. Maybe
even sooner.

"Look," I started to say, meaning to apologize because it
was the only way I knew how to try to make things right, but
Simon cut me off.

"You're right," he said. "You are the star of the show. And
right now the show must go on."

"My family. Please don't—don't hurt them."

"You've got it all wrong, Ben. If anybody hurts them, it's
you. Your actions dictate what happens to Jennifer and Casey.
They dictate what happens to everyone else you call innocent.
For a smart guy like you I would think you'd have realized that
by now."

"Listen, I didn't mean—"

"What would you say to them? If you had the chance and
it was the very last thing they'd hear. What would you tell them

that would make everything all right, at least as all right as things can be?"

Again I closed my eyes. I was already picturing both of them dead, lying discarded in some random dark basement. I'd never really believed in Heaven and I still wasn't sure, but I hoped it existed and that it was where they'd gone. I hoped wherever they were they were in peace.

"I'd tell them that I loved them," I whispered. "I'd tell them that I loved them very much."

"Seems a bit too cliché. Wouldn't they already figure you loved them anyway? Why would you want to waste it? Remember, Ben, this is the *very* last thing they hear before they die. What words do you want to leave them with before they pass over onto the other side?"

"I—" But I couldn't say anything else. I wanted to, but my voice refused to work.

"Just think about that, Ben. Think about what you'd say to them. Because it's possible that might happen soon. It all depends on you. It all depends on how well you play the game."

I kept my eyes closed, saw nothing in the darkness anymore. Not Jen's face, not Casey's.

"Now get onto to the expressway and head south until you get to 80. Then head east."

"Where ... where am I going?"

"You know I can't tell you that, Ben. But hey, what the fuck —you are the star of the show, right, so you should be treated like it. Okay then, here's where you're going."

I opened my eyes. Stared through the windshield into a new kind of darkness.

"It's a place you've been to before. A place you should be very familiar with."

This was a darkness that had lights, contained people, yet for some reason I couldn't see any of those people.

"A place even your wife and daughter have been before. A place they should be very familiar with. Have you guessed it yet?"

I couldn't see any of those people, and I knew that while none of them were dead, none of them were alive either.

"Lanton, Pennsylvania." There was no grin, not even a sneer, to Simon's voice. "That's right, Ben. You're going home."

FORTY-FIVE

Half past midnight, I was maintaining a steady speed along I-80, keeping up with the traffic but not going over any more than I had to. The last thing I needed right now, the very last, was to get pulled over for speeding. Wouldn't that state trooper feel special then? Probably win himself a medal or something.

I had the radio turned on hoping to hear snatches of the news, waiting until there was further word on what it now seemed CNN had everyone calling me. But there was hardly anything mentioned, only one quick report that the Anonymous Bomber was in FBI custody at this very moment.

Yeah, I thought, sure.

Nearly two hours after leaving the deserted parking lot, I had already entered Indiana, was passing the exit for the University of Notre Dame. The cell phone on the passenger seat started vibrating.

"Listen, Simon—"

"It's not Simon, Ben. It's Carver."

At once I sat up a little straighter in my seat. The cruise control was on and I hadn't touched either pedal in almost an hour, but now I lightly tapped the brake, began keeping steady pressure on the gas.

"What ... what do you want?"

"The Kid's been working like crazy trying to find a connection. Looks like he might have come up with something." Carver paused. "I know you're in Indiana now. I think you should come back here to Chicago."

"I can't. I have to continue. I have to finish the game."

"If that's what you want to do, fine. But can you at least tell me one thing?"

"What's that?"

"Does the name Howard Abele mean anything to you?"

FORTY-SIX

I turned off at the next exit, pulled over to the side, stopped the Impala right before the stop sign. I put the car in park, turned on my four-ways, and waited.

The phone began vibrating almost immediately.

I ignored it.

Two minutes later—the phone having continued vibrating nonstop, Simon not giving up—headlights splashed me as a car turned off the same exit. It could have been anyone driving this late at night, but I knew who it was even before the sedan pulled up directly behind me.

I picked up the phone and answered it.

Simon said, "What the fuck do you think you're doing?"

"Making a rewrite."

"A rewrite? What the fuck does that mean?"

The sedan's back door opened and my one-eyed escort climbed out. He slammed the door, looked once around the area, then headed my way.

I said, "It means something's come up and I'm changing the script."

"What are you talking about?"

"A special guest star appearance. You know, the stuff that really makes ratings soar."

I disconnected the call and lowered the window right as my escort approached.

"Pardon me," I said. "Would you happen to have any Grey Poupon?"

He said, "What the fuck do you think you're doing?"

"You sound just like Simon."

"You really want your wife and daughter to suffer, don't you?"

"They're already dead."

"They will be if you keep pulling this shit."

Another pair of headlights splashed us from the top of the off ramp.

I asked, "Do you have a family?"

"What?"

"A wife and children. Do you have any?"

"What do you care?"

"I feel bad for them."

The man saw it in my eyes and stepped back and turned toward the oncoming vehicle, reaching for his weapon.

"Tell me," I said, "what was the very last thing you said to them?"

The vehicle—an SUV—came to a sudden screeching halt. The front and rear passenger doors opened and two men stepped out, both with guns in hand. The one killed my one-eyed escort first, shooting him in the head, while the other opened fire on the two bent FBI agents in the sedan. By then I was getting out of the car, stepping over my dead escort, hurrying toward the SUV.

At first I thought one of them was Carver but then saw it wasn't. Same build, same skin color, but a fuller face.

"Are you Larry?"

"That's Larry," the man said, indicating the driver. "I'm Drew."

The other man stepped forward, offering his hand. "I'm Ronny."

"Nice to meet you guys," I said.

I went to get in the SUV's open back door but stopped when Ronny grabbed my arm.

"Ditch the phone and the glasses."

"I need the glasses to see."

He just stared back at me.

I tossed the phone on the ground, glanced at the Impala, then said, "I'll be right back."

I hurried back to the car, leaned in, grabbed one of the T-shirts from the bag, started to lean back out but stopped. My gaze had settled on the glove compartment, and one side of my mind told me to forget it, that whatever I was thinking was crazy, while another side told me it was the best idea I'd ever had.

I returned to the SUV with the glasses off and wrapped in the shirt.

Both Drew and Ronny were frowning at me.

"Trust me." I secured the shirt bundle on the roof of the SUV, made sure it was snug, and then stood back. "Now what?"

Ronny said, "Now we get the fuck out of here."

FORTY-SEVEN

The closer we got to the city, the more my anger grew. Initially I had taken what Carver told me without letting my emotions get in the way. That was how I was able to remain relatively cool and calm back at the exit. But now here in this SUV, along with Ronny and Drew and Larry, my anger had turned into rage.

Howard fucking Abele.

I remembered the first time I'd met him when Jen invited me over to the mansion, how he'd refused to shake my hand, claiming he was in a rush for a meeting. Then the second time, almost three years later, when I tried shaking his hand again and asking his permission to marry Jen. Then the third and final time, at Claire Abele's funeral, where he pulled me aside and offered me the check for half a million dollars.

I had never seen or heard from him again. Jen had refused to even talk to him the few times he tried contacting her. She wanted nothing to do with him, had even gone so far as telling Casey he was dead—something that always hurt me, because it meant our daughter would never know any of her grandparents, what with my parents already gone. At least give her the

chance to meet her grandfather, if not once—something I hesitantly mentioned to Jen and which she quickly shot down,
dismissing the idea as if I was asking if she wanted mushrooms
on her pizza. In the past two years I hadn't even thought of
Howard Abele. He'd become nothing more than a ghost of the
past, forever trapped in the back of my consciousness. I never
once thought I'd ever see him again.

Now it looked like that time would come quite soon.

"How much longer before we get there?" I asked. It was
almost three o'clock in the morning and traffic was light.

"About an hour," Ronny said. He sat with me in the back,
Larry and Drew up front.

"And Carver?"

"He and Bronson and David will meet us at the location.
He wanted me to fill you in on everything first."

"Like what?"

"The reason we're going all out on this. It's the very first
time we've had confirmation of a contracted game. Carver's
hoping this man will give us some answers."

"Answers to what?"

More than anything else, Carver wanted any and all
contacts Howard Abele could provide. Anything that would
take them closer to the key players involved. The Kid was able
to track down the pages when they were posted—he had begun
to sense a pattern, one that would change at any given time but
which was somehow still predictable—but he could never get
much further. Attempting to determine where the pages originated from was close to impossible. Attempting to determine a
server was more likely but just as difficult. What they wanted
but could never get were names, locations, anything that would
help track down who was paying to watch. The people who
were in charge were in charge for a reason—they were smart,
well connected, and knew how the system worked. They no
doubt had a dozen hackers just like the Kid keeping others

(just like the Kid) at bay. Interference pages would come up almost all the time, trying to scramble the code the Kid had managed to break, and then the site would be gone. This would sometimes take minutes, sometimes hours, sometimes days.

In the past three years they'd never had any vital information about a player until they'd already exited the game. At that time the entire operation shut down. As far as Carver could tell, those players had been random selections from the pool of American society—at least from the selections they'd come in contact with; there was no doubt in his mind the same operations happened in other countries around the world.

The first was Ronny Kersic, forty-three years old, who'd driven tractor-trailers for a living. His wife and two children lived in Maryland. He'd woken up in a shed just outside of Zapata, Texas, a few miles from the Mexican border. A small black cell phone just like the one that had been shipped to me was waiting beside him when he opened his eyes.

The second was David Resh, thirty-nine, who had worked as a bartender at a place in Georgia. He'd woken up near the train tracks in Sarles, North Dakota. Unlike Ronny, whose wife and two daughters had been held captive to ensure he did everything Simon said, it was David's wife and girlfriend both who'd been taken. His wife was thirty-seven. His girlfriend, a server at the bar, was twenty-three. In his game he'd been listed as the Man of Unfaithfulness.

The third was Bronson Lam, twenty-three, a high school dropout who'd been supporting himself and his family by selling drugs in the city of Canton, Ohio. He'd found himself one morning in Porthill, Idaho, near the Canadian border. When Simon contacted him, Bronson learned his parents had been taken.

Drew Price had just turned forty, worked as a plumber in Queens, and had woken up in Kenton, Oklahoma. His girlfriend and four-year-old son had been taken.

Larry Vaughn was thirty-two, a farmer in Missouri who had lost his wife and three kids to Simon's game. On the weekends he liked to go to the racetrack and would watch the stock cars speed around and had, at one time, even envisioned himself becoming a professional driver.

Carver had intervened in all their lives. Had learned everything he could about them and helped them understand there was no outlet to the game. As far as he and the Kid could determine, nobody had ever pulled the strings for them to be chosen. They'd simply been Americans doing the American thing, which was trying to live day by day, and then all at once that was gone. Everything was gone.

"But even though you wanted to go on," Ronny said, "Carver had the Kid check you out."

The Kid brought up a lot of information—where I'd gone to school, where I worked, where my wife worked, where she'd gone to school. The Kid crosschecked that information. He crosschecked again. And again. For the longest time nothing came. But Carver told him to keep at it, that someone was definitely pulling strings. And so the Kid continued, his computers working furiously to find a connection. One finally came.

Howard Abele's name appeared more than once during the search. The Kid learned that for the past couple years my family was being watched. Howard Abele had hired a company that in most major sectors did not even exist to break in and install visual and audio recording devices around the house. In the living room, the dining room, the kitchen. The bedrooms and even the bathrooms.

Once the Kid was able to establish the connection, he started looking into Howard Abele. Ran everything he could. Learned about all the properties he'd bought and sold in the past forty years. Learned about all the companies he had stock in. The man was worth close to one hundred million dollars and had been doing well for most of his life. Until just recently.

In the past three months the Kid found that a sizable amount had been depleted from his accounts. What was close to ninety-five million dollars. That money had seemingly disappeared, supposedly transferred to an account that the Kid quickly found did not exist … anymore.

"So you're not one hundred percent sure he's really involved," I said. The initial shock of hearing we'd been watched for the past few years had already begun to wear off—especially after what I'd been living through the past week.

Ronny shook his head. "Not one hundred percent. But come on, Ben, use your head here."

"But … why?"

Except I knew why, or at least I could suspect—and for some reason the fact that I hadn't seen this coming was the ultimate blow, the thing that kept digging its nails into my heart and soul.

I said, "Do you know anything about a person named Caesar?"

Ronny frowned at me, shook his head.

"Do you think Carver would know?"

"I doubt it. Everything he knows he tells us. None of us keep secrets from each other."

"Fifteen more minutes," Larry said, merging now onto 41.

Beside me, Ronny began checking his weapons. So did Drew up front. Ronny reached back and grabbed a rifle and then glanced at me, asked if I had a preference in firearms.

The question was ridiculous—I had never fired a gun once in my life—but the world Ronny and the rest of these men lived in was a different world from my own. In their world, they probably carried weapons with them everywhere they went.

It hit me a second later that their world was now my own.

I shook my head and pulled the small revolver from the glove compartment out of my pocket and held it up.

"I have this."

I didn't want to tell him I intended to use it to kill Howard Abele.

Ronny took the gun, opened the cylinder. Pulled out the bullets, slid them back in.

"Huh," he said.

"Huh?" I took back the gun. "What does that mean?"

We arrived at Howard Abele's mansion ten minutes later.

FORTY-EIGHT

Howard Abele's mansion—the place Jen had once lived as a girl, what seemed a thousand years ago—was located on the western side of Highland Park. It was clustered around a number of other houses that strived to be mansions themselves but came up short. The reason for this, Jen had told me the first time I visited the mansion, was because her father owned nearly three hundred acres of the land which the houses rested upon, and he wanted to make sure his home was the biggest. Jen had claimed it made her popular in elementary and middle school, since the kids would want to visit the mansion, but come high school the kids grew up and understood just what kind of man Howard Abele truly was and took their irritation out on her.

There was a black wrought iron fence, about seven feet high, which ran the entire perimeter of the property. Along the side of the street near the edge of the property was where Carver and Bronson and David were waiting in a sedan.

We parked behind them and got out and I realized that everyone was wearing black except me. Carver shook my hand and thanked me for coming back.

"It's not like I had much of a choice," I said.

"But you did have a choice, and I think you made the right one. Oh, and while I'm thinking about it."

He reached into his pocket and withdrew Jen's wedding ring. I'd asked him to keep it safe when Simon told me to bring only the cell phone and nothing else to Navy Pier. I took the ring from him and squeezed it in my hand and closed my eyes and did everything I could at that moment not to cry.

"Thank you," I whispered.

He nodded. "Do you remember the mansion's layout?"

From what I remembered, the stone-sided mansion was only three stories, but had close to forty rooms. The ceilings on the first floor were almost twelve feet high. Priceless paintings and black and white photographs had marked the flawless walls, just as antique vases and crystals adorned the occasional table in hallways and rooms. It had appeared as if Howard Abele had spared no expense to ensure that everyone who stepped foot inside the front door—and everyone who drove past—knew that he was a very wealthy and powerful man.

I told this all to Carver and his men, and they listened carefully and then nodded when I was done. It was close to three-thirty in the morning and besides the lights along the drive and the porch, which probably always stayed on, only a few other lights were on inside the first and second floors of the mansion. Somehow it contrasted greatly with the rest of the houses in the area, which were all dark and quiet with sleep.

"Also," I said, "do you know anything about Caesar?"

"Who?"

I explained what my one-eyed escort had said, his little slip-up.

Carver said, "Interesting."

Ronny retrieved the bundled T-shirt from its place on the SUV's roof. I took it from him and opened it up and placed the glasses on my face. They were freezing but at least I could see again.

Which meant the rest of the viewers could see again too.

At this thought I purposely tilted my head down to the ground.

Carver stepped close to me and whispered in my ear, "You sure you want to do it this way?"

I thought about all the years we'd been in our house on Cherry Oak Lane, the times Jen and I had made love in our bed, the times Casey had fallen asleep on my chest while I watched TV. The times I'd snuck away to the den and shut the door, certain that it was me and only me.

I nodded. "There is no other way."

"Then let's do it."

Carver and I started walking toward the entrance gate, leaving the others behind to take up their positions around the property. We still weren't one hundred percent certain Howard was in the house. We still weren't even certain if there was anybody else in there either.

The gate was standing open. Normally to open it you needed to punch in a combination on a keypad. I thought about the first and only time I'd come here with Jen, how she'd punched those numbers in without even looking. She'd been talking to me as she did it, telling me not to be nervous, that her parents were going to love me.

I kept my focus on the house as we walked down the drive. The mansion was becoming larger with each step. Carver kept pace beside me. He was carrying two guns, I was carrying one, but for some reason I still didn't feel safe.

The front door opened before we even stepped up onto the marble porch. It was tall and massive and made of oak and it swung inward. Both Carver and I stopped at once. Carver already had one of his guns out before I even considered reaching for mine.

A woman stood in the doorway. She was small and she was thin and she smiled a smile that was not at all pleasant.

"Please," she said, "put away the guns. You don't need them."

Neither of us moved. Neither of us said a word.

"It's cold," the woman said. "Please, come inside. Mr. Abele's been expecting you."

FORTY-NINE

The woman introduced herself as Olivia Kemp. She said she was Mr. Abele's nurse. She looked to be about fifty. Her dark hair was turning gray and she had it pulled up in a bun. It made me think of the woman from Hickory View, only I didn't consider this woman an innocent.

She shut the heavy door behind us. The rush of the wind outside stopped immediately, only continued to bat invisible fists against the windows.

Olivia Kemp asked, "Would you like some coffee or something else to drink?"

I said, "Just tell us where he is."

She led us down a hallway toward the back of the mansion. There was no carpet, only wooden floors, and her heels clicked and echoed. Carver took up the end and I kept glancing back at him. He hadn't put his gun away. For some reason, this didn't seem to surprise or worry Howard Abele's nurse.

Thinking of this, I asked, "You said you're his nurse, right?"

Without turning back, without even shifting her head, she said she was.

"Why does he need a nurse?"

She didn't answer.

We continued walking, turning one corner, turning another. I was trying to remember the rooms I'd seen before, the leather chair I'd sat in while waiting for Howard Abele the first time I met him. I'd never seen Jen's bedroom upstairs, had no idea what had become of it.

"What happened to this place?" I asked, because something had dawned on me. The paintings and photographs on the walls, the vases and crystals on the tables, they were all gone. Nothing marked the walls now, nothing filled the empty corners of the hallways.

Either Olivia Kemp didn't hear me this time or she chose to ignore the question. She just continued walking, her back to us.

I glanced back at Carver. He still had his gun out, looking everywhere around him as he walked.

Finally the woman stopped in front of a door. She opened it. Stepped back and motioned us to enter.

"No," Carver said. "You first."

There was mostly darkness beyond the door. I say mostly darkness because there was some light in there too, very faint. Also there was noise, what sounded like low and monotonic beeping.

And, though I couldn't be certain, what sounded like a faint echo of Carver's voice.

Olivia Kemp said, "Very well."

A few seconds later, inside the room, her words echoed.

She started forward. I followed. The presence of the gun in my pocket was very strong. My mind kept forgetting it was there, so focused now on being back in a house I never thought I'd ever visit again.

The moment I stepped into the room I felt an increase in temperature. The beeping was a bit louder too. For a second I couldn't place the noise but then I remembered hearing something very similar only two days before: walking the corridors of Hickory View, smelling the stark and dry disinfectants.

My eyes adjusted to the darkness and I made out that the room wasn't very large. The source of the light was coming from one of the walls. Large monitors stretched from one end to the other. At least a dozen in all, if not more, stacked upon each other. It was impossible to tell the exact count because a number of them were turned off.

Those that were turned on showed two separate pictures.

One of those pictures was the inside of a car. The image was dark and I could just make out the seat and steering wheel, as the camera had been positioned from the passenger side foot well. I stared at it for only a moment before realizing that the inside belonged to the Impala.

The other picture, I realized a second later, was showing the same very thing, only slightly distorted. It was almost like a picture within a picture. The reason for this didn't occur to me until I once again remembered the camera in my glasses.

Without any conscious thought I raised the index finger of my right hand and placed it directly over the bridge of the glasses. A few seconds later, on about six of the monitors—not to mention on the monitors that were now showing double—the tip of the finger appeared, creating darkness.

Behind me, the slow and steady beeping continued.

Behind me, a sick and raspy voice spoke.

"It's delayed some. But mostly it keeps real time."

A few seconds later, the voice repeated itself from speakers stacked next to the monitors.

I turned around.

Howard Abele lay in bed, which took up the other half of the room. His body was covered with a sheet. The only light was the soft glow of the monitors on the other side of the room, reflected off a long window. It was enough to show just how thin and pale he'd become. A tube ran around the length of his face, feeding him oxygen. Machines were set up around his bed. Some had glowing lights on them—yellows, greens, reds—some of which were blinking.

I'd only been in the room for less than thirty seconds but already I could feel the inevitable promise of oncoming death. It was thick in the air.

"Well," Olivia Kemp said, "I'll leave you three gentlemen alone."

A few seconds later her voice repeated itself. She turned toward the door and took a step forward, paused for Carver to step out of her way.

He didn't. Instead he raised his gun, motioned her toward the other corner.

"Stand over there. Keep your hands where I can see them."

Seconds later it was all repeated, Carver's voice coming in crystal clear from the speakers.

"Honestly," Howard Abele said. He started to reach for something beside him on the bed. Carver shouted at him to freeze. "I want to sit up. I need to press the switch."

All that was repeated too.

"Go ahead," Carver said.

The old man picked up the device and pressed a button. The back of the bed began to rise. Howard set down the device and picked up another, began punching buttons. The soft light began going out.

"Olivia," he said, "be a dear and turn on the lights."

I waited the few seconds to hear this repeated but there was silence. Only the wind howling beyond the window. Evidently Howard Abele had turned off the speakers as well.

Keeping her hands out in front of her, she started toward the bed. Reached up and flicked on a lamp. It wasn't the brightest but it lit up the room enough for me to see that the old man had become even more shriveled than I'd first thought.

He just sat there, staring back at me with what had once been piercing eyes.

I heard myself ask, "What the hell happened to you?"

"Cancer," Howard said, and coughed. It was a rippling cough that reminded me of what I'd heard across the corridor from Phillip Fagerstrom's room. Olivia started to walk toward him but he slowly raised a hand, waving her off. "Lung cancer, if you can believe it. Never smoked a day in my life, except the occasional cigar."

I didn't say anything and just stared back at him. I told myself I couldn't take my eyes away from his, not until he looked away first.

Carver said, "We're going to need you to give us some information."

The old man didn't take his eyes away from mine when he smiled. "Yes, I'm sure you do. Or at least you think you do. But I'm not going to give you any such information. Neither is Ms. Kemp. We know our place, just as I'm sure you both know yours."

The machines surrounding him continued beeping.

Carver said, "That's not an acceptable answer. We will get the information we need. We're not leaving until we do. Now, tell us who Caesar is."

Howard Abele kept his gaze straight on me for another couple moments before shifting his eyes away.

"So you're Carver Ellison—the Man of Honor. They warned me about you. Said you might be trouble. They know you're here, you know. They called not too long ago, said you might be coming. I pretty much figured it while I was watching. I told them not to bother coming to the rescue. I told them you both wouldn't be a problem."

Despite the sick and raspy voice I could somehow still hear the man who'd denied me so many years ago. His body was decaying, he was almost dead, yet somehow the confidence and power that had always been there still resided.

"Who is Caesar?" Carver repeated.

The old man shifted his eyes back to mine. When he spoke, there was pride in his voice.

"Caesar is a great, great man. He has a vision for the future that is unmatched by anyone else. He will change this world in so many different and wonderful ways. I envy the fact I will not be around to see it."

He smiled and motioned to the chair beside his bed.

"Caesar was here, you know. He heard I was sick and he came here, sat right down in this chair. He leaned forward and took my hand and he asked me what he could do for me. I've been a loyal member of the Inner Circle for the last twenty years, and Caesar appreciated that. And to show his thanks, he asked what he could do for me, and ... well, Ben, what do you think I asked him to do?"

There were so many things I wanted to say right at that moment. So many questions. So many actions that whipped through my mind, like me pulling out the gun and shooting him in the face, or rushing forward and choking him. But all that I heard myself say was one simple word.

"Why?"

A smile spread again across his withered face. He started chuckling but it turned into another coughing spasm.

"You still don't get it, do you? You don't get to ask me why. You never get to ask me why."

Behind me, Carver had begun murmuring something. I glanced back and saw him holding a finger to his ear. He said a few more words and then pointed the gun at Olivia.

"Is there anybody else here?"

Her lips pursed, she shook her head.

"We're going to check anyway."

He stepped into the room and motioned her over with the

gun. She didn't move at first but instead glanced at her boss, who closed his eyes and nodded. With this approval she started toward the door.

Carver said to me, "Ronny's coming in for backup. We'll be around."

Howard Abele chucked again. "Do you really think you have a chance against them? Against all of us? You cannot even begin to imagine how powerful we are."

Carver ignored him, stared directly back at me. "Do whatever the hell it is you need to do with this asshole. Then get out."

Olivia Kemp had already entered the hallway, was standing there waiting. Howard started chuckling again, this time saying, "You think he can do anything? This is a man of wax here, didn't you know? He's worthless."

Without a word or even glance the old man's way, Carver left. When he closed the door behind him, he did it so quietly the door didn't even make a sound.

After a long moment of staring at that door, my hands clenching in and out of fists, I turned back around to face my father-in-law.

FIFTY

Howard Abele had stopped chuckling, was now only smiling at me. With his left hand he waved to the chair beside his bed, the chair Caesar had supposedly taken when he had visited. The action was stunted and appeared to cause him much trouble, and he noticed me noticing.

"Yes, I've become quite weak. Can hardly even stand, let alone walk. It's this damned cancer. Doctors thought it would take me years ago. But I'm still here. Now please, have a seat. We have never had a real man-to-man talk, you and I."

I walked over and pulled the chair away from the bed, at a good distance where I thought I could sit and not be forced to smell the cancer reeking off his body. Also, I was afraid that if I got too close I might just continue with my initial thought and strangle him to death. But I couldn't do that, at least not yet. First I needed answers.

Before I sat down I pulled the gun from my pocket. It was warm and heavy. I stared at it for a moment before Howard Abele chuckled again.

"Are you going to shoot me? Are you going to *kill* me? I don't believe you will. You're not strong enough."

"Is that what killing is, then—strength?"

The machines continued beeping by the bed, at least three or four of them, all different beeps from different machines but spaced out just right so that it was a constant rhythm.

Howard Abele didn't answer. He just sat there, a crooked smile on his face.

"Why did you do this? You set this entire thing up. Why?"

"I still don't understand what makes you think I should answer you. The two of us live in different worlds, Ben. Two worlds that are so different they are galaxies apart."

"Your daughter and your granddaughter. You did this to them too."

His crooked smile turned to a scowl. "That's where you have it wrong. Jennifer Abele *used* to be my daughter. She isn't family anymore. Neither is the child you both named Casey."

Hearing him speak my daughter's name made me want to raise the gun right there and then. But I kept myself in check. I did my best to remain calm, to remain patient, and just shook my head.

"So they're nothing to you, just like that? Because she went against your wishes and married me?"

Howard Abele said, "Do you know what I am? I am the *paterfamilias*. I am the father of the family. I have absolute right over my household and children. If I wanted, I would have every right to kill my children, even my wife. And Jennifer Abele—well, she was just like Julia. I actually said this to Caesar and he agreed with me."

Hearing him use Jen's name in the past tense was almost too much to bear. I kept staring back at him, squeezing the gun in my hands.

"Who is Julia?"

"Julia was Emperor Augustus's daughter. She was ... disobedient. In the end she infuriated her father so much he denounced her in public and banished her for the rest of her life. You see, to run a proper empire you cannot bend the rules. Everyone must do their part, and if they do not ..."

He shook his head slowly, seemed to shrug.

"Jen married me because she wanted to," I said. "She didn't have to listen to you. She was an adult."

I caught myself using Jen's name in the past tense and went to take it back, but Howard Abele was already shaking his head.

"You still don't get it. It doesn't matter if she was an adult. She was still my daughter, which meant I had complete control. And marriage? By the time Jennifer was eleven I had already made an arrangement with a business partner of mine, also a member of the Inner Circle. She was to marry his son Jeremy. Getting them together was no easy task, but once they were finally together ... it didn't take long for Jennifer to see they were meant to be. And so what if he was cheating on her? I cheated on my own wife countless times. Half the times she knew about it, half the times she didn't, but it never mattered, and eventually Claire came to understand. She understood the nature of the beast, so to speak. She understood her place in our marriage, how she was never to question or disobey me. She even argued about the arranged marriage and I ended up beating her for it. But then ... then she broke the final straw by giving you permission to marry my daughter."

"How does that—" I started to say but stopped. In the silence there was the beeping of the machines, the sound of the wind, the slight rasping coming from within Howard Abele's lungs. "You killed her, didn't you? You ... killed your wife."

"Like I told you, I could do whatever I wanted. Besides, she was no good to me anymore. She failed to understand the system. I gave her more chances than she deserved, and she forfeited every one." The old man coughed his raspy cough and said, "None of this sounds familiar to you, does it? Weren't you ever paying attention in any of your World History classes? The greatest civilization ever to rule this planet was the Roman Empire."

A faint echo of something Simon had said to me rose in my mind, but I ignored it and asked, "Why are you telling me this shit?"

"To be honest," Howard Abele said, "it's not for your benefit. It's for theirs." And with his weak hand he pointed at my face—only I knew it was the glasses he was pointing at, the camera in the middle. "Not everyone who watches is a member of the Inner Circle. So they must be reminded of the true reason behind all of this. Because these games are only a small part of what's going on. They're merely … entertainment. But these other people, the ones who like to watch for the fun of it, they must understand soon this world is going to change, that it needs to change, and if they wish to survive, they must give full allegiance to Caesar."

I was slowly shaking my head. "You are fucking insane. You know what you sound like? You sound like some extreme Islamic fundamentalist spouting off what will happen if we don't all bow down before Allah."

The old man stared back at me, his expression grave. "*Terrorists?*" he said. "You equate us to *terrorists?* We are nothing like them. Those people, their goal is to destroy the world. We … we are trying to rebuild it."

"Why did you have cameras placed in our house?"

The old man sighed. "The cancer hit me right away. I wasn't strong enough to go to work anymore. I was forced to start working from home. But then I began letting my business managers run the show. I was still making money so I didn't care. But I was bored."

"You were bored."

"That's right. And I wanted to see what my 'Julia' was up to. It was fun to watch. It was especially fun watching you. I always liked watching you. Whether it was sitting on the couch watching TV or jerking off to the Internet, you were always entertaining. Almost more entertaining than the games."

"So you've watched the games before."

"Of course." A pause, followed by another rasping cough. "Like I said, I've been a member of the Inner Circle for years. Back then it was different though. Back then they just locked the players in a room and brought them children or animals every once in a while, forced them to copulate. Other stuff too, which I'm sure you can imagine."

I shook my head.

The smile crooked appeared again, and Howard Abele asked, "What are you thinking right now?"

"That all that is … disgusting. That *you're* disgusting."

"Am I? First I'm insane, now I'm disgusting. But let me ask you this: Is what you've been doing all your life not disgusting? Looking at naked women having sex with each other, putting their fingers and tongues in their cunts and assholes. That's all right then?"

"It's"—I cleared my throat—"not the same."

"Not the same?" He chuckled again. "You actually believe it's not the same? That's rich."

I said nothing. Forced myself to keep staring back at him but ended up shifting my eyes to the long window beyond the bed.

"That's what I thought," Howard Abele said. "I had you checked out after the first time Jennifer brought you to meet me. I had a team of investigators bring me everything they could about you. It was bad enough that you came from a poor family, that you'd never done anything with your life and never would. But the incident your freshman year at college was what stuck out most. Not that you did nothing while that girl was being beaten, but that you confessed to the police later you wanted to help. It just proved to me that you were weak. That you would never even begin to understand the new system of the world, the vision Caesar has been working on for decades now. And that girl? That girl no doubt deserved it. Had you just watched for the simple pleasure of watching, I might have actually come to like you. But you said you wanted to help her. And even though you said that, you still did nothing."

I was still staring at that window, at the darkness beyond. "Are they dead?"

"Who?"

"You know who."

"To be honest, I don't know, and I don't care. This game has nothing to do with them. It's all about you."

At that moment, somewhere in the house, a sudden salvo erupted: four solid cracks of gunfire followed by a second or two of silence, then a continuous series of *crack! crack! crack!*

I was up immediately, the gun gripped now by two hands, and started around Howard Abele's bed. The gunfire continued and I glanced down at the gun in my hands.

Shit, I thought.

Howard Abele began chuckling. "Looks like you have trouble. Does that mean you're going to stand by like a statue and watch?"

Standing now facing the door, my back to the window, I said loudly over the gunfire, "What did you mean it's all about me?"

The smile appeared again. The old man actually looked genuinely happy that I'd asked, despite what was now happening inside his mansion.

He again raised a hand—his left this time—and motioned for me to come closer. Keeping my eyes on the door, gripping the gun tightly, I took first one step, then another, and leaned down. When he spoke his voice was a harsh whisper that seemed to put the gunfire in as much importance as the machines beeping around him.

"When you know you don't have much longer to live—

when the doctors have even given you a set amount of time—
you start to question everything you've ever done. People like
to say they want to know if they've made a difference but that's
bullshit. People don't care, at least not deep down. They only
care about what they missed out on. What the one thing was
that could have really made them happy. They want to fulfill
whatever desires they hide in the deepest and darkest part of
their hearts. So I started thinking, trying to decide what would
make me the happiest, and I came to you."

He started coughing then, harder than ever before. The
gunfire continued, more sporadic now: a few cracks here, a few
cracks there. None of it sounded like it was coming toward us
though, so I knew we still had time.

"Me," I said. "Why me?"

"Because I liked watching you. You were always self-
conscious about yourself, even when you were alone. Even
when you were jerking off at the computer. Those were the best
moments, by the way, right when you came and you made that
sigh. God, it was perfect. That was when you became the most
real. When you became the most human. And I wondered to
myself, how would you do if you played the game?"

The gunfire continued but it had somehow become background, just like the machines beeping and the wind screeching
against the window behind me.

"I don't believe you," I said. I kept my gaze centered on the
door. The gun felt very heavy now in my hands. "There has to
be more to it. You didn't spend all that money just to put me
through this hell."

"But I did spend all that money. I spent nearly my entire
life's savings so they could do it my way. It's entertainment.
That's all it ever is. It's what keeps the world spinning. You were
the only one I could think of, the only one that I enjoyed
watching the most. I told them I didn't care what you did, that
I had no real request. Well, except for what happened at

Hickory View. Phillip Fagerstrom used be a classmate of mine. He was a closet faggot and I hated him. I found out he was still alive and wanted to see him die. I would have preferred you killed him yourself, but it worked out just as well. Come now, I'm sure you've learned something valuable from all of this."

Footsteps sounded out in the hallway, frantic, and I heard Carver shouting at me. Moments later the door burst open. He came in, guns in both hands, and started to say something. Then his eyes grew wide and he aimed both guns at me.

"Ben," he shouted, "down!"

He started firing before I even had a chance to hit the floor. The gunfire which had momentarily become background invaded my world again, each crack so loud they were deafening. It didn't occur to me until a few moments later that it hadn't been Carver who first opened fire. No, through the sudden melee of noise I realized that somebody else was firing too. I was crouched behind the bed, my hands over my head, and what felt like stones were raining down on me. Then the chilling kiss of wind began assaulting me and I quickly glanced back.

The window had shattered. Out in the darkness a man wearing all black was falling to his knees. An assault rifle dropped from his hands as he landed in the scattering of glass shards.

Carver hurried forward, keeping his guns aimed. Now that the wind had found an entrance to the mansion it was pouring in, chasing away the touch of warmness and stench of decay.

"What's happening?" I heard myself say, over the howling of the wind and what I only realized a moment later was Howard Abele chuckling on his bed.

"Company," Carver said. He made sure the man was dead, then took his rifle and extra ammunition. He pocketed both of his guns and checked how many rounds were left in the rifle. "We need to split."

"How many?"

"No idea. We managed to take down six. Well, now seven."

Somewhere throughout the house, another salvo started up.

Howard Abele continued chuckling. The sound somehow overrode the wind and gunfire. During the three times I'd met him I never once saw him smile, let alone laugh, and here it seemed as if he just couldn't stop.

I stared down at him. He was smiling back at me.

I said, "I need a few more minutes."

"Fuck no." The rifle now in his hands, Carver started toward the door. "We need to go now."

"Hold on," I said, and leaned down very close to the bed. In Howard Abele's ear I whispered, "I have learned something. Reality TV isn't about the people starring in it. It's about the viewers. It's about what they see. Seeing is believing, right? What really happens doesn't matter at all."

For the first time confusion passed over the old man's face.

He said, "I don't … understand."

"Of course you don't."

And stepping back, I pointed the gun at his face and pulled the trigger.

FIFTY-ONE

There were six chambers in the gun, all filled, and I used each and every one of them. The gun kicked in my hand with each shot. I may have scrunched up my face, may have screamed something unintelligible; I can't remember exactly. All I know for certain is once I pulled the trigger a seventh time and heard the dry click I turned at once and headed for the door. Carver was waiting there, the rifle aimed down the hallway. Behind me, Howard Abele may have tried saying something but it was lost in the wind.

"Is it clear?" I said to Carver. He nodded and I stepped out, shutting the door behind me. I tossed the gun on the floor. Somewhere down the hall there were a few more rounds of gunfire.

Carver pulled one of his guns from his pocket. He handed it to me. "Now do you think you can handle the real thing?"

The gun Carver handed me was a nine-millimeter. He'd checked the magazine, told me there were five bullets left, and that if I wanted to shoot something, I better make sure I had a safe place to take cover.

"Are you ready?"

"Yes," I said, though the word was simple and small and I think it was lost behind a sudden wail of more gunfire.

"Make sure the safety's off," Carver told me, and when I stared down at the gun, he reached out and flicked something on the side.

Then he hefted the rifle and turned and we started down the hallway.

Back the way we came less than a half hour ago, the mansion had transformed itself in a very bad way. Some of the bare walls were now marked with bullet holes. Bits of glass and mirror and plaster covered the wooden floors. We passed a body wearing all black. His eyes closed, his mouth open, blood coming from his chest.

Carver stepped over him like he wasn't even there.

A few seconds passed without any gunfire and for some reason this felt wrong. Carver sensed it too. He stopped his slow and steady pace and then just stood there, listening.

Silence.

"Does that—" I started to say, whisper really, but Carver snapped his head back, gave me a glare which caused me to shut up at once.

We listened.

More silence.

We started forward again. I tried to keep my gun aimed to the side, so it wasn't pointed at Carver's back, but it was difficult. I had to keep reminding myself that this one was full of live ammunition.

We rounded a corner. More bullet holes in the walls, more plaster on the floor. Carver did a good job of keeping his footsteps silent. I tried my best to follow his example but found it even more difficult than keeping the gun away from his back.

Then we came to two more bodies, both lying supine just outside an opened door.

Carver stepped over them just like before, like they weren't even there, and aimed his rifle into the darkness of the room. He stood there for a moment, then continued on. I tried to do the same but I couldn't take my gaze away from the motionless bodies and the darkness of the blood.

Footsteps sounded out ahead of us, rough and heavy footsteps, and I jerked my head up. Carver had stopped, was aiming the rifle down the hallway. A figure appeared around the corner and then halted, bringing up a gun, and there was a tense moment when I was certain another cacophony of gunfire would start up. But then I recognized the large bearded man as Ronny Kersic and released a small breath.

"Anything?" Carver whispered.

Ronny shook his head. He raised one gloved finger and mouthed the words *One more.*

"Where?"

I felt the gun even before the hand gripped my shoulder. Then all at once I was jerked back and an arm wrapped around my neck and I could feel his body behind me. With a heavy voice he shouted, "I'll blow his fucking brains out."

Carver spun, raising his rifle. Ronny, maybe fifteen feet behind him, slowly started forward, his rifle raised and aimed too. Aimed right at me.

"I mean it," said the man holding me as a shield. "I'll kill him. Don't fucking move."

Carver took another step forward and then stopped. He was maybe ten feet away, maybe eight. Ronny stopped as well. Neither of them lowered their weapons.

The nine-millimeter was still in my hands but my hands had become stone. I could neither move them nor my body. My eyes were wide, my mouth was open, yet I couldn't seem to make a sound.

"But he's the star of the game," Carver said.

"Game's over," the man said. "This bullshit's gone far enough. They don't care about him"—the gun jabbed the back of my head—"they don't care about anybody else. It's you, Carver. They want you taken alive. So drop your weapons."

Carver said, "How about you go fuck yourself instead?"

"You're making a big mistake," the man said. Then to me, "Drop the gun."

But I couldn't drop the gun; my hands were still stone.

"Drop it," the man said, jabbing his gun harder against my head, and I dropped it at once. Shame hit me a second later and I cursed myself for doing such a stupid thing.

"The game's not over," Carver said. He hadn't moved and was still keeping the rifle aimed. I found myself staring at the dark hole of the barrel, wondering if I would be able to actually see the bullet when it was shot. That was me right then: Benjamin Anderson with a gun to his head, not thinking about his wife or daughter, but rather if he'd catch a glimpse of the bullet before it smashed into his face. "The game's never over."

"It is now," the man said.

"No," said a new voice, this one coming somewhere behind us, "it isn't."

Another deafening gunshot, so loud that I could actually feel my ears beginning to bleed. The solid presence of the body close against mine slipped away. The arm around my neck loosened. I took in a deep breath, then another, and scrambled forward. I tripped over my own feet and hit the floor and rolled over. For some reason I expected the man to still be standing there but he had already dropped to the floor. The place where his head had once been was now a mess. Blood was everywhere, splattered on the floor and the bare wall. Behind him stood David Resh, who had taken his gun and placed it right to the side of the man's head and pulled the trigger.

My ears continued ringing. Something was heavy in the air,

something I'd only later learn was cordite, as well as the dead man's piss. My body continued to shake. I spotted the gun I'd dropped and tried reaching for it but found that I was shaking too badly.

A hand fell on my shoulder.

I jumped, may have even cried out.

Carver's voice, faint through the ringing in my ears: "Let's move."

I just sat there, staring at the dead man, at all the blood, and did everything I could not to cry.

FIFTY-TWO

The foyer where Olivia Kemp offered us coffee or something else to drink was a mess. More glass and plaster—and even some blood—marked the wooden floor and bare walls than in the hallways, which made me think this was where the gunfire had originated. The heavy oak door stood open, letting in the wind. Bronson Lam stood over another dead body, waiting for us.

"Where's the old woman?" Carver asked.

Bronson shook his head. "We lost her."

"Fuck."

Carver turned and glanced back at us—Ronny walking in front, me in the middle, and David bringing up the rear. The nine-millimeter was back in my hands but my hands were still shaking.

"Somebody's coming," Ronny said loudly, raising his rifle, but Bronson told him to stand down, that it was Drew. The man was hustling up the drive, up onto the porch, and stepped inside. He was breathing heavily, his cheeks flushed, shaking his head.

Carver said, "What's wrong?"

"Larry," Drew managed. "He's—he's dead."

A large piece of plaster lay on the floor close by Carver and he kicked it at the wall, shouting, "Goddamn it!"

Nobody else said anything. The wind beyond the door continued to howl.

"We have to leave," Carver said. The rifle hung on a strap over his shoulder. He had his hands on his hips and was staring down at the floor. "We probably woke up the goddamned neighborhood and we can't wait for the police."

We stood in a circle around the one dead body. It felt strange, watching these men talk and act this way while before they'd been truck drivers, bartenders, drug dealers, plumbers. They'd never been in the army, had never been officially trained for this kind of action, but Carver had done a good job, had made sure they knew all they needed to know to survive the game.

And coming here tonight they knew it would be a trap, that Simon would send his men. That had been the idea, after all, to let Simon's men come. That's why before Carver took Olivia Kemp and left me with Howard Abele he made it sound like only Ronny was coming in for backup, to make Simon and his men and all the viewers believe our numbers were small. Which they were—our numbers were very small—but Carver's men had waited out beyond the perimeter for Simon's men to show up, had gotten a number of how many there were, and then, as Simon's soldiers raided the mansion, Carver's soldiers came at them from behind.

Ronny asked, "What about the woman?"

"Fuck the woman," Carver said. "David, did you get the hard drives?"

David nodded.

"Then we got what we came for. Let's go."

As one solid group they turned and started toward the door. I was the only one that didn't move.

"Ben," Carver said to me, turning back, "what the hell are you doing?"

"I can't leave yet. I need to finish this."

"It's too late. We don't have time."

"Then you can go on without me."

"Fuck," Carver said again. Had there been another large piece of plaster around he no doubt would have kicked it. He turned back to his men and told them to get the car and SUV ready, that they were leaving in five minutes. Then he walked back toward me. "Three minutes, that's it. Is that going to be enough time?"

"I don't know."

"Tough. That's all you're getting. And if you don't kill the motherfucker, I will."

As much as I wanted to be able to clearly see what happened next, I didn't want anyone else to see, so I took off my glasses and set them on the table beside the stairs. Next I ran down the hallway, squinting so I wouldn't slip on shards of glass or trip over any dead bodies. Carver stayed close behind me, the rifle no longer strapped over his shoulder but back in his hands. He wasn't taking any chances, and I could tell he was pissed that I was drawing this out.

But I couldn't help myself. I needed to put closure on this for my own sake, if not for Jen and Casey's.

We came to the room where Howard Abele had been watching me for the past five days, where he'd probably been watching me and my family for the past three years. Everything we'd done, every happy moment, every sad moment, every moment where only a look passed between us and nothing more, had been on camera, had maybe even been recorded so Howard Abele could go back and rewatch his favorite parts.

It was especially fun watching you ... I always liked watching you.

My hand was on the knob and I was already opening the

door before I got the feeling that something wasn't right. But then the door opened and the shooting started and I hit the ground again—but this time it wasn't fast enough. This time one of the bullets got me right in the arm and pain exploded all over my body.

Carver fired immediately. I was crumpled on the ground, my left hand gripping my right shoulder, feeling the warmth of my own blood. I was sure that I was going to die, that I was going to lose so much blood and pass out, that with my right arm still gripping the gun I raised it and just started firing. This gun felt different than the revolver but my mind couldn't make the correlation why until there were no more bullets and I was still pulling the trigger and asking myself why nothing was happening.

The gunfire had stopped, both mine and Carver's and Olivia Kemp's. She'd been in the room with Howard Abele when I opened the door, standing close to his bed with a gun, and when she heard me she turned and started shooting. Carver took her down at once, her body jerking from the rain of bullets, and then she was on the floor, a lifeless crumpled doll oozing blood.

Carver bent and started inspecting my wound. My ears were still ringing, the pain was still exploding throughout my body, yet beyond all this I could hear the howling wind. The howling wind and Howard Abele, chuckling away from his place on the bed.

"It's fine," Carver said. "You're lucky. It just grazed the skin. Nothing like this."

He raised his right arm to show the blood coming out of the space just beside his chest.

"Shit," I said, jumping to my feet. Now that I'd had it confirmed I wasn't going to die from lack of blood, the pain had quickly dissipated. It stung like hell but I knew I would live and that was good enough. "Are you—"

Carver shook his head. "The bullet's not in there. But I need to get this wrapped. Do what you need to do and do it fast." He stared at me for the longest moment, relaying the simple fact that what had just happened here was all my fault, and while we both knew it he wasn't going to hold it against me. He took the gun from my hand, ejected the magazine, loaded a new one, handed it back to me and said, "You've now got two minutes."

He started back down the hallway. I watched him, listening to the wind and Howard Abele and my own mind telling me to just follow Carver and get wrapped up too, that I didn't need all this shit.

Instead I turned and entered the room. Closed the door behind me. Howard Abele was still chuckling as I approached.

"Very well played before," he said, shouting so his raspy voice could be heard over the wind. "But I'm guessing there are live bullets in that one. Are you going to kill me for real this time?"

The revolver had been full of blanks. I had no idea what Simon had expected me to do with it, but for some reason I hadn't been surprised when Ronny told me. Just like I told Howard Abele, what really happened didn't matter, just as long as the audience believed it did.

Now it was different. Now there was no audience, was just the two of us. Now what happened really did matter.

When I'd initially fired the revolver, I had tilted my head at the last moment as well as my hand so the flame and muzzle flash and residue from the discharge didn't blind the old man. Not that I didn't care to blind him, but I always knew I was coming back here, and I wanted to make sure he could still see when I did.

"I told you before," Howard Abele said as I stepped up next to his bed, "you're not going to shoot me."

"No?" I placed the barrel of the gun against his right kneecap. "Then what do you call this?"

I pulled the trigger.

The scream that emitted from Howard Abele's mouth was almost too satisfying. He writhed around on the bed, his face scrunched up in pain, trying to reach for what was left of his knee. My mind kept telling me to stop, that I didn't want to become this person, and I kept telling my mind to shut the fuck up.

"They amputated your own daughter's finger," I said. "God only knows what else they've done to her. Not to mention what they've done to your granddaughter."

I leaned over and placed the barrel of the gun against his left kneecap.

"Beg me to stop, Howard. Beg me to stop like Jen begged them to stop."

"Stop," he said, or may have said through his pain—it was difficult to hear his voice over the wind and the machines beeping their rhythmic and innocuous noise and a new sound that should have been familiar but for some reason wasn't.

I waited another moment, just watching his face, and then pulled the trigger again.

More screaming, more writhing on the bed, and still that new sound persisted, and after a few seconds I realized what it was.

A cordless phone lay on the table on the other side of Howard Abele's bed. It kept ringing, and I knew who was calling and I didn't want to speak to him but still I walked around the bed and picked up the phone, punched the talk button and placed the phone to my ear.

Simon said, "I figured you would come back to see Mr. Abele. It took me a moment to understand why you ditched the glasses, but then I remembered—there were only blanks in that gun. I'm actually surprised you figured it out. I'm guessing you came back now to finish the job?"

"I am finishing the job," I said. "I'm doing to him exactly what you did to my family."

"Your family—"

I disconnected the call, dropped the phone to the floor beside me.

"Do you want to play a game?" I asked the old man. "It will be fun."

He didn't answer me, still thrashing around in pain.

"Oh wait, that's right," I said, now turning away from him and stepping over Olivia Kemp's body to inspect the machines surrounding his bed. "It's not up to you whether or not you want to play the game. I'm the viewer, after all. It's my decision and I want to be entertained."

I followed the cords and found the one with the tube connected to it, the tube that was feeding Howard Abele his much needed oxygen. I started to reach for it but then something else caught my eye. A power strip on the floor, its little protection indicator light glowing red, all the outlets used up to keep these machines running.

The cordless phone I'd dropped on the floor started ringing again.

I ignored it and grabbed the power strip's plug and then thought better of it, decided instead to press the red button glowing on the strip itself. The moment I hit it the red glow went dark and the machines stopped beeping.

"Here's the object of the game," I said, leaning close to Howard Abele so he could hear me. He was still crying and I had to slap his face a few times to get his attention. "It's simple really, something anyone can do. Just press that button again so the machines start back up and keep what's left of you alive. You do that and you win. You don't and—well, you're a smart guy. You know the nature of the beast, so to speak. I'm sure you can figure out how this system works."

Howard Abele didn't seem to hear me, instead focused on all the pain streaking through his body.

The phone continued ringing from its place on the floor. I stepped away from Howard Abele's bed and picked it up.

The first thing Simon said to me was, "Don't you want to save your family anymore?"

"My family's already dead." I walked to the door and turned around, just watched the old man twisting around on his bed. "The game's over."

"No, Ben, your family isn't dead. And the game most certainly isn't over. One last part and then it will be."

"Are you *telling* me this? More Simon Says bullshit?"

"That portion of the game's changed. This here has become much more … well, entertaining."

"Fuck you." Still staring at Howard Abele, still watching him die. The little pain that had been in my shoulder was now gone. I felt nothing at that moment. Even the hope I'd been keeping alive in my heart and soul all this time had snuffed out. "They're dead. I know they're dead."

"Oh really," Simon said.

It sounded like he stepped away for a moment, then a new voice came on the line, Jen's voice saying, "Ben? Oh God, Ben, is that you?" She sounded like she was about to cry, sounded like she was already crying. This was followed a couple seconds later by Casey's "Daddy?" and I could actually see the tears in my little girl's eyes, I could see them falling down her small and perfect face. "Daddy, please make the bad men stop."

But then their voices were gone, followed by what may have been screaming, though it was impossible to tell for sure over the shrieking of Howard Abele and the wind. Then Simon was back, Simon who always had a grin in his voice, a grin on his imagined face, but who sounded completely and utterly serious right now as he asked:

"Do you want to see them again?"

I didn't answer and continued watching Howard Abele.

"Well?" Simon said. "Do you?"

"Yes," I whispered.

"Then follow directions like a good boy and you will. I know you don't have the phone anymore—we traced it back to that off-ramp exit—but you still have the glasses, and that's the only way we're going to make this work. Remember, Ben, we're friends now, and we trust each other. As long as you have the glasses on and I and everybody else can see where you are, that you're coming in the right direction, then everything will be fine."

"And what"—I swallowed, my throat suddenly dry—"what direction is that?"

"California. Smith River. Right back here to the Paradise Motel. It's where Jennifer and Casey are. It's where they've been this entire time."

Howard Abele had given up trying to reach for his knees, had given up pretty much everything and just lay there now, tears all over his face.

"You're lying," I said.

"Am I? Well that's just something you've got to decide on your own, because it's the only way this game is going to end. You're going to come here with Carver. I want him too. He and I have some unfinished business to work out, especially after tonight. You and Carver, nobody else, and we'll know if you try to fuck around."

Simon then went on to give me directions. It was over two thousand miles, but as long as Carver and I kept driving nonstop we would make it without any trouble. Also, he said, they were going to call off that press conference the FBI was supposed to have regarding my escape. They were going to change the story a bit, say how I did in fact try to escape and got killed in the process. They were even going to give the Anonymous Bomber a name, create him an identity, so anyone recognizing the blurry image as Benjamin Anderson could stop wondering.

"And as an extra bonus," Simon said, "we've been rerouting the 911 calls for the past fifteen minutes. Should give you some extra time, but not much, so let's not waste it."

"That's impossible. You can't … you can't be that powerful. You just can't."

"It's not me, Ben. It's Caesar. He has more power than you could ever imagine. And right now he wants this game to come to an end. So yes, Ben, for your sake, I certainly hope it's possible, because as of this moment you have forty-eight hours."

"And then"—I had to swallow again—"then I get my family back?"

On the bed, Howard Abele turned his head to look at me, beseeching with me with his eyes to help him.

"Of course," Simon said. "Only remember when I asked you before who you loved more, your wife or your daughter? I expect to have an answer by the time you arrive."

Howard Abele, still staring at me with tears in his eyes, mouthed something I couldn't make out.

"Why?" I asked, my voice cracking on that one simple word.

"Isn't that obvious by now? Because when you get here you're going to have to tell me which one you love more. The other one? Well, the other one you're going to kill."

PART III

PARADISE LOST

FIFTY-THREE

It's impossible to guess how many viewers there were at the beginning. Besides Howard Abele and all the rest of the Inner Circle, how many others had paid thousands and thousands of dollars to be given a direct link to watch my family's suffering? One hundred? One thousand? Had they watched it all at home, in their dens while their wives or husbands read or watched TV or cooked in the kitchen, while their children did their homework or talked on the phone with their friends? Or maybe they'd logged onto this at work, knowing that their company's firewall would never pick it up because this was a site that shouldn't exist, a site that didn't exist, and anybody catching wind of it wouldn't find anything wrong if they were to try to look it up as well. Maybe they took their laptops and holed up in some hotel, where room service would bring them whatever they wanted. They put DO NOT DISTURB signs on the doors and logged onto the Internet and just watched and enjoyed the show while at the same time sneaking drinks from the mini-bar.

But once the Man of Wax supposedly shot a cop in Chicago and then was connected with an explosion down in

Ryder, Illinois, how many more signed up? Those in the Inner Circle probably didn't have time—or the money—to spend watching every game that took place, but there was just something about the Anonymous Bomber that was familiar to them, something that they had a hunch about, and so they contacted whoever it was they needed to contact. And what were they told? Sorry, as it always is with supply and demand, the normal price has gone up considerably, would you like to hear the new rates?

As my one-eyed escort—or Jerry, or the fucking idiot, whichever you prefer—had said, this had turned out to be one hell of a game.

So how many people across the country, across the globe, were glued to their computer screens when I raised the revolver loaded with blanks and started firing at Howard Abele's head, I can't say. Just as I can't say how many people there were when I finally left Howard Abele's room and walked back through the hallways, stepping over bodies and plaster and glass. As the Abele Mansion hadn't been a known destination in the Man of Wax's game, there hadn't been any cameras around, no options to switch to a certain page to get a different viewpoint.

No, the only point of view was the one I saw, and for roughly fifteen minutes that point of view stayed constant. Staring at what was half a blank wall, half the stairs leading up to the second floor. Even now I wonder about those people logging onto the game right when that happened, having heard so many good things but then being forced to just stare at the wall and stairs. I wished I could have kept it like that, kept them watching it for hours (which no doubt a good majority of them would have done), but I couldn't, not after my deadline of two days.

And so this is what you would have seen had you been one of those wealthy and powerful people in the world who had the dark desire to watch other people suffer; this is what you would have seen in the early hours of Sunday morning:

The stationary view of the wall and stairs shifting all of a sudden as the glasses are placed back on my face. Then the steady and constant bounce as I go looking for Carver.

I find him in the kitchen and explain to him about Simon, about the final part of the game, and how Simon wants him to come along too, demands it actually. And Carver, with the middle section of his body wrapped up, shakes his head, tells me no way. We argue about this for a while, the sound actually pretty good, the microphone in the front corner of the glasses picking up everything.

But Carver relents. He understands there is no choice in the matter. I'm going back to Smith River, California, regardless of what he does, and maybe Carver knows this and feels some kind of pity. He patches up my shoulder and then we're headed outside. The wind is still cold but not as strong, not as brutal, as before. We walk down the long drive, listening to the silence around us. Just as Simon promised, the 911 calls are being rerouted, giving us the extra time we need.

We decide to take the sedan. I wait in it while Carver explains the situation to the rest of the men, how they're not supposed to follow. Minutes later Carver's in the car, doesn't say a word, and we pull away.

We leave Ronny and David and Bronson and Drew (as well as Larry, dead) behind. We leave Howard Abele and Olivia Kemp and whoever else invaded the mansion behind. We leave everything behind, saying nothing to each other, just driving in silence.

The sun is already rising by the time we cross the Mississippi and enter Iowa, but it's to our backs, chasing us like we're in a race. I'm the first one to drift off, slumped over in my seat, not reclining back because Simon wants to constantly see where we're going, not the sedan's ceiling.

Continuous highway, cars and trucks and more cars. Buildings and billboards and lights and more buildings. Clouds in the sky, the sun as it passes over us, more clouds.

Carver makes a stop just outside Iowa City to gas up. I'm still asleep, my head tilted just so that the audience only sees the gas station parking lot and nothing more. Then Carver gets back in the car and we continue driving.

In Omaha, I wake and we switch, so now it's me driving, the audience with a good view of the dash and the steering wheel. One would think this is boring stuff but just as Simon says, the promise of what's to come whets the audience's appetite, keeps them watching miles and miles of highway, of an endless horizon. They're holed up in their dens or offices or cubicles or hotel rooms watching and wondering everything I'm going through, because surely they've been told already what the final part of the game will be, what the Man of Wax is expected to do once he reaches his destination.

In Cheyenne, where I'd stopped and it first started to rain at the beginning of the game, we stop again to gas up. This time we go inside, grab some water, some snacks, then ask for the key to use the bathrooms around the side. There is no key, the woman behind the counter tells us, and I go first, enter the darkness until I find the switch and flick on the lights. Take a piss, not caring at all that everyone else who wants to is watching me pee, and then zipping back up and washing my hands, stepping back outside as Carver goes in to do the same.

Then it's back in the sedan, Carver driving this time, the day wearing on, the sun heading closer and closer to the horizon. Neither of us has talked this entire time. We haven't played the radio. There have just been the sounds of the car, the sounds of the road, the constant rush of wind every time one of us turns down our windows to smoke.

Maybe we do this on purpose, wanting to bore the living shit out of all the viewers, hoping that their minds will wander and decide to do something better with their time. Certainly I don't want them to still be watching when I finally get to California, when I make my way up the highway toward Smith River and the Paradise Motel.

Of course, the majority of the audience probably knows this already and has walked away from their computers, gone to watch TV, check email, pay some bills, screw their significant others, do some shopping or laundry or both. They've already calculated how long it's going to take me and Carver to reach our destination. They may even have alarms set on their watches or cell phones, may have notified the front desk to give them a wake-up call. They don't want to miss what's going to happen at the end of this game, because just as the Almighty Caesar has supposedly decreed, this has the potential to be an all-time classic, and they don't want to miss out on the grand finale.

All the rest in between is simple build up, just drawing out the suspense. Highways and cars, deserts and trees, clouds and stars. Pit stops for gas, for food, for pissing and shitting.

This is what each and every one of the viewers saw as they watched from their special and secret places.

The following is what actually happened.

FIFTY-FOUR

What seemed like a century ago I had woken up in room six of the Paradise Motel, my family gone, no idea where I was or how I had gotten there. That had been seven days ago, and here I was now again at the Paradise Motel. Only I wasn't in room six. I wasn't in any of the rooms. Now I was crouched on the beach side of the motel, Carver beside me, a rifle in my hands as the dark sky began to soften bit by bit from the rising sun.

We'd been here for close to two hours already, watching the motel closely, keeping tabs on the manager's office and the two other rooms whose lights hadn't gone out since we first arrived. Ronny and Bronson and David were with us, all spread out on different parts of the grounds. The night was silent, just the sounds of the early morning waves crashing against the beach, the occasional whoosh of traffic on the highway, the few early morning seagulls cawing from their perches.

Ever since we arrived I'd been going out of my mind with anticipation. Jen and Casey were in there, in one of those rooms, and I was being forced to stay crouched here in the dunes. That was why Carver wanted me close to him, because he knew my want, my need, to take off toward the motel, calling out my wife's and daughter's names. For seven days they'd been so far away from me, so far they might as well have been dead, but now here they were and I was being held back.

We were waiting for first light before we moved in. This had already been established with everyone, especially me. As far as Simon and everybody else was concerned, Carver and I were still on I-80, probably entering Nevada by now. We still had until about five a.m. Tuesday morning to reach the Paradise and none of the people here were prepared for us yet, and why should they be?

And so we waited, crouching in the sand by the tall grass, watching the motel.

The Paradise was U-shaped, the bottom part pointed directly out at the ocean, the two arms facing inland. There were no windows on the beachside, no sliding glass doors that opened onto small private patios, which seemed strange for a beach motel. There was, however, a kind of boardwalk that stretched out from the back, where weatherworn plastic chairs and tables sat upright and vacant. Between the boardwalk slats, weeds and grass had begun to sprout, looking as if they'd had all summer to grow and were now losing the will to live.

Ronny and Bronson were stationed on the other side of the motel, David across the highway with a sniper rifle. We'd kept in radio contact this entire time, though everybody had been mostly quiet. One guard was pacing the parking lot, going back and forth between the arms of the U. Occasionally he paused to light a cigarette. From where we were crouched we'd seen the red glow of the tip a few times already. There was also at least one person in the manager's office. That would most likely be Kevin, who'd called me early Monday morning to give me my wake-up call.

There were two other rooms with lights on, but there was no way we could get close enough to see how many people were inside. One of those rooms, I knew, had to contain Jen and Casey.

Back home, the sun had already been up for close to three hours. People were getting up to take showers, to make breakfast, to get dressed for work. Life continued as it always does, a constant cycle that never stops. But here on the beach near the northern tip of California, the sun was just beginning to appear.

I kept glancing at Carver beside me. We hadn't said anything for the longest time. Finally his eyes shifted to meet mine and we stared at each other. He nodded, touched his throat microphone.

"Everyone in position?"

Some light static from my own earpiece, then Ronny's voice, confirming he and Bronson were in position. David's voice followed a second later, confirming the same.

Carver glanced at me once again. I had to squint to see his face clearly enough. I hadn't had my glasses in the past six hours, and while I'd gone longer without them, I didn't think I could go much longer. I needed them, because I didn't want to have to squint when I saw Jen and Casey again. I wanted to be able to look at them without any trouble and tell them just how much I loved them, how much I missed them, and how I would never let anything like this ever happen again.

"Okay," Carver whispered, "we'll go once David's ready. David, the target in place?"

A pause, then David confirmed that yes, the target was in place.

"On your mark," Carver said. He had a rifle strapped over his shoulder and now hefted it. I glanced down at the rifle in my hands, surprised by how comfortable I now felt holding it.

For a moment it was like time had stopped and the world held its breath. The waves continued to break against the shore, the sporadic traffic continued to drive up and down the highway, and the guard standing in the parking lot went to light himself another smoke. We watched him from where we were crouched by the beach, maybe fifty, sixty yards away. The tip of his cigarette glowed red as he sucked in all that nicotine. He never had a chance to blow it back out though, because in that moment David fired one shot. The rifle had a silencer, its dull clap drowned out by a tractor-trailer roaring past on the highway, but we heard the sudden intake of breath as the guard's body jerked, then fell to the ground.

Carver, his hand to his throat mic, said, "Now."

FIFTY-FIVE

As the world continued spinning and the waves continued breaking and the light of the sun became brighter and brighter by the second, we rushed forward until we were almost touching the Paradise Motel.

It was Ronny and Bronson's job to hurry into the parking lot where the guard had fallen to pick him up and carry him away, where they deposited his body in the sand and tall grass. Then they started around the front of the motel again, moving carefully right up on the walkway, peeking into the windows, trying to determine if any of the rooms were occupied.

We'd already established the ground rules: as long as whoever they found wasn't my wife and daughter, they were free to be killed.

Carver and I went straight to the manager's office. There was a door in the back of the office, a screen door, where light from inside suffused onto the small cement porch that contained a plastic patio chair and table. On the table was a glass ashtray. In it was a dozen stubbed out cigarette butts.

At that moment, on the other side of the motel, Ronny and Bronson were busy going from one room to the next. As Ronny would later tell me, almost all the curtains were closed in every window. There were only two rooms that had their lights on, and those were rooms two and five. They snuck up to each dark room and listened but there was no sound, not even the soft murmur of conversation, and they backed away.

With a steady hand Carver gripped the screen door. We'd already worked out how this was going to go but now he glanced back, stared at me for a few long seconds as if asking if I remembered. I nodded. He continued opening the door. We knew nothing about this screen door, whether or not it was going to screech, but whatever the case we needed to act fast.

Only a little sound was produced as Carver opened the door, just a slight hydraulic hiss, and then Carver was rushing inside, his heavy boots somehow quiet as they stormed over the linoleum. I followed a second later, and I found myself in a back office, which smelled of beer and weed and sex. This last didn't make sense but then we turned a corner and there they were on the floor, a man and a woman, just lying there naked on two stacked mattresses. White sheets covered their bodies. The one was definitely Kevin but the other I couldn't make out, her face buried into her pillow. Beside the bed were crumpled condom wrappers and balled-up tissues.

Carver walked toward them slowly, his rifle aimed, until he was standing right next to Kevin's side of the bed. With his right hand, he pulled out a switchblade from his pocket, flicked it open. Kevin continued to sleep, his eyes closed and his mouth open, emitting a slight snore. Carver extended the knife until the tip touched Kevin's Adam's apple. Kevin's eyes opened for a second, as if blinking open in sleep, and then realization hit him that this wasn't a dream and his eyes opened wide and he was just staring up at Carver, then at me, then back at Carver.

He made a noise, something that sounded like "huh?" and his legs started to kick. Carver pressed the knife right into Kevin's throat. Kevin's body jerked, stayed very still. He just stared up at Carver as Carver leaned forward. The girl still lying with her face in the pillow hadn't moved at all, and for some strange reason I wondered if she was dead.

Carver whispered, "Where are they?"

Sleep had been chased from Kevin's system and now he was wide-awake. His scarred face had flushed. He glared back at Carver, his chin raised because if he lowered it any the tip would cut deeper.

"Fuck you," he whispered harshly, defiantly, and Carver cut his throat.

For some reason I expected Kevin to die instantly, but it took him awhile. Convulsing on the bed, gurgling blood, trying to breathe in air—it was so much that it caused the girl lying next to him to sense something was wrong and sleepily raise her head from the pillow. She saw what was happening immediately and started to scream. I was there a moment later, the rifle now strapped over my shoulder as I put my one hand over her mouth, my other hand on her shoulder to keep her in place. She still tried to fight me but by then Kevin was almost dead and Carver took his knife away from Kevin's throat, the blade now dripping blood. Kevin gurgled for just a few more seconds before stopping altogether.

Next Carver pointed the knife at the girl's throat, shook his head, whispered, "Shh."

She stopped struggling but continued to shake.

"Are you going to scream?" Carver whispered.

With my hand still on her mouth, I felt her head as it moved from left to right and back again.

Carver looked at me and nodded once. I took my hand away.

"Now," Carver whispered, leaning down across where Kevin lay dead in a growing pool of his own blood, "where are they?"

The girl continued to tremble. "You … you're going to kill me."

"That depends on you. I asked him a question and he refused to answer it. Now are you going to follow his example?"

The girl didn't say anything, just began sobbing. Carver looked at me again and I saw the irritation in his face. He extended the knife even closer toward her throat.

"Do you want me to kill you?"

A soft sound, almost lost within her sobbing: "No."

At that moment outside, David had rushed in from where he'd been positioned on the other side of the highway. He started helping Ronny and Bronson, who had already determined that the only rooms occupied right now were in fact rooms two and five. How many were in each room was impossible to tell, but now that David was here with his silenced rifle, they started toward room five.

"Okay," Carver said, staring right back into her eyes. "Then answer my questions and I won't kill you. I promise that."

"They … they'll kill me."

"Not if I kill them first."

Ronny tried the knob for room five. It wasn't locked. David stood in front of the door, his rifle raised. He glanced at Ronny, at Bronson, at Ronny again. He nodded. Ronny turned the knob and pushed the door open, and David stepped inside.

Carver said, "Now tell me where they are."

"Wh-Who?"

"The woman and the child. The ones being held captive. What room are they in?"

There were only two men in room five. The bed had been taken away and the entire place was filled with tables. On the tables were a half dozen computers. This was the base for the game, where the cameras in the player's glasses and car and wherever else transmitted to and then the transmission was broadcast out over the Internet. Two men, each no older than thirty, sat on folding chairs working at these computers. Neither of them had time to move or say a word before David stepped in and shot them both. Bronson followed, hurrying over to check the bathroom, while Ronny stayed out on the walkway, keeping an eye on room two.

The woman shook her head. "No," she sobbed. "I—I can't."

Carver pressed the knife right against her throat. She released a sudden but breathless scream.

"Then where's Simon?"

Besides the two bodies, room five was empty. The three men started over toward room two. They set up the same way as before. Ronny tried the knob but found that this one wasn't going to turn. He nodded at Bronson, whose job it would be to kick down the door. Bronson got in position. He glanced at

Ronny, at David. Both men nodded. Bronson kicked it open, and the two other men entered, their guns raised.

The woman having told us all she knew (which wasn't much), Carver returned his knife and then raised his rifle. The woman made a soft noise, something that sounded like *please*, and he shoved the butt of the rifle right into the side of her head. She dropped at once. This time she was facing up and I managed to get a good look at her, even in the dark.

She was the girl who'd dropped off the package Monday morning. She was the one chewing strawberry bubblegum. She was the one who gave me the automatic thanks after I signed my name.

Carver glanced at me, said, "Let's move," and we started toward the front.

FIFTY-SIX

We hurried through the small waiting area of the manager's office and hit the door that took us out into the inner section of the U. The pickup and van were there like before, but now there was another car, too, a sedan just like the one that had driven me from the police station in Chicago.

Across the sand-speckled parking lot, the door to room five stood open. There was sound to our left and we raised our rifles but first David appeared, followed by Ronny, then Bronson. They were shaking their heads.

"Empty," Ronny said.

Carver put his finger to his lips, shushing Ronny and the rest of them before they spoke another word. We both started forward, passing by room one until we got to room two and the others.

"That's because he's not in there," Carver whispered.

The three men were bunched up on the porch, each holding their weapons at the ready, making it nearly impossible to push through.

"Who?" Bronson said, stepping back to get out of Carver's way, but he must have said it too loudly, giving away his position, because before Carver could shush him again or pull him back, gunfire erupted from inside room three. The window shattered; glass rained everywhere. Bronson's body convulsed just like Howard Abele's on his bed.

Before any of us could rush forward to where Bronson fell or begin returning fire, room three's door opened and a man stepped out. All of us raised our weapons but none of us opened fire.

We couldn't, because the man wasn't alone.

He was holding a small boy in front of him, a small black boy. With his other hand the man held a gun straight at the boy's head.

"Anybody moves, anybody breathes, and I'll kill him." There were four of us but the man kept his attention solely on Carver. "It's been a while, hasn't it, my friend?"

Carver was silent. The boy in the man's arms began crying.

"Shh," the man said, stroking the boy's head with the barrel of his gun. His eyes never left Carver's face. "Come now, Carver, be civil. Say hello to your son."

FIFTY-SEVEN

For the longest time nobody spoke. The only noise was that of the waves, the traffic, the squawking of spooked seagulls. And the boy crying in Simon's arms.

Then Carver said something, a murmur I couldn't hear.

Simon said, "Say it again, Carver. I don't think your men heard you."

Carver cleared his throat. "Stand down."

Standing there on the walkway, my rifle aimed right at Simon, I watched Ronny and David both glance at each other. Neither one moved.

"Goddamn it," Carver shouted, "stand down!"

Ronny was the first to lower his rifle. David followed a few seconds later. I just stood there, the rifle stuck in my hands.

"Drop them," Simon said.

Neither Ronny nor David moved.

Simon said, "Fine, then I'll kill him now," and pressed the gun right into the boy's head. The boy screamed even louder.

"Do as he says," Carver said. "That's an order."

It didn't look like either man was going to follow that order. Then, all at once, Ronny's rifle fell to the ground.

David glanced at him, stared a moment, then dropped his rifle too.

"All your guns," Simon said.

First Ronny pulled a nine-millimeter from the waistband in back of his pants. David slowly took out a gun that was strapped to his ankle. They tossed those on the ground as well.

"Ben, now it's your turn."

For the first time Simon looked at me. And, for the first time, I looked at him. Really looked at him. He was just a regular guy. Standing no taller than six feet, a full face and short dark hair. Like anyone you'd see on the sidewalk, at the grocery store, at church. He grinned as me, his teeth white and straight.

"I know you don't want to but neither did these two men, and see how helpful they were? Drop the rifle, Ben. No, on second thought, throw it up here."

It was the last thing I wanted to do, and to be honest I didn't think I could. As much as I told myself to let go, my hands refused, until finally, after a couple of seconds, first my right hand relaxed its grip, then my left hand, and before I knew it I'd tossed the rifle.

"Good," Simon said. "Now, Carver, be a good boy."

"Let him go."

Simon shook his head. "Not yet."

"This was the deal. You trade me for my son."

The entire time the boy continued to cry. He was squirming in Simon's arm but Simon was doing a good job keeping the boy between himself and the rest of us.

Simon's eyes shifted from Carver to the rest of us. He smiled and said to Carver, "Your men don't even know, do they?"

Carver said nothing.

"All this time you've been telling them, what, that your son was really dead?"

Again Carver said nothing.

"Don't get me wrong," Simon said to the rest of us, "there was a dead baby in that toilet. But it wasn't Carver's son. Carver didn't know that at first, but he eventually found out. He understood that we kept his son alive—or at least I kept teasing him with the idea he was still alive."

Silence.

Simon smiled again. "Every time I had the chance, I reminded Carver that his son was still alive. His wife, well, she unfortunately is no longer with us. We found a much more, shall we say, profitable use for her. We have video of it too, Carver, in case you never saw it." He paused. "Did you ever see it?"

"Let him go," Carver said.

"All this time," Simon said, "you've been trying to get to me because I have your son. And all this time you've been lying to your men, haven't you? Telling them that their families were already dead so they would leave the game." He shook his head. "Tsk, tsk, Carver. For a man once named the Man of Honor, that's not very honorable at all."

"Give him to me."

Simon shifted his eyes to the rest of us again. "Don't get me wrong. By now your families are gone. Well, except yours, Ben. They're still around, but you're still out of luck."

"What do you mean?" I asked, but before Simon could respond Carver shouted, "Give me my son!"

Simon said, "By the way, Carver, your son is quite a bright boy. Do you know what his first word was?"

The boy continued to sob, but his sobs were less vicious now. He seemed to be losing wind, staring at Carver like he actually recognized his father, ignoring the gun aimed at his head.

Simon repositioned the boy on his arm, rolled his shoulder, grinned again.

"It was *entertainment*. How do you like that, Carver? We sat him in front of one of the games and he pointed at the screen and said, *Entertainment*. Like I said, very bright boy you've got here. Knows his stuff."

Carver said nothing.

Simon sighed. "Oh well, if you're not going to play nicely, maybe you shouldn't play at all. But I'll give you one last chance. Simon says *catch*."

The boy screamed again as he went airborne, Simon throwing him at Carver. Carver started forward, shouting and shooting at Simon who had begun firing the gun. Carver's rifle gave three consecutive kicks before he threw it aside and lurched forward to catch the boy.

I'd seen what was happening even before Simon said his final word. I started moving at once. The moment the boy was in the air I pushed past Ronny and David, my head down and my shoulders up because I knew that any moment one of the bullets would tear through me. I hopped over Bronson and continued forward—four more steps, three more steps, two more steps—and I reached Carver just as the rifle fell and he grabbed the child. He lost his balance and started to fall back but I made it to him just in time. I gripped hold of his shoulder and his arm and kept him steady and on his feet.

I expected the boy to still be crying out, to be screaming, but he had fallen silent.

A moment later, held now in Carver's arms, I saw the reason why.

FIFTY-EIGHT

Again, nobody spoke for the longest time. The ocean, the traffic, the breeze, even the seagulls spooked once more by the sudden volley of gunfire—all that was constant but had become more than just background. Blood pounded in my ears. I'd been certain there for a second that I was as good as dead. But no, the only ones dead now were Bronson lying on the walkway, and Leon Ellison lying dead in his father's arms.

"Carver?" Ronny's voice, fighting to make its way through the silence. "Carver, you okay?"

Carver sat on the ground where I'd helped lower him. My hands were still on his shoulder and arm. I could feel him trembling. The sun was higher now on the horizon, giving this area of the world just enough light, and I finally saw his face. I saw the tears. I saw the pain. I saw the anger and the frustration. Mostly though, I saw the hate.

And I saw he wasn't looking down at his son. He was holding his son like he was never going to let go, yes, but his eyes were on something else.

That was when another noise fought through the silence. One

that must have been going the entire time. It reminded me of being back in Howard Abele's mansion, sitting there beside his bed. The chuckling of a dying man. Now that dying man was Simon. All three of Carver's bullets had struck him in the stomach.

The man wasn't wearing a vest; the abundance of dark blood was enough to confirm this. He had fallen and managed to prop himself in a sitting position against the wall, right between the opened door of room three and the window of room four. He sat there, chuckling, blood dribbling from the corners of his mouth.

His gun lay only a few feet away. It wasn't within reaching distance, and as long as he didn't have himself wired to any explosives, we were okay for the moment. Still I found myself standing and walking toward him. Bending to pick up the gun and continuing on. It was only a few feet and didn't take long at all, yet somehow I felt as if I'd walked a mile.

I crouched down next to Simon, who grinned back at me. His chuckling died in his throat, had become coughing instead. I pointed the gun at his face.

"Where are they?"

"Who?"

I jammed the gun into his eye. "Where are they?"

"Have you"—cough—"decided"—cough—"which one"—cough—"you love more?"

Silent, I kept the gun jammed right into his eye.

Simon coughed again. "Then how about"—cough—"the very last thing"—cough—"you'd say to them?"

I took the gun from his eye, pressed it against his shoulder blade, and pulled the trigger.

He didn't scream. He barely even reacted. But he was in definite pain; I could at least see that from his eyes despite him trying to hide it.

After opening and closing his mouth several times, he

managed to say, "Finally"—cough—"you grew"—cough —"some balls."

"Where. Are. They."

His eyes shifted from me for just a moment, shifted from me to glance at something across the parking lot.

"You fucked yourself, Ben," he said, and coughed some more. "You should have stuck"—cough—"to the plan. Carver's son"—cough—"arrived early, but …" And he slowly shook his head, grinning at me with a mouth full of blood.

"You told me they were here the entire time."

"I"—cough—"lied."

I glanced behind me. Carver still sat with his son. In his arms the child was nothing more than a bloodied mess. Ronny knelt beside him, trying to talk to him, but Carver wasn't listening. David had started over to where I was crouched with Simon. He carried his rifle again.

I said to him, "Can you go check the rest of the rooms?"

He nodded.

"You're"—cough—"a day early." Simon started to speak but had to stop, had to cough up even more blood. "How?"

"Misdirection," I said, glancing once more over my shoulder. David had whispered something to Ronny and they had split up, both now carrying their rifles at the ready, David crossing the parking lot to check the rooms on that side, Ronny checking the rooms on this side. Carver had set his son on the ground, very gently, and was now getting to his feet. Looking back at Simon, I said, "The public falls for it every time."

The grin appeared again on Simon's face. "The public"— cough, cough—"is stupid."

I didn't say anything. I didn't want to agree or disagree with him. I didn't want to tell him anything else, either. He didn't need to know about how in Cheyenne, at the gas station, when I stepped into the darkness of the restroom, I wasn't alone. That the Kid was waiting in there too. That in the five seconds or so of darkness I handed over my glasses and he punched the lenses out so he could see. And then the lights were flicked on and he took a piss, washed his hands, making sure not to look once at the mirror. Then it was back in the sedan, where not Carver joined him minutes later but Drew. Both were dressed in the same kind of clothes Carver and I had been wearing when we first started. They pulled away, got back onto the highway, neither saying anything to each other, the Kid not once looking at the rearview mirror or anything else which would give away his reflection. And Carver and I went to the airport, got on a private jet the Kid had paid an arm and a leg to secure for us, and we flew the entire way to California, where Ronny and David and Bronson were waiting to drive us up the coast.

Carver stood behind me. He said nothing for the longest time. Then, in a voice that didn't quite sound like his, he asked for the gun.

"Wait," Simon said, coughing up more blood. His entire front was covered in it. His time with Carver was apparently over, and now his attention was focused on me. "Why"— cough—"painting?"

For a moment I was taken back to the time when I was six years old and watching my father paint the backdoor. Standing there and asking him why he always painted. And my father taking a moment and resting on his hunches, wiping the sweat from his face, taking a deep breath. Telling me that every time he painted something old, made it look new, it was like he was helping fix the world. Just, he said, helping fix the world one brushstroke at a time. He had asked me then if I wanted to help and I'd nodded enthusiastically, saying yes, and he'd smiled and handed me the paintbrush and pointed to a spot near the bottom. And I'd painted it, had painted it clean. I never mentioned that moment to my father, not even when he was on his deathbed, because as time wore on and I got older and understood the world a little better, I realized that the old stuff, the nasty stuff, would always be there, right underneath the surface, and no matter how many times you painted it, all of that stuff would still be there. Yet at the same time I suspected my father knew this too. He understood it but didn't care.

But I wasn't going to tell Simon this. It was none of his business, and besides, I had more important things on my mind.

I jammed the gun back into his eye and said, my teeth clenched, "Where is my family?"

Simon smiled, blood between his teeth. "Gone"—cough—"like the"—cough—"wind."

Carver asked for the gun again. I continued to ignore him, keeping the gun where it was.

"Who are you, anyway?"

Simon's grin grew even larger, rivulets of blood streaming from the corners of his mouth. "My name"—cough—"is Benjamin Anderson." His free eye shifted up to Carver. "My name"—cough, cough—"is Carver Ellison."

Carver leaned down. He took the gun from my hand. I glanced up at him, wondering just what the hell he thought he was doing, but he wasn't looking at me. Instead he was staring back down at Simon.

"Who is Caesar?" Around us the waves crashed, the seagulls squawked, the traffic continued. Ronny and David continued searching the motel, testing knobs, kicking in doors, their rifles raised, checking every space of every room. "Tell me who he is and I might let you live."

Simon grinned again, even more blood in his mouth. He said, "Give unto Caesar"—cough, cough—"what is Caesar's."

"Yeah?" Carver said, nodding slowly. He cocked the gun and aimed it back at Simon's head. "When I finally meet him, I'll give him this too."

And he shot Simon in the face.

FIFTY-NINE

Carver dropped the gun and turned away. After a while I stood up and turned away too. Carver had gone to kneel next to his son again. Simon could have been bluffing but I didn't suspect so, not in this case. This was something that Simon had been planning for a long time, his own form of entertainment. After all, sometimes the audience doesn't need to be a huge number of people, but just one. Sometimes one is all it takes.

Across the parking lot, up on the walkway by room seven, David kicked in the door. He started to enter but stopped, turned back. He shouted at us to come over there.

I was moving before I even realized it. I sprinted past Carver, past the van parked in front of the room, up the steps and onto the porch. David stepped in front of me, held me back with both hands.

"Whoa," he said. "I'm not—I'm not sure you want to see this."

I tried pushing him away but he kept holding on, his fingers digging into my shoulders. "Get the fuck off me," I said, and David stared back at me, shaking his head, now whispering, "Ben, you don't—"

"Let him go."

This was Carver, quickly approaching from behind. Ronny was with him. David held onto me for a second longer, then let go. I pushed past him into the room seven, the room right next to the one I'd woken up in a week ago.

I stopped at once.

The room had been cleared. No bed. No table. No chair or dresser. Just two wooden caskets on the floor, looking like something out of a western. On one of the caskets was printed **WIFE OF WAX**. On the other casket, **DAUGHTER OF WAX**.

"Jesus God," someone breathed behind me. I never found out whether it was Ronny or David. I know it wasn't Carver, because Carver had come up beside me, his rifle in his hands.

"Ben?"

I didn't answer. I just continued staring. I thought about the question Simon had been asking me all week, who I loved more, Jen or Casey. And now here I was, standing here with a decision to make, a choice between my wife and my daughter.

"Ben?" Carver said again, and I started shaking my head, still staring down at the caskets, at the words printed there.

I whispered, "I … can't."

Carver must have motioned something to Ronny and David because seconds later the two men entered the room, walking past us toward the caskets. Ronny went to the casket on the left, the one with **WIFE OF WAX** printed on top, while David went to the casket on the right, marked **DAUGHTER OF WAX**. They bent down and inspected the outside of the caskets, before standing back up.

"This one doesn't look like it's wired to anything," David said.

Ronny nodded. "Same here."

A moment passed. Carver said my name again. I just continued shaking my head, continued staring.

Carver said, "Okay, guys, we're going open them up."

Ronny and David glanced at each other, then bent over the caskets, worked their fingers under the lids.

"On three," Carver said.

They looked up at him, waiting.

Carver opened his mouth but paused, glancing at me once again. "Fuck it," he said under his breath. Then to his men, "Just do it now."

As one, they lifted the lids of the caskets.

SIXTY

Except if you were one of the hundreds or thousands of viewers watching this particular game, you wouldn't have seen any of that. All you would have seen was the passing deserts and distant peaks and sagebrush of Nevada. Signs for Carlin, for Battle Mountain, for Golconda.

In fact, no doubt almost all of you were somewhere else at that time. Playing with your children. Counseling your employees. Teaching your students. Speaking to a board of investors. Prepping yourself for surgery. Any number of things.

You had the time figured out, knew how long it would take before the Man of Wax and the Man of Honor reached their destination. Only then would you slip away from the world you've lived in all your life, smiling and saying the right things at the right times to the right people—only then would you take off your mask and go to your computers. You had been anticipating this moment, had been dreaming about it.

Only you found that, at the appropriate time, the page was gone. Completely blank. Surely this must be some kind of mistake, some technical error. You made calls, you sent emails, you tried finding out what had happened, but you got no answers.

A few may had guessed it already, though. A few who had nothing better to do with their time and just watched the highway along with the Man of Wax. Sitting on their couches or in their desk chairs, drinking coffee or sipping beer, lounging in their underwear and sometimes masturbating if the mood hit them just right. These few would have been the only witnesses to what happened at the end. How the car made another pit stop off of 80 in Fernley, Nevada. But the pit stop was not at some gas station or fast food restaurant, but just some random parking lot. Maybe those few watching noticed this right away and sat up a little straighter in their chairs. Maybe they kept their eyes glued when the glasses were taken off what was presumably the Man of Wax's face. Maybe they watched as the glasses were held up and a hand appeared in front of the camera, a hand that proudly flipped all who was watching the bird. Then the bird and the hand disappeared and the glasses were snapped in half, breaking the transmitter.

Maybe—and here's where we really have to hope—they even had the volume turned up on their speakers and could clearly hear the Kid's voice right before the screen cut to black.

"Game over, motherfuckers."

EPILOGUE

It's been four weeks since that first morning, the morning the game officially started. It's been three weeks since our little raid at the Paradise Motel. Three weeks since I stood in that room and watched them open the caskets.

They were empty, both of them. For the longest time nobody said a word. Then I broke down, fell to my knees and just started crying.

Eventually I got myself together. I wiped at my eyes, sniffed back more tears. Stared down into each casket, then glanced up at Carver, who hadn't left the room yet, unlike David and Ronny who went to gather all the computer equipment to later give to the Kid.

I said, "What does this mean?"

Carver stared down at the caskets. "It means they're still alive."

"But how … how do you know?"

"I don't," Carver said. His eyes shifted to meet mine. "Neither do you. But like you told me in Chicago, we can't give up that hope. It … it's the only thing they can't take away from us."

When interrogated the girl gave us nothing, not even her name. It seemed the act she'd pulled with Carver before was just an act. She'd been scared, maybe, but she'd just woken up and couldn't think straight. She refused to tell us anything, especially who Caesar was. In the end Carver broke her neck and left her dead body next to Kevin's.

We debated about calling the police, the media, even taking some pictures, but decided none of it would matter in the end. Besides Bronson and Carver's son, we left the rest of the bodies to be cleaned up by someone else. In the manager's office Carver wrote a note on Paradise Motel stationary that said, *Caesar, I'm coming for you.* He tacked the piece of paper to Simon's bloodied chest.

So we left the Paradise Motel. With Bronson and Carver's son wrapped in the motel's white sheets in the back of the van, we drove and we drove and we drove. Eventually we came to the place Carver and his men sometimes stayed. First we buried Bronson in the backyard. Then Carver asked the rest of us to leave him alone for a while. We went into the house to give him his privacy, but still I watched him from the second floor. I watched him bury his son all by himself. I watched him say a prayer. Then I watched him break down crying.

Drew Price—who'd been standing in for Carver—showed up later that day. The Kid never did show up. He went back to his basement decorated with posters of Terry Gilliam films and continued his work. Fighting the good fight, he's told me over the phone, but I'm not so sure anymore.

Two days later the Kid informed me that my house back in Lanton had burned down. I'd wanted to return to it at some point and take whatever I could that would forever remind me of my family—Jen's quilt she'd knitted one year, Casey's worn copy of *The Little Prince* or her *Shrek 2* poster— but now there was no point. The house's demise, the Kid said, was reportedly from an electrical fire, which killed the family living inside. Where the bodies came from and how they managed to pass as us I'll never know. But for those who cared, Benjamin Anderson, his wife Jennifer, and their daughter Casey were dead.

To add insult to injury, Lanton had recently lost another painter. My old friend, Marshall Gibson, and his wife Lydia, died in a car accident Tuesday evening one week before. The same Tuesday I was busy driving through Nevada.

The only good news the Kid could provide was that Casey's preschool was still standing.

After hearing all of this news I had gone outside to be alone. Eventually Carver came out and sat down beside me. He didn't speak. Finally I cleared my throat and asked the question I'd been holding back.

"Just how deep does this go?"

"What do you mean?"

"You know what I mean. You told me back in Chicago this wasn't some conspiracy. That it was just a bunch of people having a good time. But now with Caesar? And about how this guy is going to soon change the world?"

For the longest time Carver didn't say anything. Then he looked at me, took a deep breath, and said, "I have no idea."

The next day Carver had a black eye.

"Who gave you that?" I asked.

"Drew. I can't say I blame him. I deserve it. I've already talked with the rest of the guys and now I need to talk to you. I've been putting it off long enough."

"About what?"

"How I owe you an apology. I … I wasn't completely honest with you—with any of you."

"Ronny told me none of you keep secrets from each other."

"I'm not proud of what I did. Simon … he just kept taunting me with the idea that my son was still alive. I never even knew for certain that he was. But I wanted to believe it so badly that it became true to me, and I decided I would do whatever it took to get him back."

"And now he's dead," I murmured, and instantly hated myself for saying it.

Carver stared hard at me, his eyes cold, before he nodded slowly and whispered, "Yes, he is."

There was a long silence, and then Carver asked me if I wanted to stay with him. He said he couldn't promise me anything, but he would try his best to help me find my wife and daughter.

"But what if they're already dead?"

"Do you believe they are?"

I said nothing for the longest time. Then I told Carver I might as well stay with him and his men because it didn't look like I had any choice. He said that wasn't true, we always had a choice, and right then I had an idea. Carver wanted to get me trained but I told him there was something I needed to do first. I explained my idea, then we talked to the Kid via Skype to get his opinion.

"Might work, might not," the Kid said. "I mean, if he wants to do it, I'll post it wherever I can. What the fuck."

Yes, what the fuck.

I've been writing for six days straight now. Only stepping away to eat or move my bowels or sleep. But I don't like sleeping, because I toss and turn too much. I keep thinking of where Jen and Casey might be right now, how scared and confused they must feel. It's been hell to relive that particular week of my life but I figured I had no choice. This story needs to be told, needs to be posted wherever it can be posted across the Internet.

I keep thinking about the quote from Edmund Burke, about how all that's necessary for the triumph of evil is that good men do nothing. The only problem I see is that there are no real good men in the world, not really. We're all flawed, each and every one of us, we're all imperfect.

Yet somehow, evil hasn't yet triumphed.

So why am I writing this? You might think it's so that these people can be exposed for the scum they truly are, that the proper authorities will finally do something about it. But that's not it at all. It's impossible to point fingers and tell who these people are. They're out there, yes, they're everywhere, but just like Carver said, stopping them is impossible. It's a virus that will continue to spread and there is nothing that can be done about it.

But this isn't for those people. This is for Sandra and Leon Ellison. This is for those residents and employees at the Hickory View Retirement Home. This is for James Henley and his wife and their unborn twins. This is for Gerald and his family, for Juliet. This is for each and every person who has either died or suffered for the sake of not just my game, but for all the games. People who never had a choice in the cards they were dealt, who were brutally moved around the game board of life as disposable pawns for the sake of entertainment.

Mostly though, this is for Jen and Casey.

Simon had asked me what the last thing was I'd say to my wife and daughter if I had the chance. I had told him it was that I loved them and it still is. But I've also come up with something else. Not the last thing I'd say to them, but the first thing I'll tell them when I finally see them again. After I've hugged them and kissed them and wiped their tears away.

For Casey, it's that recently I've been going outside every night and looking up at the sky, asking aloud, "Has the sheep eaten the flower or not?" And while I haven't yet heard the five hundred million bells, I know they're ringing. At the moment, I think that's enough.

As for Jen, it's this:

Last night I dreamed of Michelle Delaney again. As always

I'm at the college party and bored, ready to leave. I go outside, start back to my dorm, but then hear her screaming, crying for help. And I rush around the building to find her there with her boyfriend, who just continues beating her and beating her and beating her. It's all like it always is, the night and the leaves and the chill of the wind. Just like when it first happened.

Except this time it's different.

This time, I take a step forward.

The story continues in *The Inner Circle*, the second book in the Man of Wax Trilogy, available everywhere.

ABOUT THE AUTHOR

Robert Swartwood is the *USA Today* bestselling author of *The Serial Killer's Wife*, *No Shelter*, *Man of Wax*, and several other novels. He created the term "hint fiction" and is the editor of *Hint Fiction: An Anthology of Stories in 25 Words or Fewer*. He lives with his wife in Pennsylvania.